This is How a Heart Breaks

M. J. Parisian

Dedication

For the men in my life…
Toby, Evan, and Blake
The keepers of my heart.

Part One: Faith

Life with Grace

The Choices We Make

September 2 at 8:13 a.m. || 21 Comments

Life begins at the end of your comfort zone.

We've all heard that before, but how many of us are actually living by that motto? Raise your hand if you avoid people who challenge you or compel you to think differently. How about that conversation with your spouse that can wait until tomorrow when they're in a better mood? The diet you were supposed to start yesterday?

I get it, I really do. Status quo is far easier than shaking things up and doesn't require more energy.

Living your dream life requires some good, old-fashioned courage. It takes the kind of courage a soldier has walking into battle. The kind of courage a woman needs to live with stage IV breast cancer. The courage required for every mom with a teenager. Hell, even asking for a raise requires a certain amount of courage.

It isn't easy, but nothing worth having has ever been easy. It takes faith to trust yourself and stand up for the life you want.

Do you have that kind of faith?

You chose this life. All the beautiful, crazy, and mundane things in it.

You. Chose. That. Your life is a compilation of every thought, decision, and acceptance you've ever made.

And at any time, you can pick up a pen and begin rewriting your story.

So what are you going to do with that?

Are you going to continue on this path that may or may not lead you to where you want to go? Or are you going to courageously take a chance on a life that you truly want?

Life is what you choose.

Choose wisely.

Sometimes what you're afraid of doing is the very thing that will set you free…

Chapter One

It was 6:15 a.m., and I had already made one major decision today: I wanted out of my marriage.

After a night of tossing and turning in the spare bedroom, I dragged myself to my bakery and wrote a letter to my husband, Barry, informing him the marriage was over. I knew we would both be busy with work that day, and I didn't want the weight of this thought sitting in my heart. Once it was out there — on paper at least —I felt a bubble of hope start to rise through my body. Rays of light finally pierced through the dreary cloud that had been hanging over me.

The silver lining.

Two dozen lemon scones were cooling on the wire racks, and the first batch of blueberry muffins were already baking, with another tray waiting on the counter. Tina Turner was blaring on the speakers as I rolled out the remaining dough for the cinnamon rolls. I had fifteen minutes before Shelly showed up with her over-caffeinated energy and white skinny jeans. Fifteen minutes to replay every explicit detail of last night. Fifteen minutes before I would have to resume my role of wife, mother, and baker.

A trickle of sweat trailed down my back as I raced around the kitchen. Part hangover, a dash of guilt, and a sprinkle of hope. Attempting to shake off these thoughts, I washed my hands and grabbed some Motrin out of my bag. I checked my phone for any messages and swallowed the pills with a swig of lukewarm water sitting on my desk. Stevie Wonder slid into the next track as the timer beeped for the muffins. A blast of heat enveloped me as I swapped out the trays, letting the batch cool before taking them off. I smiled as I thought about last night.

I knew it was wrong.

I knew I was flirting with disaster.

I didn't care.

It honestly shocked me how easily a night of friendly flirting and pickleback shots almost ended up with broken vows. One of us had the common sense to stop it from going too far, but it wasn't me, and I felt giddy about seeing him again.

My phone chimed as a text came through, but I needed to get the cinnamon rolls sliced and into the pan. I looked at the clock and noticed that Shelly was late — again. Another text chimed. She was probably letting me know she overslept, as usual.

When she finally pushed her way through the kitchen door, eyes wide as saucers, a police officer followed in right behind her.

He tipped his hat, but frowned. "Ma'am," he said. "I'm looking for Lynette Sinclair." His eyes showed no compassion.

My throat was dry. "That's me," I said, wiping my

hands on my apron.

He cleared his throat. "Ma'am, your husband, Barry, was rushed to the hospital this morning. He was found shortly after six this morning when one of the partners arrived at the office."

Shelly's hand went to her mouth. "Linny, go," she said. "I'll take care of everything here. Just go."

I looked from one to the other not comprehending what was happening. "I don't understand. What happened to him?" My voice cracked.

"Ma'am, I don't have any details. We called your residence and your mother said to find you here," he said. "I was told to take you to Memorial."

The music suddenly sounded ridiculous, and my stomach rolled at the thought of what I did last night. I ripped my apron off, grabbed my bag, and followed the officer out through the front without saying a word to Shelly.

Sitting in the police car, I took out my phone and noticed the texts were all from my mom. She was trying to warn me.

The total weight of the shame began hitting me in waves. Five minutes ago I was replaying every detail about last night, and wondering how much further I could take it next time. I thought about my letter, folded in my purse, wondering if it would ever see the light of day.

Was he dead? Did he even come home last night? I never saw him, but I had gotten home so late and slept in the spare room.

My face heated with guilt as the police officer peppered me with random questions. "Look, can we not have the small talk right now?"

He nodded and stared straight ahead, lips tight.

"I'm sorry," I said. "I just can't answer your questions right now."

I stared out the window, seeing the hospital ahead. I tapped out a simple text to my mom.

ME: *Heading to Memorial now. Will keep you posted.*

MOM: *Prayers are with you!*

Oh, Mom. Ever the faithful, doting mother. Like prayers would help any of us now.

Chapter Two

I had felt every minute pass as I stared at the clock in the waiting room, clinging to the St. Jude medal my mom gave me for Mother's Day this year. "He's the patron saint of lost souls," she explained in a whisper. "I thought you might need a little help—you know—in finding your path."

I could sense the blank look on my face wasn't the reaction she was going for, but I was speechless. How does one respond when your mom called upon saints because your soul is lost? My mother had always been true to her faith, while my beliefs tended to ebb and flow with various events in my life.

The necklace sat in the box for a couple weeks, but eventually, I acknowledged that my life was a shitshow. It had been around my neck ever since. I had a failing marriage to a man who refused to admit we should divorce, and I was still in love with Gordy, a man I had been trying to forget about for months. I owned a bakery that needed my attention twenty-four-seven, and had two of the most beautiful kids on the planet who needed a mom who didn't talk to herself all the time. I was swimming in a pool of my own misery and didn't know how to get out of the deep end.

My stomach burned at the thought of Gordy, and I

berated myself again for last night. Gordy could *never* find out about last night and what almost happened. Guilt flooded over me in waves. I knew Gordy was trying to save his marriage, but every part of me wanted to reach out to him right now. I wanted him to comfort me and tell me everything would be okay. I wanted him to tell me he'd be back. That was all I wanted right now. Last night proved how lost and confused I had become. A woman I didn't even recognize in the mirror anymore.

How could I do something so reckless and selfish? How low must I be feeling to take such a risk?

The phone rang on the receptionist's desk in our waiting room, jolting me out of my thoughts. When I got to the hospital this morning, they let me see Barry for two minutes before they took him for more testing. Then, a nurse led me to another waiting room by the outpatient surgery. She explained he was having angioplasty and I would be notified when he was done.

He was so pale when I saw him earlier. Of course, the lighting and hospital gowns would make anyone look ill, but fear reflected in his eyes. I had never seen that look on his face, ever. Not even when Charlotte was born with the umbilical cord wrapped around her neck and she came out pale blue.

I figured I had to have some brownie points for wearing St. Jude's medal, so I started to pray. "*Everyone returns to faith when faced with a challenge,*" my mom always said. But this challenge felt too immense, too real, and far bigger than anything I could handle on my own.

I didn't want my marriage to Barry any longer, but I certainly didn't want him dead either.

Texts were blowing up my phone from my mom, my best friend Gracie, and even Barry's partners. The only one I responded to was Gracie. She had a knack for knowing me better than I knew myself, and she wasn't afraid to tell me to buck up. Gracie had been through her own hell and back this past year with her husband's scandal, and now she seemed happier than she had ever been. Even though she didn't know about last night, somehow Gracie knew I'd be beating myself up now.

I turned my phone off and slid it back in my purse. I noticed the letter there, unread, and knew I'd never be able to give it to him now. I unfolded it and began to read the words I had written so early this morning.

Barry,

I know you think the "glue" that holds this marriage together will weather the storm that we're in, but I don't believe that's true. I feel like counseling might have helped us six months ago, but now I just feel like I want to move forward—without you—

"Excuse me, Mrs. Sinclair?"

The receptionist from the waiting room stood in front of me, eyebrows raised.

"The doctor will meet you in the conference room

across the hall," she said. "I can take you over there now."

She stood there, waiting for me to gather my things. I'd give anything to have a few more moments of limbo where I didn't have a husband. I knew I couldn't run and hide, and I'd probably go to hell for thinking this, but I wanted St. Jude to help *me*, not Barry. *I* wanted to be saved from all of this mess.

"Mrs. Sinclair? Are you okay?" Her forehead wrinkled with genuine concern. I sighed as I grabbed my bag and stood.

"I'm fine," I said. "Just a long morning."

She led me out of the waiting room and across the hall. The room was small, stuffed with three chairs and a tiny end table stuck in the corner. "You can have a seat, and the doctor will be right with you."

I slumped in the closest chair and waited for the doctor. A few moments later there was a knock at the door and he entered.

"Mrs. Sinclair," he said, reaching to shake my hand. "I'm Doctor West, and just left your husband who is resting comfortably." His eyes met mine, and I felt calmer instantly. I had never met this man but I felt safe in his presence.

I nodded, feeling shaky. "How is he? Will he be okay?"

He nodded. "Luckily, your husband is a strong man."

I nodded again, feeling like a bobblehead doll.

"The tests showed some blockage of Barry's left

coronary artery. We performed angioplasty and inserted two stents. He's in recovery now and doesn't seem to be in much pain. You should be able to see him shortly." He spoke in short, clear sentences, but I wanted more.

"Okay, how long will he be here?" In my head, I wished for weeks of recovery.

"Actually, that's more good news for you. We will keep him overnight for observation, but he should be free to go tomorrow," he said. "I will be sending someone from our practice tomorrow morning to go over a diet and exercise plan he will need to add into his daily routine."

Tomorrow? My mind was spinning. He'd be back home tomorrow, and I would have to take care of him. "Thank you, Doctor West, for everything," I managed to say before he left.

I pulled out my phone and texted my mom, who was still home with Charlotte and Trevor.

ME: *Barry will be fine. Home tomorrow.*

MOM: *Oh thank God! How are you? Have you been getting my texts? Kids are fine. Charlotte just got home from school. Trevor is watching a video.*

I smiled. Trevor was *always* watching a video. Where Charlotte needed to be doing something constantly, Trevor only needed two things: snacks and a TV.

> ME: *I'm waiting to see Barry in a bit and I'll come home. He will need some things for overnight.*
>
> MOM: *Ok take your time. I'll let your dad know he's okay.*

I rolled my eyes. As if my dad would even care about anything other than his business.

Next, I texted Gracie, giving her the same information. I knew she was going to come to the hospital if I didn't let her know something soon. Waiting patiently was not one of her better qualities, a point proven by my ringing phone.

"Hey Dunham," I said, answering. When we were in high school, there were three girls named Grace, and the teachers would use their last names if there was more than one in a class. Ever since then, I have called her by her last name.

"So he's okay? Was it a heart attack?"

She sounded more worried than I did. "It was, and they had to perform angioplasty to open one of his arteries. He should be able to come home tomorrow though."

"Are you okay, Linny? You sound so tired." I struggled to hold back tears at the sound of concern.

"I'm good," I said. "Just been through a mess of

emotions this morning, and I'm still not sure how I feel."

She sighed on the other end. "Is there anything I can do right now? My mom made a casserole for you and the kids, and I got a bottle of Riesling for you."

"Honestly that sounds perfect. I'm going to stay here for a bit, but I'll need to come home and get some things for him I'm sure," I said. "God Dunham, this is such a mess."

"I know, Linn, believe me I know. I'll drop the stuff off soon, but call me later if you want some company."

A different nurse knocked and opened the door. "Barry is okay to see you now," she said.

"I gotta go Gracie," I said before disconnecting. I stood, making sure I had my bag, and let the nurse lead me back through the double doors to outpatient surgery.

The recovery room was one giant space with five beds on either side. Each bed had its own curtain for privacy, if you want to call it that. I could hear people whispering behind their curtains as the nurse led me to the last bed on the left.

My hands were freezing and my heart was beating out of my chest. I didn't know why I was so nervous to see him, but the nurse was holding the curtain open for me, a smile plastered on her face.

"You have fighter in here," she said, winking.

Barry was hooked up to several machines, all of them beeping, showing his heart rate and blood pressure. He had a loopy smile on his face as he looked at me.

"There's the love of my life," he drawled.

Turning around, I looked to see who he was talking about. I cringed, realizing it was me. The nurse giggled.

"The medication is still in his system. He's feeling no pain."

I nodded. "So, it sounds like they found you just in time this morning," I said. "The doctor says you're a lucky man."

His smile reminded me of the Joker from Batman. "I'm lucky because of you," he said.

The nurse put his chart at the end of the bed. "I'll just let you two lovebirds visit for a bit. He needs to lie very still for the blood vessels in his groin to seal." She looked directly at him. "No sudden movements or dancing, young man."

I sat down in the plastic chair beside his bed. He reached for my hand, an IV taped to his own. He continued to look at me like he did when we first met at a party during Christmas break. He'd always said I was the brightest person in the room. He laughed at everything I said as if I were a stand-up comedian. He followed me around all night, making sure my drink was full. No one had ever given me that kind of attention without wanting something else, but he was completely genuine that first night. The first time his eyes held mine felt as if the earth shifted on its axis, and a warmth spread throughout my chest. I remembered a small nod from him that confirmed he felt it too.

This was how he was looking at me now. Gone was the look of resentment and annoyance. I had forgotten he could look at me any other way.

"So," I said, "are you in much pain?"

"Not anymore, now that you're here," he replied.

He was starting to creep me out.

"Linny, I had a vision this morning. I know why I couldn't let go of this marriage."

"Barry, I think you still have some medication in your system," I said gently. "You're not making any sense."

"No Linny, listen to me." He started to sit up, but then remembered the nurse's orders. "My thoughts have never been clearer. I love you, and I'm going to spend the rest of my life proving that to you."

I pulled my hand away, thinking this was a cruel trick. He was going to sit up and say "GOTCHA" at any moment.

"I know you're thinking this is crazy after the last few years. Hell, I would've wanted a divorce from me too if I were you, but Linny, I mean it. I see how wrong I've been."

"But Barry," I said. "I know you've been through a lot, but am I supposed to forget the past few years because you see the light now?"

He sat there staring at me with love in his eyes. The goddamn things were *twinkling*.

"You know what? This isn't a conversation for right now," I said. "Let's get you home and healthy again."

"Linn, listen to me," he pleaded. "Do you remember the one reading we had at our wedding? The one about love is patient... love is kind? Go home and read that for me. I know it hasn't been easy, but if you can read that for me I would really appreciate that."

He was killing me. Slowly. Five hours ago all I wanted was a divorce, and here he was quoting readings from our wedding, and the one thing I knew for sure was that my love wasn't that patient, and it certainly wasn't feeling very kind.

The nurse pulled the curtain back. "I hate to interrupt, but we need to finish up a few things before we move him to his room for the evening."

I stood and faked a smile. "It's fine," I said. "I was just leaving to get some things he will need for the night."

Barry continued to smile at me. "Uncomfortable" was an understatement. "Do you know what room he'll be in when I come back?"

She looked at her chart, "Room four twenty-eight. But he won't be in there until five o'clock, at least."

That gave me some time to process this day. "Okay, I'll come back then," I said.

"Give the kids hugs from me," he said, tearing up. The nurse tipped her head and gave me a lopsided smile.

"I will," I said. "Try to get some rest this afternoon."

response.

"I almost did it with Jimmy at Lakeside last night." I cringed as I said the words out loud, but immediately felt better getting it off my chest. Her eyes grew wide. "And this morning before I heard the news, I wrote a letter to Barry asking for a divorce."

She took a deep breath and blew it out slowly. "Wow. Not what I was expecting," she said. "Are you and Jimmy a thing now?" Jimmy, Charlie's brother, also happened to be Gracie's high school crush. He was a younger, hotter, version of Charlie.

"No, last night was just a big mistake, and he was the one to stop everything. Thank God. I was just lonely, and he was sympathetic enough to listen to me last night after you and Charlie left."

"Why didn't you tell me you were so unhappy last night? I would never have left you," she said.

"I know," I replied, sipping the wine. "I started feeling sorry for myself and didn't want to leave."

"You certainly kiss a lot of guys for being married."

"Fuck my life," I whispered. "The only good thing I've ever done is raise two children who, hopefully, don't know what a psycho their mom is. Promise me you'll never tell Gordy."

"A, it's not my story to tell, and B, don't be so hard on yourself, Linn. Barry hasn't made your marriage easy, and I think last night was more about you reaching out."

"Oh I was reaching," I snickered.

She covered her ears. "I don't want any details!"

"Stop it, we didn't do anything," I said. "Just some groping."

"Linny, I swear, I'll leave if you keep going."

She seemed serious, so I let it go. Neither one of us said anything for a moment, both lost in our own thoughts.

"So what are you going to do?" She asked the million-dollar question. *What was I going to do?*

"I don't have a clue. My choices are to go against everything I've wanted for *years* and stay in this loveless marriage, or to leave my husband who just had a heart attack and is begging me to give him a second chance." I drained the glass and set it down, feeling the warmth spread throughout my limbs. "I'm pretty much screwed either way."

Gracie grabbed the chocolate and broke off a square. "Do you think there's a third choice?"

"Like what? Grab the kids and move to Florida?"

She sighed. "I don't know Linny. I just feel like this all happened for a reason."

"Jesus, Dunham. I don't need your mom's wisdom right now. I have enough guilt on my plate to last me this lifetime."

Gracie's mom, Julia—a best-selling self-help author—was one of the kindest people I knew. Gracie seemed to be following in her mom's footsteps by starting a blog and working on a book of her own. I hadn't told her yet, but Gracie's last post was the reason I wrote that letter to Barry.

"I'm not trying to make you feel guilty, Linn. I just want to help you through this," she said. "You've been unhappy for so long, and it's about time you make some choices that are going to help you down the road."

I shook my head, not wanting to hear what she had to say right now. "You said no judgements."

She moved closer to me and took my hand in hers. "I'm not judging you and I don't want you to feel that way," she whispered. "You just tell me what you need from me right now."

"Honestly, I think I just need to go to bed," I said, squeezing her hand. "I'm hoping to wake up and this was all a bad dream."

She smiled. "I know that feeling all too well," she said. "Do you need help at the bakery for a few days?"

I laughed. "Are you offering your baking skills? Because you and I know that wouldn't work."

"Okay, what about the kids? Can I help there?"

"Actually, my mom is coming in the morning to get them off to school, but would you be able to help in the afternoon? I'm not sure how long Barry will be at the hospital or if he'll even come home tomorrow."

"Now *that* I can do," she said, standing.

I turned off the fire, and we both carried the wine and snacks into the house.

"I really am sorry about your shitty day," she said, pulling me in for another hug. "And I'm sorry for not saying the right things."

"You're fine," I said, holding back tears. "I really think this day has brought too many emotions to the surface, and I need sleep."

"Okay, I'll get the kids tomorrow, just let me know what time."

"Sounds good," I said. "Thank you for coming over."

"Anything for you," she said, walking away.

I shut the door and leaned against it. It felt like a cliché, something you'd see in the movies, but as I slid down to the floor and broke into sobs, I knew this was real.

I knew in my heart that I'd wake up tomorrow and would have to deal with this mess of a life.

Chapter Four

Ever since I was a little girl, baking has always been my thing. To this day, the aroma of Duncan Hines brownies will take me back to the age of eight when my mom first allowed me to use the oven by myself. Of course I was too young, but my begging was relentless. Some girls were good at sports or school, but I've always been drawn to the kitchen. My mom would make me finish my homework before I started a nightly ritual of what to bake, and she always knew that I would end up in a bakery somehow.

Being in my bakery's kitchen, surrounded by the smells and sounds, is a comfort I can't find anywhere else. A week after Trevor was born, in a fit of sleep deprivation, I found my way here to Bab's at five in the morning to make a batch of blueberry muffins. I could've made them in my own home, but coming here was my refuge then, as it is now. There must be a psychological reason I'm drawn to this place, and it should concern me that there is no other place I'd rather be, but it doesn't. For me, this is home.

I finished the rolls, muffins, and scones for the morning and knew Shelly would be in soon. The cinnamon rolls were winning the daily contest of Best Smelling this morning, but the glazed lemon scones would win the award for Most Photogenic. Every day I played the baked goods beauty pageant in my head, secretly wondering if I was crazy. The blueberry muffins were the proud recipient of Miss Congeniality five years running. Nothing's more likable than a classic blueberry muffin with a crumble top.

Sleep came in bits and pieces last night as I tossed and turned thinking about yesterday and its turn of events. I thought about what Gracie said and wondered if there was a third option for us. It was so set in my head that I would be out of this marriage, and now I just felt trapped. A part of me wondered if I would ever get my own life back.

Shelly bustled through the door as if she were being chased. "Hey, you're here," she said, surprised.

"Well the goods aren't going to bake themselves, Shelly." The snarky comment escaped me before I could stop it, but I had expected her to show up early to help bake this morning.

"Oh jeez, did you need me here early? Oh! And how's Barry?"

This was how her brain worked, a constant need to catch up to the next thought. Instilling a little forward thinking has been my goal when I hired her a year ago, but working with Shelly was similar to teaching time management to a teenager. Both felt like losing battles.

"Barry is going to be okay," I said. "He had a procedure done yesterday on his heart and should be coming home today."

"Wow, that's scary, but I'm glad he's going to be okay," she said. "You must have been worried sick."

In that moment, I looked at her, and realized Shelly knew nothing about me at all.

"It was a long day, but hopefully life will get back to normal soon," I said. "By the way, I'm wondering if you'd be able to come in a little earlier for the next week or two. I'll need to be home to help him, and then come in after the kids are at school."

"Actually, I was going to talk to you about that this morning," she said, sliding an apron over her head. "My mom surprised me with a trip to Key West for a couple weeks. She is going down tomorrow and wants me to join her the next day," she said. She meticulously lined up the scones on the serving tray, clearly unaware of the alarms going off in my head. "She even bought me a ticket. *Total* surprise." She nodded vigorously, as if it was the best gift ever.

"Yeah," I said, flatly. "That's a total surprise to me too."

"Oh hey, is it okay?" She stopped what she was doing and finally looked me. "I guess I figured you could run this place with or without me."

I took a deep breath. "Well, I guess it doesn't matter if it's okay or not. It sounds like you're going."

"Yeah but... I was hoping you wouldn't care or anything," she said. "I mean, I can't *not* go."

"You know what? I'll even give you tomorrow off. That way you can pack and get everything done."

My thoughts were clear, cutting. Just like my marriage, I wanted to be done with Shelly. I knew today was going to be her last day, and I would have to find someone new to help me manage this place.

My mom had always said I could make decisions like no other, and once it was made, there was no changing my mind. "Life isn't always black and white, Linny," she would say to me when I would write something off or start something out of the blue. "Sometimes there is a grey area," she'd add.

This vacation of Shelly's was a sign to me that I needed to find someone new.

"I have a friend who's staying at my place for a couple weeks while he gets his life in order. Do you want me to see if he can help out around here?"

My head snapped up. *Could she actually hear what I was thinking?* "Um, this friend of yours," I said, trying not to sound desperate. "He's only in town for a short while?"

"Well, I think so," she said. "It's complicated, but he isn't getting along with his family right now, so I told him he could apartment sit for me while I was gone. He's from Traverse City."

"Has he ever worked in a restaurant? Could he come in today?" I didn't want to get too excited, but this would totally save me if it panned out. We both had our hands full with trays for the display case. I took a deep breath and let the scent of maple and brown sugar calm my frayed nerves.

"He's worked at Starbucks for a while now. He was making coffee when I left."

She quickly pulled her phone out of her back pocket and tapped out a message. How that phone even fit in the pocket to begin with is beyond me. There wasn't much wiggle room in her jeans.

"He said he can be in after he showers," she said, sliding the phone back in her pocket. I couldn't help but imagine Shelly sitting down and shattering the screen.

We managed to fill the cases and start both coffee makers before turning the "closed" sign to "open." Even though Shelly had her flaws, I would miss her knowledge of my store and easy demeanor. Customers loved her energy and bright spirit, but it was the same spirit that let her just decide to take a vacation without any notice. I could only hope that her friend could fill her shoes and help me around the bakery, but the way my luck was going, I wouldn't bet any money on it.

Grabbing a mug of hazelnut coffee, I left Shelly to handle the front of the store while I went back to start on the mini-quiche and oatmeal cookies. The world would be a better place if everyone knew how to make oatmeal cookies.

My thoughts drifted to Jimmy as I beat the eggs with a wire whisk. Was he thinking of me? Did he regret what happened or did it bring a smile to his lips? Would my life ever be something I recognized?

I knew answers wouldn't come to me this morning.

Life felt out of control at the moment, and for a self-proclaimed control freak, that is not a good feeling.

If only there really was a recipe for a happy life...

Chapter Five

Every now and again, a customer will come into the bakery and I can feel a vibe from them—like we knew each other in a past life. It doesn't happen often, but when it does, it feels like magic.

It was this way with Aiden.

He stepped through the swinging door as if he hung it himself. Wide-eyed, he scanned the kitchen taking it all in, and he gave a low whistle. "I've died and gone to heaven," he declared.

Wiping my hands on my apron, I walked over to greet him. "You must be Shelly's friend," I said, regretting not asking his name was earlier. "I'm Linny Sinclair."

He gave me a hearty handshake. "I'm Aiden Nash," he said, smiling. "And I will do whatever you tell me if I can work in this kitchen with you."

"That's quite an introduction." His enthusiasm caught me by surprise. "Wash your hands over there and grab and apron," I said. "This interview won't be like any you've ever had."

His smile grew wide, and he bounced over to the sink. "You know," he said raising his voice over the running water and mixer, "I've never worked in a bakery before, but I was a barista for the past two years at Starbucks, so I have some experience."

"So you're good with customers, then?"

He was wrapping the tie around his waist and knotting behind his back. "Customers are everything," he said, smiling. "I knew they were coming to Starbucks because it's the standard, but I always made sure they came back because of the service."

It was rare to find someone his age that actually cared about customer service. He rolled up his sleeves and eyed me like I was performing magic, looking for the sleight of hand.

"Let's start by rolling out some dough for the mini pies," I said, sliding a rolling pin in his direction. "It's Friday Pie Day tomorrow, and I have the dough rolled out every Thursday morning." Giving him a ball of chilled dough, I explained how to start rolling it out from the middle out, adding flour when needed. He picked up on it quickly, shaping and molding the dough into perfect even circles.

"I can't believe I'm here and doing this," he said, smiling. "Shelly always sending me Snaps, and I've followed your Instagram from the beginning."

His personality was so inviting, I couldn't help but feel like he'd be the perfect addition to the bakery. Not that it should matter, but he was good looking too. Short, perfectly-styled brown hair and large brown eyes. He wasn't overly tall—at least five-nine—but he dressed as if he walked out of a J-Crew catalog.

"You're rolling that out like you've done that

before," I said. "So, tell me Aiden, what brings you to Frankfort?"

His expression dropped a bit. "I still live at home—been going to junior college for the past year—and it's just gotten to a point that I don't think I can stay there anymore. I'm not exactly living up to their expectations and wanted to get out of town for a few weeks. I'm taking online classes this semester, so I'll be able to keep up with school no matter where I end up."

"Won't your family worry about you? Do they know where you are?"

He sighed. "Unfortunately, I think they'll be relieved with my non-existence. I have a way of making them feel like they did something wrong."

"And how do you know Shelly?"

His face brightened immediately. "Actually, she's my second cousin. My dad and her mom are cousins and grew up together. Shell and I have always been more like friends than family though."

Now I understood why she felt so comfortable giving her job to Aiden temporarily. They were family.

He rolled out his third pie dough, each one better than the last. It took me a year to acquire that kind of technique consistently.

"Okay Aiden, let's get down to business," I said. "My husband is having some medical problems, and I'll need to be out of the bakery more than usual. How much time do you have available?"

He stopped rolling and looked up at me. "I am so sorry," he said. "Is everything okay?"

I paused, thinking he showed more concern than Shelly ever did. "He will be fine, but recently had a heart procedure. He'll be on the mend for about a month."

"My online courses are labs, so I can do the work whenever," he said. "Basically, I can work when you need me. I'm not afraid of long hours, and if I'm being honest, I'd rather work more and learn what I can while Shelly's gone. Our manager at Starbucks was starting to train me for assistant manager when I left, so I know I'm up for the task. As for the baking, I am a quick study."

How could I not give this kid a chance?

"You know, if you keep this up, I might not let you go in two weeks."

He blushed and flashed me the same smile I saw on Charlotte's face when she tied her shoes by herself for the first time. I felt comfortable around him, and knew he would affect the customers in the same way. Some people just had a charisma that put other people at ease. In sales, he was the gold standard. I knew this in my heart after ten minutes with him.

"Can I do the rest of these for you?" he asked, motioning to the pile of dough sitting in front of him.

"Of course you can," I said. "How long can you stay today?"

"As long as need me," he said. "There's not much to

do but sit in Shelly's apartment and watch TV."

"I will have to leave in a bit to get my husband home from the hospital. After that I'm not exactly sure what time I'll be back here. Shelly is staying till four o'clock today. Will you be okay staying that long?"

"Definitely," he confirmed. "I'll bug Shelly all day to teach me everything she knows, unless you have more things you want me to do in here."

"If you finish those, you'll be my hero," I said, washing my hands. "Also, there's a pretty good sound system if you're interested. I had it off for the interview, but you're welcome to use it if you want."

A slow smile spread across his face. "Music *and* baking? I have died and gone to heaven."

"If you're still willing to work here when I get back later, then we will discuss the pay and fill out the paperwork."

He walked to the sink, washed his hands, and started to scan the iPod for music. When he landed on Earth, Wind, and Fire it only confirmed my feeling that we were friends in a past life.

Some things you just know in your heart.

"Go, take care of your husband," he said. "I will see you later and fill out all the paperwork needed. I'm not going anywhere."

My phone vibrated with a text notification.

GRACIE: *Do you still want me to get the kids at school today?*

ME: *If you can... if not, I can get my mom.*

GRACIE: *Nope, they're mine. Just call the school and make sure I'm not arrested for child abduction.*

ME: *Good call.*

I reached to shake Aiden's hand, and he pulled me into a hug instead. "Thank you so much for this opportunity," he said.

There was no awkwardness that I usually felt being close to strangers. I had gained some weight in the last few years, and that made me shy away from physical contact. But this hug felt like someone was taking care of me. It felt like I could relax.

Pulling away, I grabbed my purse and bolted from the kitchen. It wasn't the hug that scared me, but the connection I felt with him. He understood me, and until that moment, I hadn't realized how desperately I longed for that feeling.

I blinked away tears as I tossed a goodbye to Shelly, who waved back from behind the counter. The sunshine and blue sky reminded me of playing on the beach as a little girl, and I wanted nothing but to run to a place and time when life seemed easier. Less alone. I didn't want to pick up my husband and pretend that life was going to be normal.

Even if I couldn't say the words out loud, I knew in my heart what I really wanted was a different life. A

life filled with more love.
A life filled with connections.

Chapter Six

The inscription read:

This journal belongs to my dearest friend, Linny.
At the end of the day, you can either focus on what's
tearing you apart, or what's holding you together.
Choose wisely.

September 20, 10:00 p.m.

How is it possible to be thirty years old and this is
my first official journal? I am not a journal writer.
They have never been my thing and getting my feelings
out on paper isn't what I'd call therapy. But Gracie did
buy this for me and made me promise I'd write in here
every night about what I was feeling.

As if I even have a clue.

Let's start with what I'm NOT feeling: Hopeful.

It's as if the one thing I had been fearing has come
true. I am trapped in this marriage... at least for the
time being, and my life is not my own. It's the same
hopeless feeling I had when Gordy cut things off. Oh,
how I wish I could talk to him right now and have him
tell me everything would be okay.

Barry came home from the hospital today, and I truly believe this is the most time we have ever spent together in the house. A part of me was hoping he'd be stuck at the hospital for a few more days, but it turns out his heart is 'recovering beautifully.' The doctor said, "After a few weeks at home, he should be able to ease back into his routine slowly. Of course his normal routine will need to be adjusted from here on out if you're going to keep that heart intact."

I felt like a fraud in the hospital as the part of the doting wife. He is still on his love-is-patient grind, and no one could hear me screaming inside. I wanted out of this marriage more than anything.

The kids thought it was a holiday since we were both there when Gracie brought them home from school. Their little faces brightened up and I swear Trevor was looking for presents.

Not sure what I'd do without Gracie either. She stayed at the house while I went back to check in at the bakery. Shelly and Aiden were busy prepping for the morning bake. Aiden seemed to be a natural—already comfortable with the kitchen. Shelly confirmed he was helpful all day and quickly picked up anything she showed him today.

He hugged me again when I gave him the paperwork. Not quite sure what to do about that. Feels awkward and true at the same time. Other than that, he's a keeper.

And now I'm sitting here, glass of wine beside me,

and I'm supposed to be pour my heart out in this beautiful little book. Everyone is asleep and it just occurred to me that this is my favorite time of day. That feeling of being alone, but not really... it feels safe to me. It feels like I've done my job of taking care of this family and my reward is a moment of peace. With everyone in bed I can be myself just for a moment. How rare it is that I get to just be me?

Amazing that I've never noticed this before...

The next morning, the first thing I noticed the about Aiden was the smirk planted on his face as he swung through the door. He unloaded his messenger bag by the desk and removed a framed picture. It said, "Cupcakes are muffins that believed in miracles."

It was perfect.

"Where can I hang this?" He smiled, holding it like an award he had just won.

"How about right above the iPod dock on the desk? We can find another place for the schedule later."

"Oh, trust me, I have big plans for this kitchen," he said, hanging his picture. "Or at least this space you loosely call a desk."

"Well, I'm open to suggestions," I said. "The baking area has always been my primary focus, and that's just kind of a junk space."

He shot me a look that said *obviously*. He grabbed an

apron and strolled over, singing along with Tom Petty, his eyes surveying some of the muffins I had sprinkled with sugar.

"Why do you do that?" he asked.

"I add a little sugar to the top to make them a little crispy and crinkly. It gives them a little oomph," I said.

"Muffin oomph," he said. "I like it. What else is on the docket this morning? Anything I can start for you?"

Looking around the kitchen, I noticed the first batch of banana chip muffins still in their pan. "Can you unload the muffins over there onto a display tray? The scones will be done soon and you can get those out too."

He started on the muffins even before I finished my sentence, humming along with the music.

"I have to say," he said, "your taste in music is spot on." His mood was infectious, and my shoulders started to loosen. "Who's your favorite artist or band of all time?"

Wracking my brain, the question caught me off guard. "Hmmm, let's see it would have to be a three-way tie between Stevie Wonder, Michael Jackson, and Lady Gaga."

"Stop." He froze and stared at me. "You're killing me."

"You don't approve?" It felt good to giggle.

"Uh, no, that's like the best three-way *ever*," he stopped when he realized what he said. "I mean, that's a great list."

"I love me some Gaga," I said. "And she sounds amazing in here. The acoustics makes her voice even stronger."

"You might be my sister from another mister," he said, shaking his head. "Everyone I know either likes rap or pop. Makes me want to invest in Beats."

Wiping sweat from my brow with the back of my hand, I glanced over at him as he worked. He had slim jeans on again today, and while most people can't pull them off, they looked good on him. He paired them with a gray long-sleeved T-shirt that was well worn, but still looked sharp, not sloppy. He also had an underlying sadness that was lurking beneath his looks and charm. He talked a good game, but his eyes spoke volumes to me.

"Knock-knock," Julia Dunham said, coming through the swinging door. "Hope I'm not intruding on your top-secret muffin making." Julia was Grace's mom, and I adored her growing up, despite their mother-daughter tension.

Wiping my hands, I pulled her into a hug. "Julia!" I looked at my watch. "Isn't this your writing time?"

"It is, but I wanted to check in and see how you were holding up." She grabbed a scone from the pan Aiden had cleared for me. "I wanted to pop in before you got too busy with the morning crowd."

"Aiden, this thief is Julia Dunham, and also my best friend's mom. She could show us all a thing or two about baking."

His eyes grew large. "Wait —*the* Julia Dunham? Best-selling *author* Julia Dunham?"

She held out her hand for him to shake, but he pulled her into a full body hug instead.

"Oof," she mumbled into his shoulder, limply patting his back.

"You're definitely better than the Walmart greeter, Aiden." She backed away, adjusting her shirt.

"Sorry for the assault, but I have read every one of your books. Some of them twice." He resumed unloading the scones from the tray. "You have helped me so much."

"You are too sweet, truly, but what on earth could you need from my books?"

His face clouded over with sadness for the briefest of moments. If I hadn't been watching him, I wouldn't have seen it, but it was there one second and back to normal the next.

"Everyone can use a little Julia wisdom in their lives," he quipped. The door slammed shut on whatever emotion had passed through him.

"It certainly is a pleasure to meet you," she said.

"The pleasure is mine," he replied, blushing.

"Julia, why don't we head out front and get some coffee to go with your stolen goods," I said, pulling off my apron. "I'll be a minute, Aiden."

"Take your time, boss lady," he said, sliding the muffins in the oven. "And Julia, I hope I get to see you again."

She tipped her head and her smile grew wide. "Aiden, don't you worry, I will make it a point to come see you again."

More blushing.

"So, how have you been?" she asked once we were seated with coffee and treats.

I took a deep breath and let it out slowly. "Well, I'm sure Gracie has shared with you my recent turn of event with my marriage," I began.

"She did," she said, nodding. "Health-wise, is Barry doing okay?"

"He is, and he's settled at home now."

"That's good," she said, sipping coffee. "You know, I've been digging a little online, and it's not so unusual for heart attack victims to wake up with a change of heart. They begin to see what a gift it is that they survived."

"I get that, Julia, I really do, but it's so hard to forget the years of animosity between us." I broke a piece off the corner of the scone and let it melt in my mouth. The calming effect was instant. "It's as if he doesn't remember any of it and wants to start over again."

"No one is expecting anything from you, Linny. Maybe not even Barry. I'm just looking at this from all sides. It's what I do. How are the kids handling all of this?"

THIS IS HOW A HEART BREAKS

I snorted. "Trevor thinks it's Christmas because Barry is actually home for a change. Charlotte has been quiet about all of it."

Her eyes softened. "Give it time and the answers will come to you. I promise. One of these days, you'll wake up and know what it is that you need." She sat back in her chair cradling her coffee in her hands. She belonged in a Folgers commercial. "The toughest answers take time. Your quick decisive nature won't fix this problem."

Damn, she knew me well.

I looked down at my plate and realized my scone was gone. *When did that happen?*

"And if I take my time and still want a divorce? Will I be able to live with that, Mrs. D?" It will never matter how old I am, she will always be Mrs. Dunham to me.

"If that's what you truly want, of course! That's the beauty here, there are no wrong answers. That's not to say any decision is going to be easy, though. There will be repercussions either way, but you have to figure out what *you* need. Everything else will fall into place then."

I leaned back in my chair, crossing my arms. Maybe everything would be okay.

"You always know what to say," I said. "How is that?"

"I've always seen the good in any situation, no matter how bad it is. There is always a reason something has come into our lives. Something we have to learn." She set her mug down and reached for my hand. "Our job is to figure out the lesson being taught."

Julia had lost her best friend and assistant this past summer, and I knew she was still learning too. "What have you learned from losing Jeri?"

Her eyes locked on mine. "To trust Gracie, not only as my daughter, but as my assistant." She squeezed my hand and released it. "And to trust myself, too. I'm still muddling my way through the rest. She didn't make it easy, leaving me so quickly."

"No, she didn't," I agreed.

"I do have to get back to work now," she said, glancing at her watch.

We stood and I hugged her, wishing I could talk to my own mom like this. My mom always had a way of making me feel guilty for whatever choices I made.

"I know you're afraid, Linny," she whispered, "but figuring out what your fears are will also help you understand what you need. The opposite of love isn't hate—it's indifference. The fact that this is so hard means you still care about something."

"That's exactly what I'm afraid of," I joked.

She squeezed my hand a final time and was out the door before I had the chance to beg her to stay and whisper advice to me all day.

If ever I needed a fairy godmother, this was the time.

Chapter Seven

After dinner I took advantage of my mom being over and headed back to the bakery to prep for the morning and close up. The night air was unseasonably warm as sunlight clung to the last few moments of the day, as if savoring the perfect dessert at the end of a meal. It didn't want to let go, but in a month, daylight saving time ends and darkness will engulf us at five o'clock.

The block was quiet since most businesses had closed for the day. Bob's Barber Shop was on one side of me and Queen's Dry Cleaning was on the other side. Their storefronts were traditional (okay *boring*), and Bab's sat between them like a beautiful frosting cream center. With both businesses open at the crack of dawn, I couldn't have found a better location.

The lights were off and it was quiet as I unlocked and entered my sacred space. I locked the door behind me and headed for the kitchen, only stopping to find John Mayer on my iPod. Once he was crooning I noticed my desk was organized. And not just organized, but Pinterest-worthy organization. Little baskets were hung on the right side, each serving a single purpose. The top one is for mail, the middle one is for pens and highlighters, and the bottom one has dividers with pushpins, paperclips, and tiny sticky notes. He had covered the desktop with a navy-blue gingham patterned paper, and a small vase of fresh tulips sat in the corner. He had also found two pictures of Charlotte and Trevor and hung them in frames on the left side of the space. Under the picture he brought in, he hung cork board for notes or schedules. A single sticky note was pinned to the center:

Tomorrow I tackle the files! A.

I had been smiling since I noticed it and couldn't remember the last time anyone did something like this for me. After snapping a picture and posting on Instagram (*Thank you, @ANash214!*), I found an apron and began the process of tomorrow. The easiest tasks each night are the scone and cookie doughs. I try to change it up each day with a variety, but keep the standard chocolate chip every single day. My Grandma Pauline passed this recipe to me, and it's the most precious recipe I possess. So many people have tried to replicate them, but this recipe will only be passed down to Charlotte when she's ready. The dough I could make in my sleep, and then I divide them into the serving sizes and store them in large Ziploc bags. It's a system that has served me well in the bakery. Tonight I'll save a few of the cookies and take them home to bake for the kids before bedtime.

I am so lost in the melancholy of the songs coming on that I suddenly find myself done in record time. For some reason I just want to get back home. The last batch of scones had just been placed in the fridge when

I heard a knock at the door. I peeked through the swinging door just in case it was a customer, and I saw Jimmy standing there. My stomach dropped and I stared at him, afraid to let him in.

His face was drawn in sadness as he motioned for me to open the door. He tipped his head and pleaded with his eyes, *please open the door,* they said to me. Slowly, I made my way and turned the bolt. I didn't notice him opening the door. He simply stood there, pulling me into him and shushing me. I cried on the shoulder of the man I wanted to sleep with a few days ago.

He pulled me towards the closest table and sat me down. Napkins appeared, and I wiped my eyes and nose before talking.

"You shouldn't be here…" I started to say.

"I should've been here two days ago," he said. "I didn't know what to do when I heard."

"Well there's nothing we can do. It's not like anything happened Jimmy." The words sound defensive, bitter.

"Linn, I'm not here to talk about what happened or didn't happen. I just want to see how you are. You must be so overwhelmed with everything."

In that moment, my thoughts rejected what he's saying. "I'm fine," I said. "My mom and Gracie are helping me around the house, but everything is fine. Barry is going to be good as new." The words came out so immediate, and I didn't know where they came from.

His eyes—locked on mine—weren't convinced. "Linny, it's okay not to be fine with me. I only want to help."

"No offense Jimmy, but your help can only get me in trouble." The words were cutting and came out before I knew how to stop them.

"You know that's not what I mean," he snapped. "We've been friends for a long time, and I thought you might want someone to talk to."

I started to tear the napkin into tiny pieces, letting them fall to the table in a pile like confetti. "Do you know what I was thinking of when the police officer came in to tell me my husband was in the hospital? I was thinking of us, Jimmy. You and me, pressed against the wall at Lakeside. And now I'm living with the guilt of knowing that if it were up to me, we wouldn't have stopped. I didn't want to stop," I whispered.

He continued to stare at me. "We can't change anything about that night. You were broken, and I shouldn't have let it go so far."

"This is just so complicated now," I sighed. "I just want to go back a week and change the direction of my life before it's out of my control."

"You can still do that," he said. "You just said Barry is going to be good as new, so get him through this and make your peace with him. Let him go."

"That's the joke in all of this, Jimmy." A bitter laugh escaped me. "He woke up and wants a new chance at our marriage. He wants me to give him a second chance to make it right."

The blank look on his face is comical. "What does that even mean? How can he just wake up and want a new life?"

"That's what I've been trying to figure out. He woke up completely different, changed, and I am so pissed off, I can't even think straight."

"Well, what are you going to do? Is he at home now?"

"Yes, he's home resting. My mom is watching the kids till I get back home," I said, looking at the clock above the kitchen door. "Which should be about now." I stood and swiped up the remnants of my napkin into my palm. "Do you need any baked goods?"

He stood and pulled me into another hug without saying anything. Anger boiled up as he held me. I was never going to feel this safe with Barry. I buried my face into Gordy's neck, simultaneously wanting the moment to end and last forever.

He pulled me back by the shoulders. "It may not seem like it right now, but everything is going to be okay," he said. "I promise."

If only he could keep such a promise to me. No one could.

"Thanks Jimmy," I managed. "I'm glad you stopped by, but it's probably best if we just see each other at Lakeside for the time being."

A faint smile crossed his lips as he leaned in to kiss

my forehead. "Take care Linn."

I turned back to the oven, but the echo of the bell above the door remained long after he left. That bell was a gift from my mom who insisted every bakery had to have one on the front door. It rang so often every day that I didn't even notice it until now.

And then there was just the silence.

Chapter Eight

The last batch of scones were cooling on the rack, the aroma of maple and brown sugar floating in the kitchen. The recipe was new, and I could tell by the smell that they were going to sell out. The lunch crowd lingered over second cups of coffee, and anxiety rose in my chest when I thought about going home. Barry had been hanging out around the house more now that he was feeling better, creating excruciating levels of awkwardness. The kids have buffered any of our time together, but I know I can't go on like this forever. Eventually the kids will start to pick up on the vibes we are giving off.

"Hey, Linny," Aiden popped his head in the doorway. "There's a guy out here who wants to talk to the owner."

I sighed. The last thing I wanted is a cold call from someone needing something else from me. With my bitch face on, I walked through the swinging doors. Aiden kept busy with the front counter, but I saw the left side of his mouth curved in a smile.

"Can I help you?" I asked the gentleman looking around the bakery. His initial presence startled me. He was lean, bald, and looked like he could snap Aiden in two if I asked him.

He held his hand out for me to shake. "Hi, I'm Tony." He was so soft-spoken, I almost thought he said he's stoned. I stifled a laugh at the thought and introduced myself.

"Your bakery is a great space," he said genuinely. His voice didn't match his image, and he continued to throw me off guard.

"Thank you," I said. "Is there something I can help you with?" I felt loud and larger than life standing near him.

"Do you mind if we sit?" He motioned to the corner table by the front window.

I looked at Aiden, and he smiled like a Cheshire cat. Normally, I'd tell this guy I didn't want what he was selling, but something about him made me curious. I felt compelled to know what the muscle head with the soft voice wanted.

"Sure, I have a few minutes before I have to get back to work," I said. "Can I get you something? Coffee?"

"Oh, no thank you. I'm good."

I followed him to the table and took the seat across from him. "So, what can I do for you?"

He pulled out a brochure and slid it across to me. "HOME BODIES" was written across the top in a bold red font.

"So," he started nervously, as if he's rehearsed this, but not enough. "I own a gym in town, and I'd like to start adding house calls to my services."

He paused for my reaction, but I gave him nothing. I

wanted him to get on with it.

"The gym hasn't done well yet. I mean, I just opened it two months ago, but I was hoping for a better outcome." He shifted in his seat. "I'm wondering if I'd be able to add some of my brochures around here, either on the tables or by the register maybe?"

His green eyes remind me of my dad's, and I can't help but want to help him for some reason.

"Home Bodies, huh? What *exactly* is that service?"

"Well, I know a lot of people are intimidated by coming to a gym, and I'd be willing to meet them either at their home or office—wherever they want, really— and help them with their fitness plans. You'd be surprised how many people just need a little nudge in the right direction."

The idea intrigued me.

"And," he continued, "I'd be willing to give you a one-month free trial if you'd help me out. I mean, if you're interested—not necessarily because you need it."

His face turned a dark red.

I looked out the window beside me, the mid-day sun warming the sidewalk. The words "if you're interested" replay in my head, and a closed-off space inside me opens up. Before I could second guess myself, I reached across the table to shake his hand. "You have yourself a deal. In fact," I continue, "I'll help you with some marketing ideas if you're interested. I'm pretty good at stuff like that." I sat back and folded my arms.

"Don't get me wrong," he said, forehead creased. "I'm grateful, but why would you do that? It seems like you might have your hands full here."

"That's true, my life is a mess right now," I said. "But I like this idea of Home Bodies, and I could use some help in that department myself. I think more women are like me and are definitely intimidated by going into a gym, but still need help."

He smiled. "You are *exactly* the kind of client I want to start working with, and I would love any help you want to throw my way."

"Well, I have to finish up in the kitchen, but when would be a good time to set up a meeting? I'm closed on Sundays… would that work for you?"

"Definitely, that works for me," he said. "I'm free the whole day, so pick the time that's best for you."

"How about ten o'clock Sunday morning? That way we can have the rest of our day to relax."

"That'd be great," he said. "And don't forget to have a list of health and fitness goals that you want. We will start with you, and then move onto business if there is time." He reached into his messenger bag and pulled out a thick stack of his Home Bodies brochures. "I'll leave these with you to put where you want. Thank you again so much." He turned to leave.

I stood and watched him go, wondering what the hell just happened. Health and fitness goals? I can't remember a time I had a health or fitness goal.

Probably never.

"That guy *totally* looked like Mr. Clean," Aiden said.

"He did, now that you mention it," I agreed. "He owns a gym in town and wants to get the word out, and I agreed to help him."

Aiden looked at me sideways but held his comments. He reached for the brochure and was looking at it when I went back into the kitchen.

I added the fresh scones to the display tray while I thought about what just happened. I've always prided myself on reading people and judging good character. The contradiction of his looks and personality threw me. I felt like I could trust him from the second he started talking, and that is not normal for me. People are usually suspect until proven otherwise, and trust is always earned.

So why did I fold so quickly with him? It didn't feel like attraction, but I did feel something like hope in the three minutes we talked. I shook my head and took the tray out to Aiden.

"So what do you get out of this if you're helping him?" He was being protective, which I found adorable.

"He is going to give me a one-month trial of the home training. We're meeting here on Sunday morning."

"Alone? Are you sure you can trust him, Linny?"

I laughed. "Believe me, he looks a little scary, but he really wasn't when I talked to him."

I went in back and grabbed my phone and bag. "I'm going to leave for a few hours. You can close at the normal time, and I'll cover the prep tonight."

He was still looking at me with concern, but he smiled. "Sounds good, boss lady. And if you need me to stay tonight, just say the word."

"Aiden, you are too good to me," I said. "I'll text you if anything comes up, but otherwise I'll just see you in the morning."

Chapter Nine

I left a half-hour early so I could try and compose my thoughts before Tony arrived at the bakery. It had been so long since I had even thought about goals for myself—other than bakery related—and I realized that I had let myself go. I couldn't even think of a goal other than make it through the day, just to get to bed every night.

I knew enough not to write this goal down.

The ten-minute drive to the bakery was frustrating this morning. I was blocked by road closings due to the Fall Colors Marathon, which had been going on in our town since I was a little girl. It surprised me, mostly because I had never seen it before and wondered how it was possible that year after year I had completely avoided such a big event in my own town. People come from all over Michigan and the UP to run this race. Our small town is invaded every year with all kinds of people, most you wouldn't guess were going to run a marathon. I made a small mental note to have marathon specials in the bakery next year. Maybe we should even open on this Sunday for the runners to treat themselves.

I found myself driving in a narrow lane with what appeared to be the last of the pack running the race. The orange cones divided my lane, and I had no idea how much longer they had to go, but for their sake, I hoped it was near the end.

There were two women wearing bright pink tutus slogging their way along the path. In front of them was a gentleman who appeared to have never trained for this event. His steps were sluggish and looked painful, both for him and myself watching.

I stopped at the light and watched the family and friends cheering all the runners on as they make the turn down Montgomery Street. One woman, slightly overweight and struggling, smiled brightly for one of the cheerleaders and gave him a high five, which made him cheer even louder for those behind her. Tears sprung to my eyes. I found her perseverance to keep running, just for the sake of finishing, inspiring.

I have never done anything in my life with that amount of perseverance.

Never.

And that's why I found myself deciding that running a marathon—*this* marathon, next year—was my goal.

"So have you thought about what kind of goals you would like to accomplish?"

We are seated at the same table as the other day, each with a bottle of water sitting in front of us. I suspect he is awaiting a safe but vague answer. Something like "lose weight" or "be more active."

"I'd like to run the Fall Color Marathon next year."

"Okay." He blinked. "Are you a runner?"

"Nope. I only run to the bathroom or kitchen." I laughed at my own joke, but he took out a notebook and opened up his calendar.

"Okay," he said, again. "That's quite a commitment, but if you are truly invested in this goal, we can make that happen. Are you willing to begin training three times a week starting tomorrow?"

I am shocked. He hadn't even cracked a smile about this. I assumed he would've chuckled and told me that marathons were for athletes, and that I should tackle something more doable for someone like myself.

"You're not concerned that this might be too big of a challenge?" I cracked my water and took a swig.

"You don't strike me as someone who takes anything lightly, and if you have the courage to admit that you want to run a marathon, then I fully believe you will accomplish it. Are you concerned?" His eyes narrowed on mine. "Has anyone ever told you that you can do anything you want? You don't need permission from me or anyone else," he said.

"I think I've been feeling trapped for a while, and that is the first time someone gave me my power back." Tears welled up in my eyes again. *What in the hell is going on with me?*

"Well, giddy up," he said, winking. "Don't get me wrong. You have picked the hardest goal you could possibly choose, and it's going to be hell if you find out you don't like running. But, on the other hand, when you cross that finish line one year from now, you will understand that there is nothing you can't accomplish."

"So you're saying I have a fifty-fifty chance."

"No," he said, shaking his head. "I'm saying you have a one hundred percent chance. But it could be ugly."

I nodded, uncomfortable under his gaze. "Are you waiting for me to change my mind?"

"Not at all, but I am wondering why you would have picked something so challenging to begin with."

I wondered how much I could tell him. "In a nutshell, my life is a hot mess. When I drove here this morning, I witnessed greatness coming from middle-age, overweight people who were out there running just because they could."

"I won't overstep, but the reason you want to run is also the reason your life is a hot mess. Eventually you're gonna have to face it head-on and deal with it."

"Awesome. Looking forward to that," I said.

A hint of a smile played on his face, and I couldn't help but smile too.

"So what we're going to do, at least for this month, is meet once a week. You have the option to meet at my gym and go over exercises that will help with the running, but you'll still have to hit the road or treadmill three times a week." He paused and took a drink of water. "Or, the other option is to meet like this, and we can go over what's working or not, and tackle more of the mental aspect of what you're going to do."

"I'm not gonna lie... tackling the mental is probably going to be like a marathon for you," I said.

The corner of his mouth twitched up again.

"For this first month, at least, we can meet like this. We can go over what worked, or didn't, and create the next week's goals." He wrote my name in the Sunday box for the following week. "Is this time okay for you every week? I can just go ahead and schedule them for the month if so."

I pulled up my calendar app on my phone to check the next few Sundays and the only thing we had were skating lessons on Sunday afternoons.

"Yes, this time works for me for the month," I confirmed, adding it to my calendar.

"Excellent. I will email you your game plan for the week tonight.

I took a deep breath, realizing for the first time what I have to do now. "So what else do you want from me? Do you want to go over any marketing strategies for Home Bodies?"

He looked down at his notebook again. "Do you have any ideas that don't require much funding?"

"Tony, you don't need a ton of money to create an online presence. Are you on Facebook or Twitter?"

He shook his head. "I was on Facebook for a while, but I didn't really see the point, ya know? It's like everyone is on there snooping into everyone's lives," he said. "And the whole Twitter thing confuses me."

"Well, you're going to make friends with both of them, because they are literally free marketing. There are a couple other social media avenues you can take, but let's just start with these."

He nodded and flipped the page on his notepad. "Gotcha. What's the first step?"

"Let me set up a game plan for you as well, and I'll email that to you tonight? That way we both will have what needs to be done in writing," I said. "And I will even promise my game plan for you is going to be way easier than mine."

His smile lit up his whole face. "It's not good to dread the workouts before I even send them to you. In order to succeed, you must first believe that you can."

"Isn't it enough that I committed to a marathon? I have to believe in myself too?"

"Actually, you have to believe in yourself first, then you can do whatever you want. Most people have it backwards, thinking that setting a goal is going to change their lives. It has to start with believing you can accomplish what you want to do."

"You make it sound so simple, believing in yourself."

"If it were simple, then everyone would be happy," he said. "We live in a world where everyone is on the fast track to nowhere, chasing the perfect life, and I think you might be on that same track." He looked around my quaint bakery. "This space is so full of perfection, right down to the napkins, but I can't help but see how unhappy you really are."

"You're right," I said, folding my arms. "The napkins are perfect."

He stared at me, eyebrows raised, waiting for more.

"And I'm unhappy," I admitted.

"Okay," he said looking down at his notepad. "Looks like we both have a place to begin."

"I believe we do," I said, standing. "Here is my business card with my email. I will reply to yours tonight with strict instructions for social media dominance."

"Do you always deflect everything with humor?" He was smiling, but his eyes were serious.

"Yes," I said. "And someday you'll find me funny."

He sighed. "I doubt that, but I guess I can't stop you."

This statement made me smile for some reason. I unlocked the door for him and shook his extended hand. "Here's to the beginning," I said.

"Linny, I'll be in touch. Have a good week."

"You do the same, and I'll be looking for you online."

He shook his head and smiled.

The lock clicked into place and I watched him walk down the street. He looked back once, and I turned quickly, feeling busted. There was a napkin on the floor under the table where we were sitting. I picked it up and noticed writing on the blank side.

This perfect napkin was created by YOU.

My heart swelled, and I took the napkin and pinned

it to my bulletin board in the kitchen. I felt better already and looked forward to the rest of my day.

Chapter Ten

From: Tony Trainer <trainertony16@gmail.com>
To: Linny Sinclair <linnsin16@gmail.com>
Subject: Home Bodies Week 1 Plan

Linny,

Here is your plan for week 1, plus some questions at the bottom I'd like you to answer and email back to me. Answer honestly, please. The more honest you are with yourself, the better this process with go.

Please let me know if you have any other questions.

1. Walking only this week.
   Monday/Wednesday/Friday for 25-30 minutes each.
2. There is an app called Lose It. You will download and register. It doesn't matter to me if you lose weight, but I do want you to be healthy and see what you are consuming each day. I won't be checking this unless you want me to, but you need to start treating your body like an athlete would. This first week is for tracking only... Simply track EVERYTHING you eat.
3. Come up with ONE WORD this week that will become your focus for the year that you're

training for the marathon. It can be anything, but it must mean something significant to you. Examples: Power, Faith, Journey, or Happiness. Pick something that will motivate you on days when you need some motivation. This is your word, so choose wisely.

Questions (Please hit reply and answer)

- What do you want to feel when you are done with the marathon?
- If you could change one thing about yourself, what would it be?
- Other than the marathon (which is a BIG deal), what are some other goals you're hoping to achieve by working out?
- Give me 5 words to describe yourself.

Please respond by Monday morning if possible.

Tony
231-555-7283
Allow yourself to be a beginner. No one starts off being excellent.

"Courage doesn't happen when you have all the answers. It happens when you are ready to face the questions you have been avoiding your whole life."
— Shannon L. Alder

From: Linny Sinclair <linnsin16@gmail.com>
To: Tony Trainer <trainertony16@gmail.com>
Subject: RE: Home Bodies Week 1 Plan

Hi Tony, thanks for your email. At this point I'm wondering what the hell I signed up for, but don't worry, I won't quit before I start. I signed up for Lose It and set a goal of 20 lbs in 3 months. Does that sound about right? I'll be honest, I've never been one to count calories, so I imagine this is going to be an interesting week.

I'll think about the one word as well and let you know Sunday, but I'm thinking it's going to be something like Hell.

Questions answered

- What do I want to feel when I'm done with the marathon?
  I want to feel two hands on my back, giving me a full body massage.
- If you could change one thing about yourself...
  Can "everything" be an answer? Too vague? Well, I guess I would change my DNA to that of a thin person.
- Other goals (besides the BIG marathon)...
  Honestly, I'd just like to get through the marathon without needing any kind of reconstructive surgery at the end of the race. I

would like to keep my original knees and hips
if possible.
- 5 words that describe me...
  introvert / hardworking / funny / generous /
  friend

TONY'S HOMEWORK FOR THE WEEK!!!
1. Your only job this week is to make friends with social media. You will create business accounts for Facebook, Twitter, and Instagram. You don't need to post anything yet, and when we meet next Sunday, I will show you how to use each of them to boost followers. Followers = Clients

If you have any questions, don't hesitate to text me. I'm better at text than email. And for God's sake, don't ever leave me a voicemail... I won't ever hear it.

Linny
231-555-2253

My calves hurt. My shins hurt. It was only Tuesday, but the weight of what I committed to settled on my shoulders yesterday during my first walk and it felt daunting to me now. A vision of Britney Spears with that enormous yellow snake draped around her shoulders was how the weight felt.

Like I said, daunting.

My planner looked like that of a serial killer. Scribbles of bits and pieces I'd eaten all day littered the page, and I'd spent the last twenty minutes trying to figure out how to log "a smidge of cookie dough" and other equally nutritious choices. My second glass of wine has been mocking me, daring me not to log it in, but I did, and realized that I am well over my allotted caloric intake for the day.

And today was a *good* day.

Barry had been reading Harry Potter to Charlotte every night for the past week. They were almost done with the first book, and both of them couldn't wait to see what happened next. Of course, I knew what happened next, but would never give away any wizarding secrets. I started the series when we were on our honeymoon and finished when I was pregnant with Trevor. Hearing the words again brought me back to that magical time of being so full of hope.

I was lost in thought, and it was the silence that startled me. When I looked over, Barry and Charlotte were both staring at me.

"What are you working on over there?" he asked.

I shook my head. "Nothing, really. Mostly I'm listening to you right now."

He closed the book and kissed the top of her head, a mop of curls loosely pulled into a hair tie. "I'll be right back, Pumpkin."

She followed him to the kitchen where I was sitting

and pulled herself up into my lap.

"Everything okay with the bakery?" He was digging for answers.

"Actually the bakery is having a great month. We're about five percent over last year at this time." I took a sip of wine and wondered if I could trust him. "I, uh, started a training program this week. Yesterday, in fact. And I'm just trying to figure out this new app I have on my phone."

His eyes lit up with a glimmer of amusement. "Linn, that's great," he said, genuinely. "What made you start this? You're already so busy."

"Well, this trainer came into the shop the other day and offered me a free month of training if I helped him with some marketing ideas. I didn't take it seriously, but on my way to meet with him, I just decided it was time."

"Time?"

"Time to take care of myself for a change," I said. It came out harsher than I intended.

"I know I have put a huge strain on you these past few weeks," he said. "Probably these last few years, if I'm being honest."

Charlotte started doodling rainbows in my planner, but I know she is listening. Barry looked at her as well and nodded. He grabbed my hand on the table and gave it a squeeze. "All I want is for you to be happy," he said.

Tears pricked my eyes, and I shifted Charlotte off my

lap. "I don't even know what that is anymore." I stood and dumped out the remainder of my wine and rinsed out the glass. "But I guarantee I'm going to find it," I said.

He smiled, and I noticed the spark in his eye again. Before tonight, I couldn't remember the last time he looked at me like that. That look was both comforting and concerning to me at the same time. I still didn't know if I wanted to continue this marriage or not. I felt like a fraud in my own home, and more than anything I wanted to hide from everyone. The last few years has felt like everyone I knew wanted a piece of me. Hiring Tony made me realize how much I had been sacrificing and what I wanted back.

"Why don't you go in and read something, anything," he said. "Trevor is already crashed, and I can get Char into bed." She looked up at him, eyebrows raised. "Yes, we'll finish that chapter."

When was the last time I picked up a novel? The idea had me intrigued. Felt like years, long before the bakery was up and running.

I closed my planner and grabbed my iPad out of my bag. I would have to find something to read, since I hadn't purchased any books recently. Snuggled in bed, I quickly found a title that looked like something I'd want to read. *Happiness for Beginners* sounded like something written personally for me, and it downloaded in seconds. Before long I was wrapped up in someone else's story. To be able to escape your own world for a moment and follow the path of another felt luxurious and relaxing.

The lights were off when I woke up, and I was tucked in bed. I vaguely remember Barry coming in to check on me, but he must have gone back to his own room. I could hear the waves off Lake Michigan even through the closed window. The idea of winter made me snuggle deeper into the blankets, and it was no time before I fell back into a dreamless sleep.

Chapter Eleven

It was Sunday morning, and I had N'SYNC blaring in the bakery. I had a crush on Justin Timberlake long before he was an uber-star.

I had been on a mission to stock up on many of the doughs so we had less prep time during the week. In other words, I was trying to find some more time to walk.

After completing the first week, I was hooked. My legs hadn't ached like that since I was in college and had taken a skating class. I made it through the class and noticed my legs had actually changed their shape. A lot of girls hated muscular legs, but they made me feel sexy somehow, more powerful. Pain or no pain, I longed to see those legs again.

The bell on my front door jingled, and I waited for Gracie to walk through the kitchen door.

She inhaled deeply, eyes closed, and a smile on her face. "Do you know this is my favorite smell in the whole world?" she asked. "Even better than the beach."

"Wow, that's some compliment," I said, wiping my hands to hug her.

She immediately started to sway and sing to our high school obsession.

"You can grab something out of the case up front if you want," I said. "Fresh pot is on too."

Her eyes lit up and she left the kitchen as fast as she came in. I followed her out, needing some coffee myself. She had been coming here at odd times to write while I worked. We kept each other company sometimes, but mostly we just did our work, happy the other one was there.

Poking her nose in the glass case, she plated several lemon cookies. The coffee steamed in the ceramic mugs, and I inhaled its heady scent as I carried them back to the kitchen.

"Soooo, tell me about your week," she said. "More importantly, why are you here busting your ass on a Sunday morning when this is supposed to be your only day off?"

"First, let me tell you how much I love your last post," I said. "This book you're writing sounds like I should be proofing it for you."

Gracie covered her face with her hands, smiling.

"No, really, Gracie. It's good," I said. I sipped my coffee and felt my shoulders begin to loosen. "And I'm here this early so I can meet with my trainer at ten."

"A trainer? You're working out? Linny, that's awesome," she beamed. "Tell me, how did this happen?" She bit into a cookie and her eyes rolled back into her head. "Damn you and these cookies."

"This guy stopped in last week—Tony—and asked if he could leave flyers for his personal training business in here. Said he'd give me a free month if I did, so I accepted!"

"Linn, I'm so happy for you," she said. "You're so busy already, but I know this is something that will make you feel better. It's like therapy."

"Exactly. I already feel a little better," I said. "Sore as hell, but good." I set my coffee down to wash my hands. "How's your week? Your mom's book is out in November, right?"

Gracie worked for her mom, so I knew life was going to get a lot busier for them around the holidays.

"Yes, we will be doing a major book tour in the first two weeks of December. I'm excited and terrified at the same time."

"Have no fear, you'll handle it easily, like you do everything else." I started the mixer again, needing to get the dough done before Tony arrived.

Gracie pulled out her laptop and fired it up. "I hope you're right about that. One thing I know is I'll be taking notes the entire time for when my own book comes out."

"Do you have a date yet?"

"It's too early to tell," she said, sliding on her glasses. "But I'm hoping early next summer."

I smiled, thinking of how far she has come this past year. Her life hadn't been easy, but she was making the most of it.

Would I be able to say the same about myself in a year?

Life with Grace

Book News!

October 1 at 9:47 a.m. || 43 Comments

My dearest friend is a baker. An exceptional baker. While my only claim to fame is a single batch of cookies, I have sat in her kitchen, keeping her company, singing along to a magical playlist, and watched her. Not in a creepy way... more like studying. I think if she knew I was inspecting her so closely, she would've kicked me out, so I pretended I was there for the company and atmosphere.
It's a great atmosphere. Perfect for writing.

Have I mentioned I'm writing a book? Following in my mother's footsteps, I've decided that this past year has taught me too much about life not to share with others. Everyone has baggage or problems. E V E R Y O N E. But how we deal with them is what sets us apart. Some people tackle them head on, while others take the wait-and-see approach. There is no right or wrong answer. Just options.

My original title was going to be *The Four Cornerstones,* but it just never felt like something I'd pick up and read myself. After a week in her bakery I realized the title — *the only title* — had to be *The Four Ingredients.* Our lives, like her tasty treats, are a mixture of ingredients that, when mixed in proper amounts, will produce something inspired. Heavenly, even.

My book isn't about changing your life or even creating a new one. It's about accepting the one you have—good, bad, and ugly—and figuring out how to keep the good and get rid of the bad and ugly. It's about naming four priorities in your life and giving them daily focus.

Knowing what's important in your life and bringing it to the forefront of your brain is the only way we can make any lasting changes. These four ingredients create the life you've been waiting for. Do you want to travel? Be a better parent? A better spouse? Is your job killing you, literally, from the stress? These are the questions that will get you started.
Narrowing down to just four is going to be the biggest challenge, but I will help you figure that out. So what are you waiting for?

Together we will create something spectacular...

Chapter Twelve

Another long week passed, and it was unseasonably warm on this Sunday morning. I'd been contemplating my life, sitting on the beach in my favorite spot, and listening to the waves crashing in. Our backyard opened up to Lake Michigan, and there was a bit of a drop where the grass met the beach. To me, it's always been ledge—a grassy one—but still, a ledge I sat upon, nonetheless. The day we moved into this house, passed down from his family, I escaped the chaos by sitting in this spot and watching the sunset. The grass was now worn away in this area, like carpet, and didn't grow here any longer. But a towel did the trick.

I didn't hear his footsteps behind me, mostly because I'd been lost in thought while watching the waves. He handed me a cup of coffee, then sat to join me, a small smile on his mouth.

To a passerby, we would look like two kids, feet dangling, watching the waves. The coffee was hot, but he had added the perfect amount of cream, making it a sandy brown shade. Perhaps he had paid attention more than I thought.

He was quiet beside me, but still smiling.

"Okay," I said. "What gives?"

He glanced my way and reached into the pocket on

his sweatshirt. Pulling out a folded-up piece of paper, my heart stops at the sight of it. I knew exactly what it was before it was even unfolded: The Ten-Year List

"Where did you find that?" My voice came out in a hushed whisper.

As he unfolded it, I was anxious to see the writing again. The familiar scrawl of someone who had too many strawberry daiquiris on a cruise ship.

"It was in the back of the Harry Potter book I'm reading to Charlotte, tucked tightly in between the pages."

"That's right," I said, reaching for it. "I was reading that on our honeymoon."

After a failed attempt to write on a napkin, we borrowed the paper from the bartender, who had a notepad behind the bar. "I'm a writer," she had said, shrugging.

The yellow paper appeared the same as it did back then, the book preserving the memory in its magical pages. Looking at the list now, my skin had gone cold. Barry hadn't said much, but he was still smiling like he had a secret.

"I can't believe you found this," I said.

Run a 5k.

Go camping.

Visit winery.

"Linn, I think it's a sign," he blurted out. "I think I found it because we're supposed to do these things on the list."

His eyes were watery, but his voice dripped with hope.

"Barry," I said. A dread filled me. We can't go through this list.

"Just hear me out, Linn." His voice is more determined than mine. He had already decided that this is going to save us.

I folded the list and gave it back to him. I didn't want it anymore.

"Linn, we are almost six months away from our tenth anniversary. And I know you want out," he said, running his hand through his hair. "But give me six months. Give me this time to prove that we can make it work."

The wind blew my hair out of my face in a *whoosh*. A defeated feeling settled in my chest. "And what happens if we go through this six months, and I still feel the same way? Will you let me go then?"

"Not exactly the feeling I want to focus on now, but yes, I would let you go if you still wanted out."

I glanced at the list in his hands, the memory of writing it so fresh in my mind.

Bonfire party by the lake.

Read the same book.

Adopt a puppy.

Road trip.

The list seemed trivial now. We were so young, and we created it to make sure we would never grow apart. I never saw that list after our honeymoon.

"Please, Linn. Give me a chance."

I hated that he thought this is a sign. Did he think this would erase the last nine and a half years?

***

The honeymoon was over shortly after we walked off the plane. Barry's cell phone rang while we waited for the luggage to come around the carousel.

"What do you mean they're suing us for liable?" he yelled. His face twisted in fear. Tiny sweat beads appeared in his hairline.

People were looking at us, tanned and weathered, and he was raising his voice like he was in his office.

"Shhh. Keep it down," I said.

He snapped me a look I had never seen before. Anger. Sure, I had seen his anger, but never towards me. And that look didn't belong here, at the end of our honeymoon, so full of hope.

I walked away from him, blinking back tears, and scanned the bags for the bright pink ribbon I had attached before the trip.

***

"What are you thinking?" He broke the silence. "Your eyes look so sad."

I shook the memory from my brain. "Nothing," I said. "I remembered something I hadn't thought of in a long time."

He waved the list like a winning lottery ticket. "What do you think? Can we give this a shot?"

Every fiber in me screamed *"no!"* I wanted out. I wanted space. I wanted to be alone. "I guess I could try for six months, as long as you are willing to walk away at that point if it's not working."

"And to think you used to be the romantic one. I'll need to up my game if this is the case."

I forgot he used to be funny, and I felt the corner of my mouth lift involuntarily. That was something he would've said when we were dating.

"I have to get to my meeting with my trainer," I said, standing.

He joined me and we walked up the deck stairs, with his pace far slower than mine. He looked so frail, taking the stairs slowly, one by one, but his eyes were twinkling when he reached the top.

"Little victories," he said.

How he managed to talk me into giving him six months of my life, I didn't understand. Agreeing to it felt like a betrayal to myself, going against my gut instincts, but I found myself unable to break his already broken heart. At least in six months he will be back on his feet, and I won't have to worry about his health.

We will split amicably and find ourselves happier in the long run. Maybe this time will help him also understand how different we are now than when we married.

Chapter Thirteen

"You do understand these baked goods aren't off limits, but should be moderated, right?" He was eyeing my plate, where a blueberry muffin sat.

"Balance, my dear Tony. Balance," I said. "Besides, there's no way I'll eat the whole thing."

He raised his eyebrows, still taking notes. What was he writing about me?

"I used to eat two of these, with coffee, and not even taste it. It was automatic," I said, taking a sip of coffee. "Now, I eat every bite, every morsel, as if it were my last."

These Sunday "meetings" were becoming something I looked forward to. His quiet demeanor unsettled me, and I found myself nervously talking and saying more than I ever would to someone I didn't know well. He was becoming a therapist.

"You're saying that you don't feel the urge to overeat any longer?"

"Not at all," I said. "I'll admit I still want to stuff myself silly and get rid of the feelings, but someone gave me a tip: set a timer for ten minutes to eat something. No rushing. No inhaling. Just savoring." I broke off a piece of the topping and popped it in my mouth. The brown sugar crumble melted on my tongue, and my eyes closed in satisfaction. "Did I ever tell you that 'savor' is my word?"

He shook his head slowly, smiling as he wrote that down. "Savor, huh? What is the significance for you?"

"After a week of not knowing what to pick, it dawned on me one day when my friend Gracie was here. She ate a cookie like she was making love to it," I said, laughing. "She ate that damn cookie like it was the last cookie she'd ever have."

His blank stare was so disarming. Once again, I found myself talking, just to fill the space.

"Anyways, I started realizing that I don't give anything in my life that kind of attention. Not my kids, not my work, *nothing*. I literally go through the day on autopilot and never stop to savor anything. Somewhere along the line, I stopped living."

"Interesting." His laser attention made me want to forget about savoring anything.

"Interesting good or bad?" I asked. "You'll need to work on facial expressions if you want to keep clients."

The side of his mouth lifted. "You're still here, aren't you?"

"Wow. Tony with a sense of humor," I joked. "Small, but it's there, under all those muscles."

Full smile. His downcast eyes crinkled in the corners.

He cleared his throat. "Can we get back to your word? What has changed now that you're thinking about it?"

"Everything," I said, simply. "At least on the inside.

My life isn't really any different, but how I'm living it seems to be different."

"In what way?"

"In a way that forces me to be more present. I mean, I'm still me, so it's not perfect, but I definitely notice things more during the day. Little things, like how freaking good this blueberry muffin is with coffee. Or the fact that Trevor knows every line to the movie *Cars*. Or seeing Charlotte's face light up when I pick her up from school. I've gone so long wrapped up in my own drama without seeing what was right in front of me."

"I'm impressed," he said, leaning back, arms folded. "With all your deflection and sarcasm, I expected you to be a tougher cookie to crack."

"Two points for bakery humor."

He rolled his eyes at me. "Go back to the timer when you eat. Do you find yourself hungrier during the day?"

"Not really," I said, shrugging. "I stop eating after the first ten and wait a few minutes to see if I truly still hungry. If I am, I eat, but more often than not, I find that I don't need any more food." I pushed away my plate to prove my point. "My main problem has always been eating when I'm not hungry. I'll eat because I'm bored, or mad. You name the emotion, and I'll find a coordinating food for it. I've been eating to get through the day, but now I have a better handle on it. Eating only when I'm hungry and slowing it down has given me a little control back."

"Huh," he said, more scribbling. "I may have to steal that advice for another client."

"I noticed your Facebook page is doing really well. You're getting more followers every day," I said.

"Yeah, the daily motivation advice was gold. People started sharing them almost immediately, and it's taken off," he said. He leaned back in the chair, arms folded. "Tell me how the first week of running went."

"I wouldn't call myself a runner yet, and the brief moments I did run during my walks were uncomfortable. I couldn't find a rhythm and just ended up panting even after one minute."

"Rhythm is the key to running," he confirmed, eyes still studying me. "And the key to rhythm is breath. Focus on your breath the next time you go out."

"How about you? Are the clients coming in faster now?"

A slow smile spread across his face. "I always knew the idea of Home Bodies would take off if people just got it, you know? But I had no idea how fast it could happen." He leaned forward on the table, resting on his elbows. "Granted, most of them have just signed up for the first month discount, but I believe they will stay on once they see a difference."

"Make sure you're not giving everything away," I said. "You have to lure them into a state of wanting more, so at the end of the trial, they have to keep you on. And you have to offer them something they're not getting from anyone else."

He raised his eyebrows.

"Not that, you dummy," I said. "This. What we do here. I don't get this from anyone else, and I would happily pay for it each month."

His brow furrowed. "But all we're doing is talking," he said. "Why would you pay for that?"

"It's not about talking. It's the connection, the understanding, and making me feel like I can actually do something like run a marathon."

"But you *can* run a marathon. You can do anything you want if you set your mind to it."

"Exactly!" I hit my fist on the table, jolting him. "I think most people in my life would've laughed or told me to work towards a 5K instead. You didn't even blink when I told you my goal."

"My job isn't to judge the goal or the person. It's to make the goal happen. Set a goal, see the path."

I chuckled and folded my arms. "And that's the beauty. I'm so used to my limitations I don't even know they're there, until I see something from your point of view." I sipped the last of my coffee. "For the record, most people think like me and not you. That's why they'll pay. You give them hope."

"I think you're giving me a little too much credit, but I'll take your word for it. I'm not in the market for false hope, though. If they expect to lose twenty-five pounds in a month, I'll be honest with my opinion." His watch beeped and he glanced at it. "Unfortunately, that's my cue. I have an 11:15 back at the gym."

"And I have to get back home," I said.

He stood and threw his water bottle away. "How's it going at home? Is your husband doing okay?"

"Yeah, he's doing well," I said limply.

He cocked his head. "I know there's a story there. When you're ready, that might help release some of the baggage that's holding you back."

"Yes, Obi-Wan," I said. "Whatever you say."

He stared at me with a blank look.

"One of these days, you're going to laugh at something I say."

He raised an eyebrow. "I doubt it, but I like that keep trying. Shows tenacity."

I giggled.

"Go, get out of here. Miss 11:15 is waiting for you," I smirked.

His face turned crimson as he walked out the door. He glanced back, just like the very first time, and gave me a wave.

I knew this one conversation would carry me through the rest of the day, whatever that may hold.

The dreaded honeymoon list would weigh on me this week, but how could I say no to him? What was six months in the grand scheme of things?

Part Two:
Hope

Chapter Fourteen

The leaves blanketed the ground, and I had to stay focused not to step off the sidewalk or trip on a curb. The *crunch, crunch, crunch* my feet made hitting the leaves helped me find my rhythm. Matching my breath to it was easier than I thought. I found myself enjoying the running portion of my walks more. They were still ninety seconds at a time, but the walking time also decreased.

I found myself energized and exhausted at the end of every walk.

Barry and the kids were outside when I walked up the sidewalk towards our home. The kids were jittery with excitement—over what I had no idea. Barry stood with them, holding Charlotte's hand as she jumped around, excited to see me.

"Mommy!" she exclaimed when she spotted me. "Mommy! We have a surprise for you!"

Oh God. What now?

I pulled my headphones off as Trevor ran towards me to wrap his arms around my legs. I pulled him up into a hug.

"What is all this excitement for?" I asked, kissing his cheek. He buried his face in my neck and giggled.

"Daddy said we couldn't ruin the surprise," he said.

"But I'm home now," I whispered in his ear. "You

can tell me now."

"Can we Daddy? Can we show her the surprise?" His tiny body vibrated with excitement.

Show me?

"Okay, what gives?" I set Trevor down and grabbed his hand. "What's going on here?"

Barry looked at Charlotte. "Should we show her?"

She nodded vigorously.

"Stay right here," he said, walking towards the front door. "And you might want to cover your eyes."

Charlotte and Trevor started jumping up and down. "Mommy, cover your eyes! Don't ruin the surprise!"

Grudgingly, I covered my eyes, causing more fits of squeals and giggles. I heard the front door shut and Barry laughing softly. When was the last time I heard Barry laugh? I couldn't remember.

Barry's footsteps stopped close to me. I found myself smiling, wanting to see what all the fuss was about.

"Are you ready?" he whispered. The hairs on the back of my neck stood up. Charlotte giggled again.

Slowly, I pulled my hands off my eyes. Barry stood there, grinning and with tears in his eyes as he held the tiniest puppy I have ever seen. A brown and white furball.

Instinctively, I reached for the tiny creature. "Ohhhh," I said. "Whose puppy is this?"

"It's ours Linn." He wiped his eyes. "A client of mine breeds Corgis and said this one was the runt. Said no one would take her."

I buried my face in her neck and she licked my face. Her little body shook with the same excitement of the kids. I sat on the grass and cradled her like a baby.

"Barry, have you lost your mind? We can't have a puppy with our busy schedules." Even as I said the words, I knew she was ours. There was no going back. The kids sat with me and petted her, showering her with love, faces beaming.

She whimpered and I set her on the grass. She crawled to Trevor, climbing up his legs and reaching up to give him kisses. He laid back on the grass, laughing, as she crawled up his chest and sat down.

I looked at Barry. His eyes glistened as he looked from Trevor to me. A lopsided smile covered his face and I saw a man I used to know, long before the tension and bitterness. I broke my gaze and focused on the dog again.

"Does she have a name yet?"

"The owners have called her Minnie since she was born, but they said we could change it and she'd figure it out."

"What do you think, guys? Do we want to keep her Minnie or change to something different?"

She was crawling on Charlotte now, sneaking kisses any chance she could.

"Not sure I get a vote, but I think we should give her our own name," Barry said. "Make her our own."

I snatched her from Charlotte's lap and brought her nose to nose with me. "What do you look like, sweet girl?" She kissed my nose like she was licking frosting off a cupcake. I snapped a look to Barry.

"What about Cupcake?"

"Cupcake the Corgi?" he questioned, smiling.

"Yes! Cupcake the Corgi!" the kids echoed.

"I think that is the best name we could give her. She's sweet and a little fluffy, just like a cupcake."

"Do we have anything she needs? A collar? Food?" It was amazing how fast I went into nurture mode for this creature I had just met. He was right, naming her made her ours.

"I have food from the owners, and she was just beginning potty training there," he said. "They also let me borrow a small crate for her. We can get more supplies tomorrow."

He bent down carefully to pick her up and nuzzled her to his face. "Who's a pretty girl?" he cooed. Her stubby tail attempted to wag. "Kids, let's start getting ready for dinner. I'm going to see if I can get her to go potty before I bring her back in."

I grabbed the kids' hands and walked up the steps to our front porch. Glancing back, I spied him setting Cupcake down and following closely behind her. I shook my head, watching both of them. A puppy was going to turn our lives upside down.

Maybe upside down was what our lives needed right now. The last month has proven that the straight path did us no favors, and we needed things shaken up a bit.

"Isn't she perfect, Mommy?" Charlotte was even

more smitten than I was.

"Char, this was the best surprise, ever," I said. "Puppies are a lot of work, though. We're all going to help with her, right?"

"Can she sleep in my bed?" Trevor asked, eyes lit up.

Cupcake wouldn't last ten minutes in his bed. Trevor slept like a big-time wrestler.

"Oh, honey, I think Cupcake is going to need her own bed for the time being. She's too small and would get lost in your bed. Now, what's for dinner tonight, kiddos?"

"Pizza!" they shouted together.

I glanced at Barry who was watching us. He shrugged his shoulders. Who was I to argue with pizza?

"Pizza it is," I confirmed. "Let's wash our hands, and I'll order it."

Doubt crept into my head as I let the warm water run over my hands. Could it be as easy as getting a puppy? I knew it was on the list, but this felt like we were trying too hard.

Look at us! We're saving our marriage! Who attempts to save the marriage with a puppy?

I heard tiny nails on the tile floor and looked down. A small voice in my head answered my own question.

We do. We save our marriage with a puppy.

October 20th

It is 2:15 a.m., and I can't sleep. Cupcake is whining every hour, on the hour, and wanting out of her crate. I made some tea to help calm my nerves, but this feels so much like the first month of motherhood, I want to scream.

Memories have been flooding my head from that time. Resentment, my favorite blanket, is weighing me down—even as I sit with her sleeping in the crook of my left arm. Being a new mom was emotional enough, but throw in a husband who worked eighty-hour weeks to make partner, and all hell broke loose. It was the first time I realized my dream of the perfect marriage, the perfect family, was just a lie.

An ugly fucking lie.

My mind keeps reliving our lives back then. Barry was as hands-off as a parent could be. Sometimes, he even forgot we had Charlotte if she was in her crib sleeping. Distracted. Edgy. Driven. That's the Barry I know, and I believe that's who he still is to this day. This new Barry will blow over, once Cupcake chews a hole in his shoe.

This Barry? The one I fell in love with and agreed to marry... he's just a memory now. I can't let my guard down, because I know he will go back to normal as soon as he's feeling himself again. I have to be prepared for that moment. I have to protect myself and the kids, and this little fluffball I can't stop looking at.

Chapter Fifteen

It had been a week since Barry brought Cupcake home and turned our lives upside down. Even Barry had begun to wonder if getting a puppy was the right decision. My nerves were frayed due to lack of sleep, and my mood had carried over to my family. Last night, I snapped at Charlotte for practicing her recorder—which was homework, but still. Those recorders should be practiced at school, and only with the teacher present. There isn't enough wine in our home to listen to *that* every night.

Why does a fourth grader need to learn the recorder anyway? It's a device used to torture parents.

After Barry put Charlotte to bed, he came back to the kitchen and poured me a tall glass of chardonnay.

"What is going on with you? You're snapping at Char for doing homework and completely ignored Trevor when he asked for more milk with dessert."

He had sat me down at the kitchen table and held my hand. I wanted to yank it away, but I held still for his sake. It felt as make-believe as the happy pictures you see on Facebook. I buried the anxiety, but it simmered on low in my gut.

Cupcake slept on her pillow by the back door, curled into a tiny little ball. Every now and then, her head would pop up to see if she was missing anything, then she'd sigh and curl up again.

She was lucky she's so damn cute.

"Honestly, it's that damn furball over there," I said, pointing. Barry looked over and his eyes softened.

"You're blaming three pounds of fur for this mood?" He tried to hide his amusement, but his smile gave him away.

"That three pounds of fur has kept me from sleeping through the night for the past week," I snapped. "I would snap at Mother Teresa if she walked through the door right now."

He chuckled softly. "I've missed this humor," he mused. "So what can I do to help? I never intended to make you do all the work with her."

"Barry, you need your rest to continue your recovery. You can't be up with her every hour during the night."

"She's up every hour? That can't be right," he said.

I shot him a look.

"What I mean is, she's old enough to sleep through the night now. We must be doing something wrong for her to be up so many times."

He walked over to pick her up, and she snuggled into the crook of his arm.

"That is Satan's dog, sent here to torture me."

He laughed again as he held her up to face me. "Linn, is this really the face of Satan's dog?" She blinked at me and whined.

I took her from him and she licked my nose. "You're

killin' me, Smalls," I whispered to her.

"Why don't I take her for a small walk around the block right now. Have her go potty and get rid of some energy. We might be letting her sleep too much during the day."

I took a sip of wine and snuggled her up to my neck. How I could love and hate a tiny little creature like this was beyond me.

"C'mon," he said, reaching for her. "It's Monday. Isn't your *Bachelor* show on? Don't even try to say you don't watch it anymore. I know better."

I smiled and relented, giving her a smooch before handing her over. Why did he have to be so nice to me? This trial period would be so much easier if he would go back to the Barry I had gotten used to.

"I won't be long," he said, attaching her glittery pink leash.

I sat at the table, sipping wine, watching him close the door behind them. Feeling guilty, I tip-toed into Charlotte's room.

"Mommy?" she said, popping her head up.

"Why aren't you sleeping, sweetie?" I sat on the side of her bed.

"I heard the door. Did Daddy leave?"

I leaned and kissed her forehead. "Shhh, he just took Cupcake for a little walk," I said. "He will be right back."

Her whole body relaxed. "Okay, good."

"I just wanted to tell you I'm sorry for not listening

to your recorder practicing. And tomorrow, I want you to play all the songs you've learned so far."

Her eyebrows lifted in excitement. "Really? Oh, you're going to love them!"

I made a mental note to buy more wine.

"I'm sure I will," I said. I leaned down to kiss her one more time. "But now, you need sleep."

"Okay, Momma," she said. "Thanks for coming in."

I closed her door gently, and then I peeked in on Trevor. As I guessed, he was spread out and sideways on his bed, snoring softly. Closing his door, I smiled at the difference between them. Charlotte was the classic oldest child. Responsible, quiet, and diligent rule follower.

Trevor had other plans for life. *Let me see what I can get away with*, was his motto, but he had a heart of gold. It didn't surprise me that Cupcake followed him around like he was the master.

I grabbed my wine and settled into the couch, turning the TV channels to find *The Bachelor*. How many times did Barry make fun of me for watching this show? He never had a problem telling me how he felt about it.

Secretly, I had watched it from the first season. It was rare for him to even be home this early on a Monday night, so what he didn't know couldn't hurt him. On occasion, I'd fall asleep, and he would come home to find me curled up on the couch and someone crying on TV. He'd wake me by throwing an insult my way for spending my free time watching such "stupid drivel."

"You do know that's not the real world, right?" he would say, snapping the TV off. He'd stomp off to bed, leaving me there in the hushed aftermath with only his judgement lingering. I'd drag myself to bed, silently seething, and fall asleep as close to the edge of the bed as I could manage without falling off.

For him to remind me this was on felt like a trap. Like he would come in and fall into the old Barry ways.

Only he didn't.

I continued to watch, even when I heard him and Cupcake walk through the front door. As he washed his hands at the sink, Cupcake found her way to me. She lifted her front paws on the sofa, whimpering for me to pick her up. Tail wagging, she settled into the blanket on my lap.

"You're gonna have to catch me up on this season," he said, sitting in the La-Z-Boy, sliding the leg frame open. "Is this the guy looking for a wife, or the girl looking for a husband?"

I looked at him as if he had three heads. In fact, Barry having three heads would've made more sense to me.

"Barry, I told you I'd give you the six months and work towards the marriage, but honestly, we don't have to force *everything*."

The corner of his mouth lifted, but he continued to watch the show. "Guy or girl? Who is choosing?"

"Considering there is one guy on a date with ten underdressed girls, I'd guess this was *The Bachelor*," I said. "With everything that has been going on, I haven't seen any of this season yet."

"Good, maybe we could catch up together," he said, settling further to his chair.

This felt so foreign, so uncomfortable to watch with him in the room, mostly because I already knew his opinion about it. And the girl's clothes were dropping at a rapid pace as the obligatory group pool date ensued.

"Oh my," he said. "Is this normal for all of them to be throwing themselves at him? They're not wearing much at all."

I smiled. "You haven't seen nothing yet. Wait until they drag him to the hot tub."

"Where are they? That looks like a mansion, based on the backyard."

"Just wait," I said. "This show is known for the over-the-top dates and locations. This is at the house the bachelor stays in while they are filming. Probably somewhere in Hollywood."

"Huh," he murmured. The look on his face was the perfect mixture of confusion and interest. He couldn't look away if he tried.

"You know, you don't have to be nice and watch this," I suggested. "You can watch TV in our room if you want. I'm sure there's sports on you'd rather watch."

The bachelor, Trey, was being led by the hand to the hot tub, right outside the pool area. A giant rock wall made the tub secluded for private moments such as this.

"That doesn't seem fair," Barry huffed. "No wonder all the other girls are mad. She just stole him from that Ashley girl."

What reality am I in that my husband is not only watching The Bachelor, *but invested in it?*

"The cat fights are epic. Wait until they get back to their house later. They never show their claws around him."

"This is unbelievable," he said, mouth gaping, watching the hot tub scene. "Her parents must be mortified."

"Simmer down, over there. This is only the second group date, I think," I explained. "There will be a lot more of this as the season progresses."

A smirk crossed his face and he shook his head. "I have to admit I was wrong about this show. The producers are genius."

"In what way?" He went back to having three heads in my mind.

"Think about it, Linn," he said, leaning forward to close the chair. "They're selling love. Drama. Beautiful scenery." He stood to go in the kitchen. "Who *wouldn't* fall in love in this situation?"

"Are you completely sure you didn't have a head injury with your heart attack?" I joked.

He made a face at me and walked back in with water. "I'm just saying that before I was so busy—yes, *too* busy—to pay attention to something like this. To see it through your eyes though, is somewhat enlightening. I have to admit I'm curious to see what happens on these solo dates."

"You got all that from fifteen minutes of *The Bachelor*?"

"I know I've been absent around here." He looked at me, half-smiling. "And I told you that was going to change."

There it was again. Pressure to feel something I wasn't sure I wanted. I only wanted to unwind with mindless TV and he had to make it about us again, but what he said earlier intrigued me. "You think we would fall back in love in this situation?"

His eyes locked on mine. "That's my hope."

Hope was an odd word. To me, it implied that you were so desperate, you had to wish for something else that may or may not happen. I didn't like hope. I liked facts that proved something, and I thought Barry did too. Hope was for the weak who didn't believe in faith.

The show resumed, but I was only half watching. Thoughts overtook my brain, and it became a game of picturing us on the show. Would we fall back in love away from the real world? Is this why they fell so quickly and then broke up months after the show ended? Was the world we created and worked so hard for actually toxic to our marriage?

As for Barry, he was hooked. The one-on-one date was at a lovely vineyard with a mashing of the grapes scene, and ended with an intimate dinner amongst the barrels. This poor unsuspecting girl was falling for the oldest trick in the book. She was falling in love with the image, the hope of what her future could be like.

Little does she know real life doesn't always involve vineyards or intimate dinners. The pursuit of success often derails the intimacy of a relationship, whether you're married or not. Barry and I failed to find balance in all our years together. Never in a million years, when I said my vows to him, did I think we would end up like we did. Not loving him forever didn't seem possible at that time, as I'm sure most newlyweds believe.

You buy into the dream. The beautiful, perfect, lovely dream, and then you start your life together.

Chapter Sixteen

The vibe in the bakery today was off. I couldn't put my finger on it, but I had to guess that Aiden was making me feel all jittery. He was wearing his usual smile. He appeared to have his usual upbeat energy. But something was off, he was hiding something. Overcompensating, somehow.

The new maple bacon muffins had been flying off the trays, and I was adding in another batch for today when he walked through the swing door.

"Aiden," I said. He jumped and snapped his head up. "What is going on with you today? You seem to be somewhere else in your head."

He pasted a smile on his face. "I'm fine, boss lady." He set down the empty tray and looked for another tray of goodies to replace it.

"Aiden. Stop and look me in the eye."

His shoulders drooped and he slowly turned around. The mask had disappeared, and his eyes begged me to stop this conversation. His entire demeanor melted away before my eyes.

"Whoa, what is going on with you?" I stopped what I was doing and gave him my attention.

His mouth tightened into a line as he shook his head.

"You're not leaving this kitchen until you spill it. I

can't have my best employee sending out this energy. We'll lose customers today."

He rolled his eyes and sighed. "Shelly came home yesterday."

"Okay…" I said, unsure where this was going. "Did she kick you out or something?"

"No, but I know she's going to want her job back, and I don't want to leave here," he said, fighting with his apron string. "This place is like home to me."

"Why would you have to leave here? I'm certainly not going to lose you."

His eyes locked on mine. "I thought I was just filling in for Shelly— that I'd be done when she came back?"

"First of all, this conversation doesn't leave these four walls. What is said in the kitchen, stays in the kitchen."

He blinked and the corner of his mouth lifted.

"Secondly, you are the best employee I've ever worked with. It's almost like having a partner when you're around. You instinctively know what needs to be done, and sales have increased since you started."

"I blame those damn bacon bombs you keep making."

"That's just it," I continued. "I wouldn't have been able to make those bacon bombs if you weren't here to make sure everything else is running smoothly. You saved me and my business at a time when the rest of my life was in shambles. You're not going anywhere."

Full smile, combined with his bear hug. I had grown

used to the bear hugs and actually looked forward to them now.

He blinked back tears and turned his attention back to the trays behind him. "Have you thought of doing a maple bacon scone?"

"I haven't but will definitely try those for tomorrow for a change up. I know the pumpkin chocolate-chip muffins have to get back in rotation as well." I washed my hands and got back to my muffins. "Are we good here? Do you need to get anything else off your chest?"

He turned and smiled. "Stop, or I'll hug you again."

I held my hands up. "Don't get me wrong, your hugs are legendary. I know hugs, and yours are up there, but one a day is all I need."

"I don't know what else to say but thank you," he said, grabbing a tray of lemon cookies. "I meant it when I said this feels like home, and I haven't felt that in a long time."

"I know, Aiden," I said, nodding. "I feel it too. You're supposed to be here."

He smiled and walked out to the front, and Lionel Richie shuffled on my music.

All was right with the world again.

"What's on your mind tonight? You seem so preoccupied." Barry helped with the dishes after dinner, a habit I still wasn't used to.

"Work stuff," I said, simmering about Shelly.

"I figured that," he said. "Care to talk about it? Lawyers make good listeners." That stupid twinkle was back in his eye.

"I don't know," I said. "I'm not even sure there is a problem yet. One of my employees is back from a vacation and I'm not sure I need her any longer."

He reached over my shoulder and shut the water off. "Let me help you."

A simple statement, but one he has never muttered before. I remembered a time when he was so furious with me for renting the space for the bakery without consulting with him. He told me in no uncertain terms he wouldn't help me in any way.

But now, his eyes begged me to open up. I sighed, grabbing a towel, and gave him every detail of Shelly, Aiden, and the drama that ensued today.

"So, you're sure this Aiden isn't going to turn around and go back home?"

"I would bet my bakery on it. He's lost somehow. I can't put my finger on it, but I think this job is helping him somehow."

"And Shelly appeared today, three weeks later, and expects her normal hours back? Did she give you any explanation for being gone so long?"

"Said she met a boy and didn't want to come back. She changed her ticket for a later return home," I explained.

"Is she any good for the shop?"

"Yes, of course, but not like Aiden. I have come to rely on him almost as a manager of sorts. I would never do that with Shelly."

"I think you need to keep both of them, at least for the time being, unless your employees are at will. Then you can fire her for taking time off without notifying you in a timely manner."

"But the real problem is that Aiden and Shelly are cousins. He is living with her right now."

"Oh." He ran his hand through his hair. "Business-wise that shouldn't matter. But, since you're who you are, I see the dilemma more clearly now."

"What do you mean, me being *who* I am?" I felt insulted, like I didn't have a business mind.

He was quiet, arms folded, and his eyes snapped to mine. "All I meant, was you care way more about people than I ever did. Your compassion is one of the reasons I fell for you so quickly."

I rested my head in my hands and leaned on the table. His compliments came so easily now, it threw me off balance. I struggled to respond to them out of fear that they weren't real.

"You mentioned him being manager material," he continued. "Could you make him one? An assistant manager, maybe? Give him more responsibility?"

I lifted my head and looked at Barry. "Actually, that's kinda genius," I said. "I could bump his pay a little over Shelly's give him more responsibility in the kitchen. Besides, we're heading into the holidays, and

I always hire more help during that time."

"And you're sure Shelly just wants her normal time back?"

"Yes," I confirmed. "She is taking classes and her schedule has always been the same. She's not my favorite employee, but she is dependable when she works and knows the shop better than anyone."

"I think my work is done here, then," he said, getting up. "Can I make you some tea or something?"

"I'm good," I said. "Thank you, by the way. I didn't realize how much it was nagging at me until you asked."

He met my eyes and nodded. "Thank you for opening up to me." He filled the tea kettle with water.

"You know the Keurig has a 'water only' setting," I said.

"I know," he smiled. "I like the sound of the whistle when the water boils."

Who was this man? Not only did he never drink tea before, he wouldn't have known how to use the tea kettle.

"Maybe I will have some tea," I said.

He smiled sheepishly. "I thought you would once I got started."

I wasn't sure I'd ever get used to him being so relaxed. "Are you going a little stir crazy around here? I bet you can't wait to get to work."

His shoulders dropped a little. "Oddly enough I was thinking about work today," he said, pouring water into each mug. "I haven't missed it as much as I thought I would. If I'm being honest, I haven't missed the stress at all."

My jaw dropped open. "Who are you, and what have you done with my husband?"

"I know," he chuckled. "It's the last thing I expected too. I realized this morning that it has been a week since I even checked in with my cases, and I really didn't care."

"Should we talk to Dr. West about all of this? I'm worried this isn't normal to have everything about you change so much." I wasn't trying to be rude or difficult, but for Barry to say he didn't care about his cases was like me saying I'd close my bakery. It was unheard of.

"Linny, I wish I could explain it better," he said, setting my tea in front of me. "All I can say, is when I woke up in the hospital I was a different person, and the stuff that used to be important to me just wasn't anymore."

I shook my head and blew on my tea before sipping. "The doctor said you could go back part time starting next week. Is that something you're ready for?"

I met Barry when he was in his last year of law school while both of us were home for winter break. I was a sophomore in college and knew he was older, but that didn't stop either of us. Not only was he the classic tall, dark, and handsome I wanted, but his cutting sense of humor was something I had never witnessed in another person. Finally, I felt there was someone to match me.

I was beginning to see flashes of that man—moments, really—who he was before the stress of his job turned him into someone I didn't want to be around.

His eyebrows raised as he met my eyes. "I can't answer that right now, Linn," he said, shaking his head. "I don't know what will happen when I go back. What I do know is I'm not going to lose sight of this marriage, or of you, ever again."

He reached for my hand, his eyes meeting mine for approval.

"Dad-dy, Daddy, Daddy!" Charlotte came busting into the kitchen. "Daddy, Trevor won't let me turn the video off. I don't want to watch *Sing* again," she whined.

He pulled her up on his lap. "Well, how about you let Trevor watch *Sing*, then you and I can read *Harry*?"

A feeling of being on the outside looking in washed over me. An alternate universe. My daughter melted like butter, and he winked before heading into the family room. I sat, sipping my tea and listening to Barry read to Charlotte. Eventually, Trevor found me and slid onto my lap, snuggling in as close as possible. This kid was the eternal mama's boy, content with sitting and snuggling as long as I rubbed his back.

I leaned back in the chair, relishing in the weight of him, and pulled him tighter. This was everything I had ever wanted, but I couldn't stop the feeling it could all slip away as soon as I embraced it. The word "savor" showed up and made so much of my life better, but for some reason—when it came to my family—it scared the hell out of me. Everything could go back to the way it was so quickly, and my heart would break all over again.

"Call him Voldemort, Harry. Always use the proper name for things. Fear of a name increases fear of the thing itself," Barry read from the first book, nearing the end. I wondered if any of the wisdom was sinking into Char's brain. I still felt like I learned something new every time I picked up a book.

Fear of a name increases fear of the thing itself. My memory flashed to Julia telling me that the opposite of love wasn't hate, it was indifference. That was what I feared more than anything. Not just being indifferent to Barry, but also to myself. Afraid of what it would, or could, do to me again. I had just begun to start living again and I was terrified that we would go back to the way we were. Could I possibly let myself fall down that trap again?

I snuggled Trevor even closer, letting the words soothe me. The end of a Harry Potter book always felt like a warm blanket. Safe. Complete. Savored.

More than anything else, those words are exactly how I want to feel.

Life with Grace

The Lemon Choice

November 2 at 8:28 a.m. || 29 Comments

I'm back in the kitchen with my friend, the brilliant baker. I have watched her move about, almost ignoring the fact that I'm here, lost in her own thoughts. Dancing as if no one was watching. This is a side to her I haven't seen since I came back to town. It's softer than usual, more compassionate. Don't get me wrong, she is one of the most compassionate people I know, but she doesn't let it show often.

When I asked her what was going on, she simply said, "I got a puppy."

Woof.

She is working out, working on her marriage, and now a puppy. If anyone was a poster child for life change, it was her. Extreme life makeover, I call it.

I've been through it. My mother's fans have been through it. But I've never seen it play out with someone so close to me. I want to help her through this, ride over the cliff with her, but life doesn't work that way. We have to go through our own dramas and figure out how to fix them or accept them.

Fix it.

Or accept it.

Those really are the only two choices we have when life throws curveballs at us. We can't hide. We can't outrun the problems. We can't pretend they aren't there.

We can only fix the problem or accept it.

When life gives you lemons, there are so many options. Lemon water, lemonade, and even the famous lemon cookies. You never have to sit with a bowl of lemons. The choice is always yours.

Chapter Seventeen

The bar was packed with the usual Thursday crowd here for karaoke night. Lakeside Landing wasn't the only restaurant in town, but for me and Grace it might as well have been. We wouldn't be caught dead anywhere else. Of course, Gracie had ulterior motives, as her boyfriend, Charlie, owned the place with his brother, Jimmy.

Yes, *that* Jimmy.

I hadn't seen him since he came to the bakery and I was nervous it would be awkward between us. The best part of coming here with Gracie had always been the relaxed atmosphere where we could lose ourselves for a night.

It certainly wasn't the karaoke.

She was already sitting at the bar when I walked in, blasted by a wave of heat.

"You're here early," I said, sitting on the barstool next to her.

"I had dinner with Charlie, then did some work from his office while I waited," she replied, pulling me into a side hug.

Jimmy sauntered over, a bar towel hung from his back pocket. My stomach did a flip flop remembering the last time I was here.

He flashed me a smile. "It's about time you got here, Linn. The usual?"

The usual was a martini, but I knew that my run tomorrow would suffer if I drank those tonight. "Actually, I'll just have a glass of red tonight."

He cocked an eyebrow and shrugged. "What brings you two out tonight?" he asked, pouring my wine.

"Linn and I are planning to take over the world. This is our first official meeting," Grace said.

"Cheers to that, sista." I clinked glasses with hers.

"So, it's safe to assume there won't be any pickleback shots tonight?" Jimmy flashed a smile.

I shot him a look to never mention that night ever again, even though my heart betrayed me and skipped a beat just thinking of it.

He smirked and walked towards the other end of the bar. Thank God he wasn't making it awkward.

"Jimmy will never change," Grace sighed. "But at least he's not avoiding you."

"Charlie's in back?"

"Yes, he'll be out in a while when it gets busier, but he needed to get some work done."

"How's the book coming? Nice post, by the way." I sipped my wine, letting it soothe the frayed edges all the way down.

Her smile doubled in size, lighting up her whole face. "Really good," she said. "Obviously it's still early, but it feels right."

"The title is perfection, if I can say so myself," I said.

"And giving us bits and pieces in the blog posts is genius. Was that your mom's idea?"

"Nope, that just came to me in your kitchen one day. I thought if they were already familiar with the idea of the book, they'd be more likely to pick it up," she said, sipping her own white wine. "But I don't want to talk about me. What is going on with you?"

"Oh nothing much, other than my life being completely upside down," I snickered. "I literally don't even know how to explain it because I don't understand what is happening."

"It's that bad?"

I flinched. "Not bad, necessarily. Just the opposite of what life was before the heart attack."

She giggled. "Okay, so tell me. Do you like post-heart attack Barry or not? I can't get a read on you, which is so weird, because I know you better than anyone else."

I took a deep breath and blew it out slowly. "I wish I could answer that for you, but I can't. He is doing everything right. Attentive, caring, thoughtful," I said the words and ticked them off on my fingers. "But it's like my head is certain he is in this strange *after* phase, and as soon as he goes back to work, life will go back to normal."

"When does he go back?"

"That's the crazy part. He told me last night he wasn't sure he wanted to go back," I laughed. "Can you imagine—Barry not going back to work?"

Jimmy came down and filled Gracie's glass for her. He raised his eyebrows to me, but I shook off a refill.

"I'm going to be devil's advocate for a minute," she said, turning to look at me. Her eyes looked determined. "Let's just say he's really changed, and this is all for real. What is your first thought?"

"Apprehension?" Given the last few years, I didn't have a clue how I felt about my own husband. "It's like I wake up every day and remember I'm not supposed to hate my husband. It was so ingrained in my thoughts, and I don't know who I am without that thought. Does that make sense?"

"It absolutely does." She grabbed my hand and squeezed. "But I have to tell you something, and I'm not sure how you're going to react."

"Do you honestly think there is anything you could say that would shock me any more than the last few weeks?"

"Gordy is getting a divorce." She said the words, but it didn't connect.

I had spent so many months trying to forget Gordy after he broke things off in the spring. Apparently, his attempt to save his own marriage had not worked out like he anticipated, and while forgetting him was impossible, I thought I had finally gotten over the heartache. Until now. My heart shattered at the thought of the situation I was in.

"Linn? Did you hear me?"

"I heard you," I whispered. "I just don't know what

to say about that."

"I didn't tell you to add to your pile, but he's coming home next week, and I wanted you to be prepared."

"Can I ask a totally self-centered question?" I stared straight ahead, not wanting to make eye contact.

"Yes," she answered. "He asked about you and how you were doing."

A breath escaped in a whoosh. I ran my hand through my hair. "Well, this is fucking excellent timing," I said.

"How are my two favorite girls?" Neither Grace nor I heard Charlie come up behind us, and we both startled.

"Whoa, you two are jumpy tonight," he said, pulling Grace into him.

"If you didn't sneak up behind us, we wouldn't be so jumpy," I snapped.

He looked at Grace and she cringed. "I just broke the news to her about Gordy."

He nodded knowingly.

"Is he coming home for good?" I asked. This felt like the best and the worst news simultaneously.

"He's not sure yet," Gracie answered. "He has a job interview while he's here, but he also wants to be near the kids since they will have joint custody."

I closed my eyes to process the information. Gordy was going to be free. Six months ago, this would've been the best news I'd ever heard, but now? Now, I sat here, numb, adding to my confusion. Charlie pulled me into a side hug and squeezed.

"It's gonna be okay," he whispered.

I shook my head. "I wish I could believe that," I said. "It's like I'm being tested or something." I took a sip of wine. "How long have you known?"

Grace's shoulders drooped slightly. "I found out last week. He told Charlie a few weeks ago, though." She turned to face me. "He's embarrassed, Linny. Feels like a fool believing she was going to change. I told him to leave you alone for now, but I know he wants to see you when he's home."

My heart tightened. *Could he possibly still have feelings?*

"I think I need to go home," I said.

"Oh Linny, stay. Let's figure this out," she pleaded. "I can't let you go after dropping this bombshell on you. This is why I wanted to get you out of the house tonight."

"What exactly is there to figure out? I told Barry I'd give him his six months until our anniversary, and I can't go back on that. Now you're telling me the only other man I've ever loved is free? I can't even fucking believe this is my life." I drained my glass.

Charlie gave us space and went behind the bar to help Jimmy keep up with the orders. I looked at Grace again, her eyes filled with concern.

"Fix it or accept it, right?" I wondered now if her post, her book, was about me.

"I think you're looking at this from a trapped perspective," she said. "Like you don't have any choices."

"Tell me what choices I have," I snapped at her. I knew she had seen my moods before, but taking it out on Grace was wrong.

She straightened her back in response. "Linn, I'm on your side. I want you to see you actually have some choices." She sipped her wine. "I know Gordy is throwing you for a loop, but nothing is set in stone. You don't even know how he feels now, and it shouldn't matter anyway."

"How can it *not* matter? I loved him," I said, softer now.

"Linny, you can only make decisions, *choices*, based on the here and now. You have to let the past go, and all the feelings connected to it. Yes, the timing sucks, but your life is completely different now."

"My life is a shitshow," I said.

The corner of her mouth lifted. "You always say that. I'd like to think your life is full of opportunities."

"Is Charlie aware you've lost your mind?"

Her smile grew. "Charlie knows exactly what he's gotten into," she said. "And I haven't lost my mind. You have a husband who sincerely wants a second chance. A bartender who would love to make you happy for a night. And another man who would probably want another chance with you. How do you not see this as opportunities?"

"Because I don't know what I want," I said, my voice breaking. "They're not opportunities if I have to hurt someone in the process of making up my mind." She looked past me at the stage, but I knew she was still listening. "Look, I know you're trying to help me see the positive side in all of this, but I can't help but feel pressured by Gordy coming to town. Happy, yes. Hopeful, definitely. But it makes me feel bad even thinking about it with Barry being the good husband now. I was just getting used to the idea of being his wife again, and now I don't know what to think."

She slumped farther in her chair. "I hear you," she said. "I really do. And I can tell Gordy to leave you alone for the time being. It's not like he thinks he's going to swoop into town and steal you away."

"I know he doesn't. He's very logical that way. He always balanced out the crazy voices in my head." My heart ached to see and talk to Gordy again. "I guess I don't have to make any decisions tonight." I leaned to block her vision of the stage and meet her eyes. "Thank you for telling me. Honestly. It's way better than just running into him and not being prepared."

"Are you sure you're not mad?"

"Promise."

Jimmy came and filled my glass, winking.

Gracie dropped her head and laughed. "What the hell? It's like you're a man magnet right now."

"I guess it could be worse," I admitted. "I could be attracting more puppies."

"Ohhh, how is little Cupcake?"

"A giant pain in my ass, is how she is. Why he

thought a puppy would save our marriage is beyond me."

"It's not about the puppy," she said. "It's about the list. And I think it's incredibly romantic."

I circled my hand around the sappy look on her face. "This does not help me not at all, Dunham."

She smirked. We were back to normal.

"I still think what Barry is doing is commendable," she said, sipping her wine. "And I'm the last person I ever thought would say that."

"Do you know he even watched *The Bachelor* with me the other night?"

She choked on the wine. "What do you mean he watched *The Bachelor*? Like, the show?"

"What the hell else would I mean? Group dates, hot tub make out sessions, and rose ceremonies. *The Bachelor* really isn't code for anything else."

"But of all the things you could watch on TV, you chose *that*?"

"Oh trust me, it wasn't my choice," I said, laughing. "I had settled in to watch it, and he came in after taking Cupcake for a walk. I had to explain everything to him and worried about his heart watching all those girls in skimpy bathing suits."

"I can't even imagine him watching all the stupid drama they create," she said. "Charlie watched it with me once and that was it for him. He told me there were some shows we didn't need to see together."

"That's what I'd prefer, but he's already asking me

about it. Downloaded the ABC app so he could watch the first couple episodes. He knows every girl by name and profession. Been talking about them like they're friends of ours."

She slapped the bar. "Stop," she said. "He did not get the app. There is no way the Barry I know—no matter how changed—would be invested in *The Bachelor*."

I held up my right hand. "I swear on Cupcake. He mentioned Stacy last night, and asked if I knew she was an exotic dancer. Took me few minutes to realize he was talking about the show. I thought Stacy was his nurse."

"This is the best thing I've heard in a long time." Gracie laughed easily. "You just made my week."

"You should come watch with us next week," I said. "He would love someone else to talk to about it."

"Maybe I will," she giggled. "This is something I gotta see."

"This morning he texted me at work to see if I knew there was a Bachelor Fantasy League online. He was thinking of joining."

"If this doesn't prove he's changed, then I don't know what does."

I giggled. "I guess so. At times, it's like living with a stranger though. He looks like Barry. Sounds like Barry. But the reality is he's so different."

"Is there a part of you that still loves him?"

I blinked. "Oh hell, I don't know. I think so? He's so good with the kids now, and I've never seen that side of him. He's kind to my mother when she's over, where she used to drive him crazy before. It's like he read a book on how to be the perfect husband and father. Even my dad is talking to him again."

Gracie shook her head, suddenly serious. "What if he doesn't go back to work? What will he do?"

"He said he'd look into a private practice for himself. Wants to still practice, but on his own terms. He thinks he can just work from home, out of his office."

Gracie's eyes were bugging out of her head. "I have to come over next Monday and see this for myself. I'll bring snacks and wine."

I shrugged. "I can only imagine how excited he will be." I drained my glass. "My bedtime is calling me. My alarm goes off way too early to be drinking more than one." I slid off the barstool and hugged her.

"Everything will work out," she whispered in my ear. "I promise."

I pulled away and waved to Charlie and Jimmy. "I'm going to hold you to that statement."

Walking out, the air felt refreshing after being in the warm, stuffy bar. In the past, I would've stayed long past my bedtime and regret it the entire next day. I was happy to go home and sleep without the bed spinning or wake up with the morning headache.

Perhaps we were all capable of change. What Grace said about choices made more sense than I had led on. I never wanted to accept my life the way it was, but I didn't have any idea how to change. That combination creates misery on so many levels. Once I decided to start taking care of myself—to fix myself—other things started to fall into place. The choices I made now are about helping myself feel better, run better, or simply to have more energy. To savor life. My initial instinct has always been to numb the pain. To eat it away or stuff it down, but Tony had given me a few ideas of how to stop the urges before I act on them.

Everything we do is a choice. How is it possible to be thirty years old and I'm just learning this now?

Chapter Eighteen

For the first time as parents, we headed to parent-teacher conferences together. Barry had never met a teacher, been to a classroom, or seen any of the various programs schools make parents attend.

If people didn't know me, they would have assumed I was a single parent.

His eyes inspected every piece of artwork that hung in the hallway. He was intent on finding anything of Charlotte's to prove she was a genius and should be put into a school for higher learning. I tried my best to not roll my eyes.

We waited outside her classroom for the teacher to be done with the parents ahead of us.

"I can't believe she's in second grade and I've never been to her school," he said. His eyes were no longer inquisitive. They were guilt-ridden.

I gave him my best "it's okay" smile. "Not all dads have the time to do the school stuff. The important thing is you're here now."

"You're just saying that," he said. "I know how absent I've been. I've lost so much time."

"Hey, it's the second grade," I said. "It's not like she's graduating from Harvard or something."

He gazed at a picture Charlotte drew titled "Home."

Upon closer inspection, I was slightly mortified. It appeared that Trevor was watching TV and Charlotte was cooking. Barry and I were excluded from the picture completely.

"Hopefully this isn't an accurate representation of us," he said. "Maybe we should step up our game a bit."

"Mr. and Mrs. Sinclair? Oh, hi Linny. Good to see you again," Mr. Murphy greeted us. "C'mon in, have a seat."

Barry ran his hands on everything he walked by as if seeing them for the first time. *Look at the beauty of this desk. Look at that chalkboard. Globes!*

We sat in the world's smallest chairs, and I worried I might break it. My extra weight wasn't coming off as fast as I thought it should, and I hated the fact I had to worry about crushing school furniture.

"Mr. and Mrs. Sinclair, I'm glad you were able to make it tonight," he started. "Charlotte is doing an exceptional job with the curriculum this year and is thriving academically."

Barry shifted in his tiny chair and beamed. He had never heard the words "exceptional student" or the always favorite, "gifted," when it comes to Charlotte. Teachers have always loved her.

"However," Mr. Murphy continued. "We have been dealing with a slight problem with her behavior lately, and I'm inclined to ask for your help with the matter."

My stomach clenched. Problems with behavior? That

doesn't sound like our Charlotte. "What sort of behavior problems?"

He looked down at his notes. "She seems to be having issues with the other boys in class recently. There is some minor bullying and aggression taking place during recess."

"She's being bullied?" Barry was almost out of his chair. I rested my arm on his.

"Oh, no, Mr. Sinclair. Charlotte is the one bullying. I've seen it with my own eyes, otherwise I'd dismiss it as untrue," he said. "Has anything changed within the home lately?"

"You could say that," I said. "Barry has had some health issues recently and our home life is a little different."

"Are you blaming me?" His eyes cut to mine.

There it was, the easy banter of accusation and blame showing their ugly heads in Mr. Murphy's classroom. Except when I looked at Barry, his eyes were sincere, pleading that it wasn't his fault his perfect daughter had aggression. He wasn't challenging me. He was terrified it was true. Instinctively, I reached for his hand and squeezed.

"I'm sorry about the health issues and I'm sure that's not the issue here. However, if your home life has changed even a little bit, then we could probably attribute that to the root of the problem."

"But what can we do?" My mind was spinning. I thought we were doing better with the kids, but maybe we're just screwing them up more.

"Mrs. Sinclair," he said, folding his hand and leaning back in his chair. "Children go through all sorts of phases, especially at this age. They are trying to figure out their place in the world and sometimes test the boundaries. I'm not too worried about this, but I wanted to bring it to your attention. Has she been different at home?"

I looked at Barry again. He shrugged and shook his head. "I haven't noticed anything," he said. "But I'm home more now than I ever have been in the past. I'm not sure I'd know a difference in personality to be honest."

"We've tried to keep things as normal as possible for both kids, but maybe we've overlooked something," I said.

"Again, I'm not too worried yet," he assured us. "But let's keep an eye on her and try to instill positive communication skills. Something less… *reactive*."

I cringed at the word. Barry had told me for years that I overreacted about everything.

Mr. Murphy stood, signaling our time was up. For years I've wanted to linger in the room far longer than the allotted parent-teacher time, but today I couldn't wait to get the hell out of here. I stood, the chair scraping the floor as I pushed it back.

"I trust this issue will work itself out in no time," Mr. Murphy said, walking us out to the door.

"Thank you," we murmured. Barry shook his hand

and we fled the class room.

We walked out of the school as quickly as our legs could take us. Barry still shuffled a bit, but he wanted to flee as much as I did.

"How have you done this all these years? That was horrible," he said, once we got in the car.

"It's not usually like that," I snapped. "She's always been the perfect child. They usually couldn't say enough good things."

"Do we bring this up to her? I don't want her to be known as the class bully."

"We can just start asking more questions about school and kids in the classroom. See if she wants to come clean on her own, rather than forcing it on her," I said. Charlotte didn't hold things inside, she was always excited to rattle on and on about the day's activities. In that moment, I realized I hadn't heard a peep about school in at least a week. How did I not notice this before?

My mom was sitting on the sofa with both kids watching a movie when we got home. Guilt tugged at my heart when I notice how tired she looked. Usually, my mom was the picture definition of energy, but tonight her eyes seemed to lack that spark.

Have I ignored everything in my life except my own problems?

The decision came to me quickly: Aiden would definitely have more responsibility at the bakery, and I would be home more in the afternoon when the kids got home. I needed to get this family back on track, and that started with me. My bakery was running smoothly now and being off in the afternoons wouldn't be a problem. It was just high school students after three o'clock, treating Bab's like a coffee shop—meeting for homework, or getting a treat with a latte. I loved that time of day, mingling with a different generation, but they seemed to be infatuated with Aiden from the first day. His easy banter made him very relatable and generated a younger crowd.

"Hey Mom," I said, sitting down and pulling Trevor on my lap. "Thanks again for coming over. Barry was happy to be there tonight."

She beamed. "I know how important it is for him to be a part of their lives right now." Cupcake was snuggled on her lap with my mom petting her. "He really seems to have changed for the better, Linn."

"It does seem that way, doesn't it," I said with a half-smile. "I hope for the kids' sakes it lasts."

"I hope for *your* sake it lasts," she countered. "You seem tired, tonight. Everything go okay at conferences?"

I knew Charlotte was listening and only pretending to watch the movie. "It seems our daughter is still a genius," I said. "And her teacher, Mr. Murphy, is quite fond of her."

My mom kissed the top of Charlotte's head. "Who wouldn't be smitten with this beauty?"

Smitten isn't the word I'd use. I'm imagined a few

second-grade boys would like to string her up by her ponytail.

Trevor crawled off my lap to move closer to the TV. My mom raised her eyebrows.

"Apparently, we're talking too loud for him," I jested.

My mom picked up Cupcake and held her up, nose to nose. "Grammy has to go, Cupster," she cooed.

"Cupster? Mom, she'll never learn her name if you keep giving her nicknames." Charlotte, still watching TV, smiled. I grabbed Cupcake from my mom and she whimpered.

"See? She likes the names I give her."

As my mom gathered her coat and purse, I told her I wouldn't need her after school for the rest of the week. She smiled as if I told her I was graduating from med school.

"Don't read too much into it," I deflected. "Barry and I just realized we need to be home a little more right now. The kids need it."

She winked as if she were in on a secret with me.

"You sleep well," she said. "Call if you need anything tomorrow. Maybe we can do dinner this weekend with your dad. You know how much he loves seeing the kids." My dad wasn't the most social person on the planet, so for her to suggest dinner felt like a sign that he was ready to give Barry another chance too.

I locked the door behind her and grabbed my phone

to text Aiden.

ME: *Can you come in a few minutes earlier tomorrow? I want to go over something with you.*

AIDEN: *Sure thing boss lady.*

Barry was sitting in the recliner with Trevor on his lap when I walked back in. I sat next to Charlotte and let Cupcake snuggle between us.

This moment, as simple as it was, was everything I had wanted before I had gotten married. I wanted the kids, the pets, and a husband who loved us unconditionally.

Why did it take us so long to get here? And better yet, would it last?

Chapter Nineteen

I had Taylor Swift blaring when Aiden strolled in the next morning. His face was hard to read, which made me wonder if he was worried about this meeting.

He washed his hands and threw on an apron, tying it tightly. He walked to the counter and began sprinkling his space with flour. He grabbed a ball of pie dough from the metal bowl and began rolling it out.

"I can do these," he said. "I'm better at them anyway." The corner of his mouth lifted and he winked at me. He was right. He was way better at rolling the dough than I was.

"I didn't ask you to come in early to roll out the dough, Aiden."

His eyes shot up to mine and his smile faded.

"There's that look again," I murmured. "Will you stop worrying?"

He took a slow, deliberate breath and focused his attention to me.

"I asked you here this morning because I want to see if you and I can come up with a different arrangement for work."

His brow furrowed. "I'm not following you."

"I would like to make you the assistant manager, starting today, hopefully." He blinked and looked away from me. "Unless, of course, you're going back home. I'm not sure why I hadn't already thought of that."

A stony expression crossed over his face. "No, I won't be going home anytime soon," he admitted.

"Can I intrude and ask why? It's clearly upsetting you, and maybe I can help."

"That depends. Can you pray the gay away?" He met my eyes, challenging me.

"Oh Aiden, you've got to be kidding me," I said. "Your family won't accept who you are?"

He barked out bitter laughter. A sound made only by emotions that had been simmering for years. "If who I am *chooses* to be gay, then no, they won't accept it. As if I'd ever *choose* this."

I walked to his side and wrapped him in a hug I'm certain he has needed, for years probably. He was stiff at first, resisting, then he collapsed into me with the weight of all his shame and disillusionment.

He pulled away, wiping his tears with the back of his hand. "How long have you known?"

"Since you walked through that door last month," I said. "I've never had a conversation like this, so I don't want to be offensive, but Aiden, it's not like you're hiding it. You're pretty fucking gay."

At first he smiled, then laughter started, one we both needed.

"Only you could make *pretty fucking gay* a loving endearment," he said. "Coming from you, nothing is offensive. At least, to me it's not."

"Okay, good. The last thing I want to do is piss off my new assistant manager," I said. "Plus the whole sexual harassment thing you could get me for. I don't even want to go there," I added. "Let's take a mini-break and go over what I will need from you." I ripped off my apron. "I need coffee, pronto."

He followed me out, grabbing a lemon cookie off the day-old tray. "Want one?"

"I'm good," I said, fighting the urge to bring the entire tray over.

"So lay it on me," he said. "What can I do around here to help out more?" We had settled in the corner booth with a few minutes before we got back to work.

"The first thing I need is for you to manage the evening shift to close most days." I took a sip of coffee. "Okay, every day," I corrected.

He nodded, nibbling on his cookie.

"So you have to decide if you want to come in early until lunch, and then come back for the evening to close," I said. "Or you can come in mid-morning and work till close. I always split the time up because I needed to be here to open and close, but you can do whatever works for you."

"That's a tough one," he said. "I love being here in the mornings so much, but it makes more sense to just come mid-morning and work through, right?"

"It's completely up to you, Aiden. Obviously, we can be flexible with the schedule until you figure out what works best," I said. "I will still open every day and work until three. That way, I can get the kids after school and have some family time without worrying about coming back."

"I don't know how you've done this schedule for years. It's crazy."

"You do what you have to," I said. "Labor of love."

"Okay, let's try mid-morning to close for a month and see how it goes. Do you care if I create a couple specials to get the after-school crowd in here? I think we have a huge untapped market."

"That would be awesome, and I want to add you to all the social media accounts, so you can help with that as well. You have a younger vibe that will attract different people. Plus the kids love you."

He beamed. "I speak their language."

"Ha. The only language I speak is middle age mom."

"Nothing wrong with that. I love the mamas too," he said. "Together we cover the market."

I blinked and shook my head. "So I need to either hire another morning person, part-time, or check with Shelly to see if she wants more hours in the morning."

"She will take the hours. No doubt."

"Okay, I will approach her today," I said. "Are you still staying with her?"

He sighed. "I am, but I know the space is too small for both of us. I need to find another place." He took a sip of coffee. "I was sort of waiting to come out to see if you were going to keep me on." His downcast eyes wouldn't meet mine.

My heart swelled and I reached for his hand. "Aiden." He looked up. "There is no shame in being who you are. In fact, *who you are* is amazing, and I am a better person for knowing you."

He tipped his head and rolled his eyes. "You treat me more like family than my *own* family does. I don't know how this fell into my lap but I'm not going anywhere."

"Good, it's settled. Mostly it was schedule help that I needed, but I'm sure we will work together to figure out better ways to run this joint." I finished my coffee and leaned my head back. "Do you ever feel like napping at six in the morning? I am so freaking tired lately."

"Vitamin D, boss lady," he said, getting up. "You're probably deficient. Living in Michigan does you no favors with that either."

I followed him into the kitchen, both of us putting our aprons back on. He turned and pulled me into a tight hug. "I wish you knew how much I loved this job," he said.

I held him tight, reassuring him. "I'm pretty sure I know, Aiden. Besides, we're like Batman and Robin, now. You can't leave the Batcave, ever."

He pulled away, wiping a tear from his eye. "In this scenario, am I Robin?"

"Duh," I deadpanned. "I'm too bossy to be anyone but Batman."

"True," he agreed. "Plus Robin is a cute, little

sidekick. I'm oddly okay with that title."

"Okay, Robin, finish those pie crusts. They're not going to roll themselves." He'd roll his eyes every time I said this, and I'm certain he mimicked me when my back was turned, but that was okay. I partially said it to bug him anyways.

Operation Batman and Robin was under way and would hopefully help with Charlotte and Trevor. I knew Barry would be grateful too, but I worried he'd take this as a sign that I wanted to fix our marriage, which I wasn't certain about. Still.

Maybe having more time at home would help us all figure out what we needed. Maybe "fake it till you make it" was our only hope. It's really the only thing I had going for me.

Chapter Twenty

I had read the same paragraph three times and still wasn't sure what it said. Thoughts were running through my head, and I was freezing my ass off sitting in an ice rink watching Charlotte in her skating class. Barry had stayed home with Trevor so I could try and get a feel for Charlotte and her school issues. Instead of focusing on the open book before me, my mind ran through the events of this morning yet again.

The ride here had been unsuccessful in getting any information out of her. I would pull out the golden ticket later and get her ice cream. Parenting had become a daily negotiation of getting what you wanted.

After my meeting with Tony this morning, I had felt empowered to run longer intervals in my run/walk. "The limitation is in your head, Linn," he told me when I complained that I couldn't get past running longer lengths of time. "It's all how you approach it in your head."

After my run, I realized that the advice is probably true for most things in life. We make difficult choices much harder than they need to be based on how we fret about it. Resistance at its best.

When I had gotten home, Cupcake greeted me by

peeing on the floor out of sheer puppy excitement. On the one hand, I was happy she loved me. On the other hand, she peed on the floor. Barry chuckled and cleaned up the mess, merely saying "naughty pup" to the fluffball.

On the bar was a present wrapped in brown paper and striped twine.

"What's this?" I asked, scooping up Cupcake.

"It's from the list," he said, eyes twinkling.

I suppressed an eye roll. "I don't remember buying gifts as one of the items," I said. "I didn't get you anything."

He chuckled. "It's a gift, but not really. You'll see," he said. "Open it!"

I slid into one of the barstools and set Cupcake on my lap. She rested her chin on the countertop, and Barry's eyes melted into a puddle of goo.

"You get an A plus for the wrapping," I admired. I almost didn't want to open it, it was so pretty.

"I have to give credit to the store for that. I would've come up with something more elaborate given the chance."

The twine released with a tug, and I carefully slid the tape off one end, avoiding ripping the paper. Peeking in one end, I realized it was a book.

Of course, "read the same book."

Sliding off the wrapping paper, I couldn't help but laugh. *Puppy Training for Dummies*. "I suspect this is required reading?" I laughed.

"The sooner the better," he said, pulling out his own copy.

Now I held this book in my lap, unsuccessfully trying to read while shivering in the ice rink. I set the book beside me on the cold bleachers and focused my attention on Charlotte. She loved her skating lessons so much, even though it seemed every skill took her months to master. Every instructor loved having her in their classes because she always tried so hard. A group of them were trying to spin in a circle on two feet, putting one toe pick in the ice and circling around with the other foot. Charlotte seemed to be having trouble with it, and then I witnessed something I never expected. She waited until the teacher turned her back then pretended to stumble into another skater. The skater went crashing to the ground as Charlotte stood looking down at her. *Was that a smile on her face?*

The teacher turned and attended to the crying girl on the ice, and Charlotte pleaded her case that it was an accident. I looked around to see if any other parents were watching the same group. Luckily, they weren't.

I no longer felt ice cream was going to be an appropriate negotiating tool. A long talk on the way home would be the answer. We had to figure out what was going on with our usually sweet girl.

"Charlotte, we need to have a discussion before we head home," I said. We sat in the parking lot, heat blasting from the vents. She still sat in the backseat because she was so small, but I turned to face her. A darkness entered her eyes, and she looked out the window.

"I happened to be watching when you knocked that little girl to the ice," I said as calmly as I could. "Can you explain to me why you would do that to someone?"

"It was an accident, Momma. I promise." She said the words perfectly, and if I didn't know her, I might have believed her. It was her eyes that gave her away.

"Charlotte, I saw it happen. You purposely knocked her down."

She stared at her hands, clutching a cup of hot chocolate, and her bottom lip began to tremble.

"What's going on, sweetie? Your teacher at school also mentioned you've been aggressive there, too." A single tear trickled down her cheek. "Talk to me. Tell me what's going on."

"Nothing is wrong," she whimpered. "I just get mad at people sometimes, and I do something to make them feel bad."

I was flabbergasted by the honesty of her confession. I didn't expect her to break so easily. "What do you mean, you get mad at people? What could make you so mad that you want to hurt someone?"

"I don't want to hurt anyone… I just want them to

feel bad," she said. "I'm afraid."

"But what are you afraid of?" My heart was breaking into tiny pieces listening to her. "There isn't anything you should ever be afraid of, Char."

"I'm afraid I'm going to lose you, Momma. I don't want anything to happen to you."

"Set that drink down and crawl up here, young lady."

She did as I asked and sat in the passenger seat, head down, crying.

"Why on earth would you be worried about me? I'm not going anywhere!" I grabbed her hand and squeezed. "Charlotte, tell me why you think you're going to lose me."

"It's just that ever since Daddy got sick, he's the one taking care of me. He reads to me all the time, and I like it, but you used to be the one who always took care of me, and now it's changed. I'm afraid you're going to get sick too."

"Oh Charlotte, my bug. I'm not going anywhere, and I'm certainly not going to get sick," I choked. "Daddy is just enjoying spending time with you, and I'm so happy you two get to do things together now. But I will make sure he lets me read to you every now and then. And I'll be home every day after school now."

Her eyes brightened. "For real?"

"For real," I confirmed. I wiped away her tears. "No more tears and no more being mean. Treating people badly is *never* the answer."

She sniffed and wiped her nose with her mittens.

"But what about Trevor when I'm trying to sleep and he's hitting the wall just to bother me. How can I possibly be nice to him when he's so annoying?"

I stifled a laugh. "Charlotte, you know we only had Trevor to make your life crazy, right?" I started the car and noticed she was smiling. "I mean, how fun would it be without him around to bug you? Pretty boring, if you ask me."

"But Mo-om, why does he have to follow me around all the time? He doesn't even like the same things I do. Sometimes, I think he does it just to make my life miserable."

"Sadly, that's what little brothers do. It's literally their job, but when he gets older, you'll learn to appreciate him. He'll always have your back. I promise."

"I doubt that, but I guess there isn't anything I can do about it now," she huffed.

"Haul your butt in the back seat before I get going," I said. "And don't knock your hot chocolate over."

She climbed in the back and buckled up. We turned the radio up on the way home and sang along with all the songs at the top of our lungs. I knew this phase wasn't completely over, but at least I knew how we could manage it better. By the time we got home, the tears had dried and she was smiling again.

Barry and Trevor were both sleeping in the La-Z-Boy with the Nickelodeon Channel on the TV. Cupcake popped her head up and blinked at us.

"Grab a book," I whispered. "Let's go snuggle in Mommy and Daddy's bed."

Charlotte bolted for her room. The boys continued to sleep, while Charlotte and I continued Harry's adventures.

Sundays were made for moments like this...

November 22

Thanksgiving is this week and I have nothing prepared yet. Aiden and I are bombarded with pie orders of every kind. My intention of being home in the afternoon lasted precisely one week, and while it was perfect for that week, I feel like a traitor now. Charlotte is moody, and it seems there is never enough I can do to make her happy anymore. The only thing that makes her happy is knowing it's a three-day week at school.

I would be a little excited about having Thursday off myself if it weren't for the fact that I have to do all the cooking that day too.

Work is helping me keep my mind off Barry and Gordy though, so that is good. When I'm still, like now, I let my mind wander to the dark places it likes to go. I can feel Barry hovering over me, watching me, wondering if I can fall back in love with him. His neediness is tangible, solid... the pink elephant in the room. It's stifling.

What I wouldn't give to have a moment in this house to myself and not be a mom or a wife. To have no one need me or want me to act a certain way or do a certain thing. I want to just be me without the walls of expectation that shadow my every move.

And then there's Gordy. I know he's back in town for the week, but I haven't seen him yet. I've avoided Gracie too, not wanting to put her in an awkward position, but I know I'll have to deal with him at some point.

My fear is that I will have the same feelings for him that I did six months ago. That I'll take one look at him and fall back in love with those blue eyes. The kindness. The humor. After he decided to fix his marriage, I cut off all thoughts of him—they were too painful, too empty. I had to let go at a time when all I needed him to do was stay. We both knew what we wanted, but at the same time I couldn't blame him for wanting a chance of making it right. Couldn't blame him for doing exactly what I'm doing now.

Or am I?

Chapter Twenty-One

The air was cold, damp—normal for November, but I misjudged the temperature and over dressed with too many layers. I was cooking from the inside out, like a turkey on Thanksgiving Day. I decided to take my workout to the beach like Gracie had suggested, and the distraction from the waves coming in gave me clarity and presence.

Why have I never done this before?

Few people were on the beach, giving it a feeling of being deserted. Exactly what I needed. The bakery had been bombarded this week with the pie orders for Thanksgiving, and we were baking around the clock. Aiden had been a lifesaver, and I couldn't remember what I did without him.

I was almost to the public beach, the beckoning lighthouse rising out of Lake Michigan, but I turned back before I had to pass the Dunham's. Avoiding Gordy was the only answer for me right now, to ride out the wave of him being in town and pray he doesn't stay.

My heart seized hearing my name yelled over the roar of the waves. I stopped in my tracks but didn't turn around, my heart beating out of my chest. I knew the voice. I'd know it anywhere. I turned, and there he was.

Gordy. My Gordy.

Blood was rushing to my head, and for a moment I felt faint and needed to put my hands on my knees to balance.

"Linn." He was standing in front of me.

I stood slowly, wanting to run away, but my eyes finally reached his.

"What are you doing out here?"

It dawned on me that he'd missed out on six months of my life and didn't know how much I've changed since then. The old Linny—his Linny—would never be running on a beach. Sitting with a book, maybe, but never walking or running.

"I've been trying to get back in shape," I said, not recognizing my own voice.

"Can I hug you?" he asked, then pulled me into him without waiting for an answer. My body tensed, resisting his warmth and strength. He pulled me in tighter, until I gave in and hugged him back. I allowed myself to relax in these arms that used to make me feel so complete. Now, I feel empty, confused.

"I've been wanting to call you all week," he said. "Gracie said I needed to respect your choice right now, but Linny, I don't know if I can do that. There's so much I want to tell you—"

"Stop," I interrupted him. "Just give me a minute, Gordy. I'm not prepared for this."

"Linny... it's me," he said. His brow furrowed, eyes searching my face for someone he recognized. "Why are you looking at me like that?"

"Do you have any idea how hard it's been for me since April? Do you realize how much you broke my heart?"

His shoulders fell. "I do know, because my heart was breaking too. Linn, I did what I thought was the right thing. I had to try and see if our marriage could be salvaged," he said, grabbing my hands. "Please tell me you understand."

I sighed, avoiding his eyes. "I do understand, more than you could possible know."

"What does that mean? Are you and Barry trying to save your marriage too?"

"I told him we would work on it until our tenth anniversary next year. If I still feel the same, he said he'd let me go."

"Wait, he wanted to try again? Barry?"

A bitter laugh escaped me. "Can we walk? I need to move." We turned and headed back towards my home, away from his. "Did Grace tell you Barry had a heart attack?"

"She did, but she hasn't talked about it since. Is he doing okay?"

"Yes, of course," I confirmed. "He's doing great, but he's changed since the heart attack. He's different. He's the man I married and not the one he turned into."

"What do you mean he *changed*?"

"I mean, it's like he's erased the last nine years from his memory, and he is the man he was before work took over his life. Wait—no, he hasn't erased the memories, because he is well aware of how he's treated me and is sorry." This felt impossible to explain.

"Is it for real? I can't believe this has been happening and Grace didn't tell me."

"You can't blame Grace," I said. "She's trying to protect me. She knows I'm giving this marriage a go, at least until next year."

"So are you just waiting him out? Or are your feelings changing too?" The edge in his voice cut through to my heart.

"Honestly? I don't have a clue. There are moments where I think this could actually work. Then I hear you're coming to town, and my whole life turned upside down again." I pulled out my hair elastic and shook out my hair. Everything felt constricted.

We walked along in silence, just the sound of waves rolling through my ears.

"We have the worst timing," he said. "If I could go back six months, we'd never have to hurt like this."

"You don't know that," I said. "In fact, we'd be in the same place. Gordy, you're not someone to give up on a marriage without exhausting every possibility, so don't tell me you would've done anything differently. We both know you'd do the same thing every time."

"But I want to stop you from wasting any more time with Barry," he said, his voice cracking. "I know that's the most selfish thing anyone could say to you, but it's true. I want a future with you. Yes, it's challenging with broken families, but we wouldn't be the first couple to do that."

"Gordy, stop. Just stop. I don't know what I feel right now. I can't give you any commitment, and I won't do that to Barry either. It's not fair of you to ask this of me. Not fair you're putting me in this position. Six months ago I would've jumped at it, but I'm different now. And I need to figure out what's best for me and my kids. That is the most important thing for me. I can't make any more mistakes where they're concerned."

"And Barry? Can you honestly see a future with him?"

I smiled and shook my head. "I don't know, but he's different. Obviously my guard is up, but he's actually pleasant to be around and trying so hard to do right by me."

"It sounds like you made your mind up," he said, jealousy lacing his words. "Forgive me if I'm not thrilled for you."

"Gordy," I stopped him, taking his hands in mine. "Don't do this. I gave you the time you needed, and all I'm asking is that you do the same for me. Give me that. My feelings for you haven't changed, but there is another layer I have to peel back first. I need to give this to Barry, and myself, to see exactly what is best for me."

He looked away, blinking back tears. I pulled him back into a hug, allowing his arms to envelope me this time.

"Please be patient," I begged. "I can't have you mad at me."

I felt him nod and kiss the top of my head. Oh what I wouldn't give to feel his lips on mine...

I broke the hug. "I need to get back home."

"Can I text you?" His eyes were begging.

"Let me think about it. I'm not saying no, but I need to see if it's something I can handle. I'll text you if or when I'm ready."

He nodded again. "That's fair. And I won't bug you, I promise."

"Thank you, Gordy," I said. "I appreciate you letting me figure things out."

I gave him a final squeeze of the hand and turned to walk back home. Walking away from him cut through my heart, and I blinked back the tears that threatened to undo me in front of him. I wouldn't, *couldn't* let him know how much I wanted to leap into his arms and run away.

I saw the lights glowing in the kitchen from the beach as I approached our home. Barry was at the sink washing something, smiling. I stood on the beach for a moment. It was darker now, so I wasn't sure he could see me, but this moment felt like something to me. Weighty. Significant.

As I crept closer I spied Charlotte sitting at the table, drawing in one of her art books, head bobbing in time with music of some sort. Closer yet, the TV gave away the movie *Sing*, Trevor's newest obsession. I was on the outside of my life, literally, looking in, and what I was seeing is what I'd always wanted. Happy family, beautiful home—and yet, I was out here searching for something I may never find: contentment.

Barry left the sink and stood behind Charlotte, eyes glowing with pride. She was unaware he was even standing there, she was so caught up in the drawing and music. He bent to kiss her on the head, and my heart swelled. In that moment, that one small action, I knew he had changed, that this mission to save our marriage wasn't just a whim. A shiver ran through my body, and I took the stairs up to the deck. I was home.

Chapter Twenty-Two

The second I walked into the kitchen, I sensed it. Tension. This feeling I used to carry with me all the time, which had been noticeably absent since Barry's heart attack, was now present with us. Lurking. It was like another person was here with us in the kitchen.

The kids were oblivious, as usual, gathering snacks and juice boxes from the fridge. I tried to meet Barry's eyes, but they avoided mine. He was quiet—too quiet—and fear ran through me that it was all over. He had changed his mind and the old Barry was back.

I was attempting to keep things normal for the kids. The usual dance to overcompensate, to hide the giant elephant in the room. Reactions that are too happy. Hugs that last too long. Barry was reading the paper from this morning, something I knew he'd already done by now. He was just avoiding us. Again, we are in this unworthy place of pretend.

I wanted to talk to him, open him up, remind him we are trying to save this marriage, but the kids chose this moment to tell me everything they've ever wanted to say to me. About school. About lunch. About Susie, who passed a cootie catcher in class and got in trouble. *Who still makes cootie catchers?*

After what felt like three hours, I shuffled them off

to their rooms to get their reading time in for the day, and walked back to the kitchen.

"Okay, spill it. I know I did something wrong," I said. His eyes met mine for the first time since we'd been home, and it wasn't anger or tension. It was hurt. His face was broken, and all I wanted to do is make that look go away.

He slid an envelope out from under the paper and I froze. A chill ran through my spine, and my heart raced.

"Where did you find that? I never meant for you to ever see that." I tried to explain the letter I wrote the morning of his heart attack, but nothing is coming out like it should.

"Then why would you save it?" His voice was eerily quiet and calm. "When did you even write this?"

"Barry, look at me." He was staring at the letter, memorizing the ache I had felt in each word. "I wrote that before all this happened. Before the heart attack. And I wasn't trying to save it. I cleaned everything out of my purse and threw it all in a drawer when you were in the hospital."

His eyes finally left the letter and met mine. On a normal day his eyes are soft brown, the color of melted chocolate. Today, they looked black, filled with pain. A single tear ran down his cheek and he wiped it away harshly.

"I've been thinking," he said. "I know we agreed to the six months, but that might have been unfair of me, considering how serious you were about ending this. If you still want out, if there is no hope, then let's just be done now. I can't invest four more months into this, only to have you rip my heart out."

My head was shaking no before he even said the last sentence. "No," I interrupted. "That is not what I want, and I am in this with you. Look, I'm sorry you had to see that, but that isn't how I feel now."

I reached for the letter and pulled it out of his grasp. The paper tore easily as I ripped it into tiny pieces. "This is how I feel about the letter, Barry. I'm in a different place now. *We* are in a different place now, and I don't want out, and I don't want to lose what we have started to rebuild."

His eyes were still downcast, his head resting on his hand. "I don't know what to think anymore," he whispered. "I want to believe we're better now, but are we?"

"Yes," I said, reaching for his hand. "We are in such a different place now. Can't you feel it? Don't you see we how nice it is to be at home again?"

He nodded his head and I squeezed his hand again. "I do feel it, but something happened when I saw that letter. I thought maybe you were just pretending to stay with me, out of pity."

"When have I ever done anything out of pity? Have you met me?"

A small smile crept onto his face. The slightest corner of his mouth tipped upward. "I don't know what

I was thinking," he played along. He cleared his throat and met my eyes. "You're really in this for the long haul? I'm giving you an out right now if you want it. No questions asked."

My mind snapped to Gordy on the beach last night. How it felt to be in his arms again after so many months. The ache I felt walking away from him, and I knew my answer. "Last night, during my walk, I had many of these questions. Can we really make this work? Is staying together best for the kids? These questions are always running through my head, actually." I turned the faucet, needing water. "But when I got home, I could see in through the back windows, here. And do you know what I saw?"

He shook his head, hanging on my every word.

"I saw everything I've ever wanted." My voice cracked. "You, Charlotte, and Trevor. That is my life, and the fact that you want to save all this is more than enough for me. I don't want a divorce. I don't want anyone else, Barry. I want you, this, our life."

Tears streamed down my face. He stood and wiped them away with the soft pads of his thumbs. He pulled me into a hug, both of us sobbing from the emotional undertow of this wave.

I had my answer. I knew what I wanted and I was going to fight for it.

Chapter Twenty-Three

It was a rare night for us to go out to dinner, especially as a family. As I sat at Lakeside with Barry and the kids, it was as if my two worlds had collided. This place is my escape—my safe place—to bitch about my marriage, or make out with the hot bartender in the back room.

How did I let this happen?

The look on Jimmy's face when we walked in said it all. Eyebrows raised, mouth in a perfect 'oh' shape, eyes flickered amusement.

I was screwed.

It didn't help matters that Charlie and Gordy were sitting at the end of the bar, nursing beers and watching the game.

Fuuuuuuck, said the voice in my head. Over and over again… *fuuuuuuuck*.

I did my best to keep things light at the table. Barry gave me a side-eye at one point when I played dumb on what to order.

"I thought you liked coming here," he said. "I know you used to hang out here with Grace all the time."

"I do like it here," I said. "It's just, we know so many people here."

"And that's a bad thing? Linny, you know half the

town because of the bakery."

He had me there. "I know," I relented. I had to try and salvage this night for Barry's sake.

Jimmy delivered my wine instead of the waitress. If I could crawl under the table, I would. "Barry, Linny, so good to see you all out," he said, setting down the wine.

The two shook hands. "Thanks, it's good to be out," he said. "I practically had to drag Linny here, though."

Jimmy chuckled. "Oh, I'm sure you did." He patted me on the back. "It's always great to have Linn around."

In my mind, I slid under the table.

"I best get back behind the bar," Jimmy said, squeezing my shoulder.

"You grew up with him, right?" I forgot how little Barry knew about my life before we met.

"Yes," I confirmed. "Gracie had the biggest crush on him in high school." I wanted any and all focus off of me.

"But she's with his brother now… Charlie?"

"Yeah, they both came from really bad marriages, but seem to be really happy now."

"That's good. And who is that with Charlie up at the bar?"

I didn't know if he was trying to piece together my sordid past, or if he was just interested in the people who had become my second family this past year.

I cleared my throat, fearing I may choke on the

words. I glanced over my shoulder, pretending I hadn't seen him earlier. He looked over at the same time and locked his eyes on mine. Those eyes.

"Uhh, that's Gordy, Gracie's older brother." My heart was suddenly racing, my face burning. I took a long gulp of water.

Barry didn't seem to notice the hurricane of emotion rolling through me and picked up the menu. I did the same, attempting to focus my attention elsewhere, even though I knew what I was going to order. The kids, picking up on my tension, started to pick at one another. I took my phone out and gave it to Charlotte to occupy her time. I flipped Trevor's menu over and set up a game of tic-tac-toe.

"Gordon is the biggest steam engine," Trevor mumbled to himself.

"Everything comes back to Thomas the Train," Barry chuckled.

Can we just stop saying the name Gordon? The voices in my head were at a high pitch and the urge to flee overwhelmed me.

"Mommy, someone keeps texting and stopping my game," Charlotte said.

Barry cocked his head and shot me a look that was both a question and a statement. A look that told me he knew about Gordy. What he didn't know was if were we still together.

I became very still and took a long drink of my wine. If my life was going to implode, I'd have to accept my part in that, but I didn't have to do it stone cold sober. I took my phone from Charlotte and switched it into plane mode to eliminate all notifications.

"If you need to answer the texts in person, by all means." His half-smile threw me off. I didn't know if anger was simmering or he was completely ignorant of the situation.

I continued to let Trevor beat me in match after match of tic-tac-toe, knowing his competitive nature would explode in public if I won. Barry rested his hand on mine. "Linny, it's okay," he said. He was too calm. "I knew about Gordy before. If you need some time, then take it."

It wasn't anger or animosity in his eyes. Just kindness. The same look I had seen in his eye the moment he came out of surgery. Like a switch had been flipped.

For a moment, I understood that everything would be okay, even if I didn't choose Barry in the end. He wasn't competing for me, he just wanted me to accept him.

"Barry, I'm not sure why you want me to go over there, but that isn't in our best interest now." I didn't want to tell him that my heart was in two places, but it was. As much as I'd tried to convince myself otherwise, the pull towards Gordy felt impossible to ignore when I saw him in person. "We are here, now, and don't need any more distractions in our lives." Thank God the kids were oblivious to the underlying conversation taking place.

"Just because you're choosing to ignore the distractions doesn't mean they don't exist. I've seen this before. Distractions have a way of growing."

His eyes gave away his fear. Even Charlotte stopped playing her game and looked up at him, then me. I took a sip of wine, keeping my eyes on Barry, begging him to stop. *Was this why he brought us here? To challenge me?*

A chill ran down my spine. I thought I had made my decision, for better or worse, to stay with this marriage, but Barry was fighting me on this. I could feel the tension again.

"Alrighty, order up," our waitress said behind me.

Barry broke his stare and took my phone away from Charlotte as the food was being placed in front of her. "Mommy should probably have this back now," he said.

My phone burned hot from her little hands, and I shoved it into my purse. Suddenly, my salad wasn't what I wanted. I wanted something to dull the anxiety coursing through my bloodstream. A burger with fries. Pizza. More wine. Anything to calm my nerves right now. As if she could read my mind, our waitress brought me another glass of wine. "Jimmy thought you'd need a refill."

My chair scraped the floor as I pushed back from the table. I grabbed the full glass of wine and walked back towards the bar.

Jimmy was leaning on his elbows, talking with Charlie and Gordy. "What are you doing?" My voice was sharp, accusing. "Can't you guys respect me enough to let me have dinner with my family?"

Jimmy's face dropped, eyes shooting to Gordy. "Linn, I'm sorry. Normally I just get you more wine when your glass gets low."

"Yes, when I'm sitting here at the bar with Gracie," I said. "But Barry and I are trying to have a meal out, and I keep getting signals from both of you that is undermining my marriage, which I'm trying to fix."

Gordy smirked. *He fucking smirked.* I needed to end this here and now. I would never be able to move forward with my marriage if Gordy wouldn't let me go. I had to try and convince him to leave me alone.

"Charlie, is it possible for Gordy and me to have a conversation in your office?"

Charlie's eyes grew wide. "Um, sure, if that's what you need."

I glanced at Barry before heading in back. He had given Charlotte his phone and resumed tic-tac-toe with Trevor. He never looked up.

I'd been in the back office one other time, with Jimmy, and I squashed down the wave of guilt that washed over me. The office was tiny—a desk, chair, and a guest chair—not great for an awkward conversation, but it would have to do.

The second the door shut, Gordy reached for my shoulders and turned me around and pushed me against the door. His lips were on mine before my brain registered what was happening.

This.

These lips.

His hands reached for the side of my face and a groan escaped him. My breath quickened and electricity hummed through my veins. I grabbed the back of his shirt and pulled him in as close as he could get. His entire body leaned into mine, pinning me to the door.

What am I doing?

I broke the kiss, keeping him an arm's-length away. Both of us panting.

"Why are you doing this?"

He looked at me, eyes wide. "Me? I thought you wanted this."

"Gordy, I told you yesterday, in no uncertain terms, that Barry and I were trying to fix our marriage. What part of that don't you understand?"

He rubbed his lips. "You have a funny way of saving your marriage, if this is how you do it. Tell me, do you kiss Barry like that?"

My face was burning, a bitter combination of passion and shame. "For the record, I asked you back here to tell you to leave me alone. That Barry knew about us and you would have to give me space."

"Then why kiss me like that?" He ran his hand through his hair and tried to pace within the office. He looked like a caged animal. "What fucking game are you playing?"

I sat in the guest chair and covered my face with my hands. I asked him back here to end this, and instead, I made everything worse. Destroying my own life was a gift. Gracie's words echoed in my head—*fix it or accept it*— and a calmness over took me.

"Can you sit down? You're hovering, and I hate that."

He pulled the desk chair out and moved it as far away from me as possible. He leaned his elbows on his knees, looking at the floor. "Linny, you can't kiss me like that and expect me to believe you want to save your marriage." He ran his hand through his hair and eyed me.

"First of all, *you* kissed *me*. Yes, I reacted because I've wanted to kiss you for as long as I can remember," I said. "Secondly, as confusing as this is, I truly do want to save my marriage and my family. I believed for so long that I could have it all, but I need to grow up and accept the choices I've made. I can't keep thinking *what if* with you. I can't wonder how you'll feel any longer. I have to worry about myself, and if that's selfish, then so be it. I am so sick of every man in my life wanting something from me right now. I can't breathe anymore."

A voice inside me was screaming "no!" but I knew in my heart this was the right thing to do.

"I don't want anything *from* you. I just want you, and don't deny that you have these feelings too."

I took a deep breath and blew it out slowly. He was

right, I couldn't deny it. I did want him, but I wanted my marriage more. "I don't know how else to ask you to give me space. I feel like I'm banging my head against the wall."

"Welcome to my world. I've felt that way for the last week."

I shook my head. This was going nowhere. "I'm getting back to my family," I said, standing. He stood but stayed in front of the door.

"There's only one way out of here, and I'm not moving until you're honest with me."

"Gordy, I have been completely honest with you. Do I want you? Yes. Do I also want my family? Yes. I can't have both, and right now, I'm choosing my family. There's no other way to say it."

His head dropped, but he stepped aside. I opened the door and walked through without looking back. He didn't follow me out. Barry had boxed up my meal and was paying the check when I got back to the table. His face looked drawn, tired, and he wouldn't meet my eyes.

"Ready, kids?" He stood, helping Trevor into his coat. Charlotte's eyes followed from Barry to me like a tennis match. She met mine and tried to smile. I forced my face to warm into a smile even though everything in me felt like crying instead.

Tears would come later, this I knew. Right now, I had to keep our family moving forward.

Chapter Twenty-Four

The kiss.

That *kiss*.

That kiss kept me up all night. The only thing saving me this morning was the fact that it was Sunday and I didn't have to jump out of bed this morning. Even Cupcake seemed to know I needed a reprieve from the hourly wake-up calls. I sneaked out of the house to walk her, and she'd stopped at every tree, shrub, or stick to investigate and then pee on. My mind was wandering on this walk, and I was in no hurry to get back home. I needed time to think and process last night.

Gordy was in the forefront of my thoughts again, even after all this time. I grew up with Gordy in my life by default. He and Charlie were always around, but after they both graduated, I didn't see him again until last year. Almost a year ago, to be exact. He and his family were visiting for Thanksgiving and needed desserts for the holiday. It had been so long since I had seen Gordy that I wouldn't have recognized him if it wasn't for Julia. He was taller, filled out in all the right places, and had grown into his wide blue eyes. I certainly wasn't looking for anything the day he came in, but the connection between us felt like lightening.

Bright. Sharp. Undeniable. I felt alive when he hugged me, and afterward, his eyes lingered on mine, questioning if I had felt something too.

An hour later, he had found me on Facebook.

That was how it began. Nothing more than a spark, and we never crossed any lines physically, but both of us admitted our feelings to each other. He started to find other reasons to visit his mom and always found his way into my shop. We would message almost daily, and he became a lifeline for me. A reason to get up in the morning.

Until he wasn't.

I see it now, clearly. He became a distraction in my life when I couldn't take the reality any longer. I escaped my life by including him in almost every thought that ran through my head in a day. I fell asleep thinking about encounters we had, or I'd daydream about ones we'd have in the future. When Gracie came back to town, it felt like fate to me. Like we were all going to be together.

When he broke ties with me last April, something in me broke as well. Nothing mattered to me anymore, least of all myself, and my family became a casualty from my inner war. I knew the feelings we had were real and based on friendship, but last night opened up Pandora's box of wanting all over again.

He knew it, I knew it, and worst of all, Barry knew it.

Barry said very little on the way home last night. He didn't seem angry, but exhausted more than anything. When we got home, he excused himself and went to bed. I stayed up with the kids for a bit, watching *Sing!* for the eighth time this week, while I relived my conversation with Gordy again.

And the kiss.

"Linny, you can't kiss me like that and expect me to believe you want to save your marriage..." It was a voiceover loop running through my head.

Why *did* I kiss him like that?

The house was quiet when we got back from our walk, with the exception of the coffee maker. I pulled some blueberry scones out of the freezer and placed them on a cookie sheet. Sunday morning was always better when something was in the oven.

I sat down with my journal and coffee, and Cupcake made a beeline for her bed. My thoughts were unfocused, scattered this morning, and I couldn't nail down exactly what I was trying to say. Who was I kidding? I knew what needed to be said, but I was censoring myself for the sake of this perfect journal.

This is it. I don't care who reads this, or if anyone ever does. I need to be truthful with the only one who matters... me. I have hidden everything for so long, and I finally want to put my thoughts down on paper to

185

see if there is a way out of this mess.

My heart aches for Barry, who has tried to be so patient with me. And then there's Gordy, who makes me feel alive, as if every cell in my body was made for him. I love them both, I truly do, but I know I can't go on like this anymore. Barry won't be patient much longer... I feel like he's at the end of his rope with me. I just don't want to hurt anyone, and that's the part that's killing me. Someone is going to get hurt.

This ends today. One way or another, I'm going to make my decision and live with it. I have always prided myself on making the toughest decisions in a heartbeat, but something is holding me back right now.

The floor creaked and Barry stood there, hair mussed up and in his pajamas. He had always been an old soul, making him seem much older than his age, but this morning he looked like a little boy who lost his best friend. His eyes were red-rimmed, the twinkle completely covered by sadness.

The timer beeped on the oven, and I hopped up to get the scones out. Anything to avoid looking at Barry. He poured himself some coffee while I put them on the cooling rack.

I grabbed my planner from the desk in hopes to start a conversation about the holidays.

"Any ideas about Christmas this year? I know we haven't done much in the last few years, but maybe we can do something special this year."

"Are you really going to pretend that last night didn't happen?" His eyes zeroed in on mine again. "I don't ask for much, but I am going to need some honesty from you."

"Barry—"

"Stop!" He startled me, slamming his fist on the table. "Don't say my name like that. Like I don't have a clue as to what's going on. I've always known."

"I'm not sure what you think you know, but nothing has ever happened with Gordy. I have never cheated on you."

He sighed and shook his head. "The way you look at him? How can that not be considered cheating?"

Brick by brick, the foundation of this marriage was crumbling down, and I had no way to stop it. In fact, I was the wrecking ball. I put my head in my hands, the black in his eyes overwhelming my senses. I had done this.

"Do you remember last spring after Jeri died, and you said Gracie was having a bonfire?" His voice was nothing but a whisper, and his eyes focused straight ahead, as if he were reliving a moment.

"Yes," I said. "I asked you to come join us and you never did. Just like always, back then."

"Only I did," he said. "I did come out, but when I walked around back, all I saw was Gordy's arm around your shoulder. You were leaning into him with the affection of a lover."

My heart started racing, remembering that moment

so clearly. We weren't lovers, Gordy and I, but that moment in time felt like we were. The feelings we had back then, and still now, were that strong.

My phone, sitting on the desk, beeped with a text. His eyes snapped to mine once again.

"Shall we take bets on who this is from?" He walked towards the desk.

"Barry, don't—"

"Ohhh, looky here…" he said, his voice thick with sarcasm. "It's Gracie's brother telling you he can't stop thinking about that kiss."

He turned and threw my phone into the family room. Cupcake whimpered by my legs, and I picked her up.

"Are you kidding me, Linn? *That kiss?*"

I stood up to make sure the kids hadn't sneaked out of their bedrooms. "First of all, keep your voice down. I do not want the kids dragged into this."

He was circling the kitchen table like a shark.

"Secondly, that kiss is not what you think. I told him last night, in no uncertain terms, that we were done."

He laughed bitterly. "Oh, that's precious. You're done *now*? So the last few months I've been bumbling around here trying to make you fall back in love with me was what, practice?" He yanked out a chair and sat down heavily. "Forgive me if I don't believe anything you say right now."

My phone beeped again from the family room. Barry shook his head. I couldn't stand that I had hurt him like this. Cupcake trembled in my arms, so I sat down at the table with Barry.

"If you can't believe anything I say, then can you at least forgive me? I am trying here, and I realized last night at Lakeside that I needed to be clearer with Gordy. It backfired. He kissed me as soon as we got in the office, and I pushed him away. I told him to leave me alone."

"Linny, he kissed you because you're still acting torn about what it is that you want. He can feel that you're weak. If you were truly on board, he would've sensed that." His voice was calmer now, but the words were just as sharp. Cupcake heaved a big sigh and rested her chin on my arm.

"But I am on board, Barry. I'm sorry if I didn't wake up with an epiphany and want my marriage back, but I have been catching up. We both made mistakes in the past, and I know I didn't want this after the heart attack, but things have changed. You have to know that."

"I hear what you're saying, but I think there is a part of you that still wants Gordy." He had a single tear trailing down his face. "You have today to figure it out, Linn. Forget the list. Forget our anniversary. I can't go on like this anymore, and quite frankly, I deserve better than what you're giving."

"What do you mean, figure it out?" It was as if he read my journal and knew what I had written.

"I mean, do what you have to and sort out your feelings. If you want Gordy, take him. I can't be anyone's settlement." He stood and poured more coffee. "But if you choose this marriage, I never want to hear about him again, and I never want to question your feelings, either. You have to figure out what you want."

He grabbed his coffee and went back to our bedroom, leaving me here with the million-dollar question.

What do I want?

Chapter Twenty-Five

The bakery was quiet, too quiet, but my mind couldn't handle any more distractions at this point. The voices in my head would drown out any music I chose anyway. As I sat here in the corner in the front window, I'd noticed that Aiden had found the Christmas decorations in the back and somehow multiplied them. There wasn't a space in this bakery that wasn't lit, glittered, or frosted with fake snow.

When Tony walked in, his expression said it all. He stopped as if there was an imaginary wall in front of him, mouth agape, and his eyes surveyed the storefront. The words "shock and awe" came to my mind. When his eyes meet mine, I shrugged.

"I'm gonna go out on a limb and guess Christmas is your favorite holiday," he said.

"It is, for many reasons," I confirmed. "But you can blame all this on Aiden."

He pulled out a chair, eyeing the table in front of him. I seemed to have sampled one of everything from the case, and I knew he was going to have words about it.

"How has your week been?" He opened his notebook, but his eyes were locked on mine. I was trying to read what he was thinking, but as usual, he was a stone wall.

"I've had better," I said, honestly.

"The workouts? How have those been going?" Our conversations started like this every time. Workouts first, then we tackled what worked and what could've been better.

"For the first time since I've started, I missed one of the training walks. The bakery has been crazy with Thanksgiving, and life is just upside down right now." I know his job wasn't to scold me, but I felt like a fourth grader who forgot her homework.

"It's okay, Linn," he said, calmly. "You've been working like a dog, and every now and then we all need breaks." He paused, scanning the table. "You want to talk about what's bothering you?"

I looked at the table myself and saw it. I saw the plates and wrappers that had been discarded. *Why did I do this to myself?*

He stood and began to clear the mess from the table, even my beloved coffee. When he came back, he set a bottled water in front of me. "Drink."

"Drink? Are you Tarzan now?" His face didn't crack.

"Linny, I need you to understand that I'm not here to reprimand you, but I am concerned by several things. One, you missed a workout—which really isn't a big deal in the grand scheme of things—but there wasn't a great excuse for missing it. Your life is always crazy, so I'm not buying that. Two, I walk in here and notice that you've been eating your way through the case. Again, it's not a big deal, but I think it's a red flag."

"Just the two concerns or are we going for a trifecta?"

He ignored my snark. "Three, for the first time since I've been coming in here, there isn't any music playing. No Aretha. No Lady Gaga. No Michael Jackson." He took a drink from his own water. "This is the biggest red flag of them all. The other two I can wave off to a bad week. No music? Something is wrong."

His words were pelting me like little stones trying to break through the surface. I took a deep breath and looked out the fake snow-frosted window. "I don't even know where to begin," I whispered.

"How about this morning. Why are you sitting here in silence, eating?"

"My husband gave me the ultimatum this morning. I have to figure out if I'm going to stay in our marriage and everything I've worked for— or choose someone I've loved for over a year and break up my entire family."

To his credit, Tony's only reaction was his raised eyebrows.

"And while I truly want to save my family and fix my marriage, I can't help but wonder if I'm with the right person. Either way I'm screwed because someone is going to get hurt. It's just a matter of how much damage I want to cause." I met his eyes, searching for an answer in them. "When I think about the hurt I'm going to cause, it makes me want to crawl in bed and never leave. Preferably with chocolate cake." I couldn't face him any longer and started to peel the label off my water.

He nodded and looked out the window. "Can I ask you to pinpoint for me the precise moment you decided to give your life away?"

My eyes snapped up at him. "What are you talking about? I haven't given anything away."

"Yes, Linny, you have. You've given everything to these two men and completely left yourself out of the picture."

"No, my problem is I can't give either of them what they want."

"Can you tell me, without hesitating, what it is that you want? Not from men. Not from business. But from life. What. Do. You. Want?"

"I want to be happy," I said, simply and without hesitation.

"Okay, define happy for me. Tell me exactly what that looks like in your head."

"It's teaching Charlotte how to bake my grandma's cookies. It's watching Trevor run and play with our dog. It's taking care of myself and walking. It's reading again—God, I haven't read in so long and I have no idea why I stopped. It's working with Aiden. It's meeting with you. It's watching the stupid *Bachelor* show with Barry." My eyes snapped up at him again, as the last piece of the puzzle fell into place.

Tony smiled knowingly and nodded for me to

continue.

"It's saving my marriage," I whispered.

He leaned back and folded his arms. "I didn't hear anything about what's-his-name in there."

"Because he doesn't make me happy anymore. I needed him last spring, but I'm stronger now. And my marriage is trying to get back on track. I don't need him anymore. He was the link that made me feel weak, like I couldn't live without him, but you, you have helped me see a different picture in my head of myself."

He tipped his head. "What kills me, is that you refuse see how amazing you are. You will see the flaws. What wasn't done. The size of your clothing. And you will nver get to see the good stuff. When you can finally focus on that happy list, then your life will fall into place. Right now you're chasing a feeling of 'what if,' and that never works. You're more concerned with the feelings of two men than your own. Figure out what you want, then move towards it. You have to find a reason to start living, Linny. It's harder, and definitely more uncomfortable, but in the end, you get what you want. Happiness."

I sat still, stunned at the words he was saying to me. On one hand, I was offended that he could fold my life into such a little box, but on the other hand, it was truth. He didn't say anything that didn't ring true. I had stressed and worried about how both of these men would react to what I wanted, but never solely looked at it from my perspective. I never put myself first.

"Say something," he said.

"I don't know what to say," I said. "You make me feel like anything is possible. That happiness is attainable. I've lived for so long settling for the way things are, and I never understood that it's in my hands to change it."

"Be the change you wish to see in the world," he said.

"I'm not gonna lie… your use of quotes freaks me out a bit," I said.

"It's a gift," he said, shrugging one shoulder. "So, I think we need to have a game plan for today. Then tomorrow morning, you start fresh with your new perspective. If you keep hanging out in this limbo, you're going to undo all the good we've accomplished, and it's time you started to live out your word."

"Savor…" I said. "But that means I have to cut ties with Gordy today. I probably can't do that through a text, can I?" It surprised me how calm I was about it. The decision was made, and I just had to execute it.

"Nope," he said, closing his notebook. "That's a face to face, and you will be clear, direct, and unemotional about it. It doesn't matter how you felt in the past. You said it best… you don't need him anymore."

"You are a cold-hearted man," I said. "But everything you said is true. I already feel calmer, just knowing the decision is made."

He stood and slid into his Northface coat. "Have you seen my numbers on Facebook? I'm up to three thousand followers." His face glowed with pride.

"I love the question of the day you're doing on there," I said. "You're making a difference with people."

"Thanks, it's so cool to see people making the connection with what they're thinking and how they're feeling." He leaned in for a hug, something he's never done before. "Good luck today," he whispered.

I nodded into his shoulder, feeling so much gratitude towards him.

"I'm gonna go shower and try to get all the Christmas off me now."

"Look at Tony, making a joke. Is that a crack in that tough exterior?" I nudged him in the shoulder.

I followed him to the door and noticed the crinkles in the corner of his eyes. A genuine smile.

Locking the door behind him, I watched him walk to the edge of the curb, turn and smile. Turning around, I viewed the store through fresh eyes. Different eyes. He was right, Christmas threw up in here, and it was too quiet. Music first, then I would text Gordy to see when he could meet with me. Getting that out of the way was key to starting fresh tomorrow.

Chapter Twenty-Six

After texting Gordy and agreeing to meet at 3:00, I called Barry to make sure he could take Charlotte to her skating lesson and also include Trevor. I wanted to meet Gordy at home, on my turf, so he could see what I had chosen, and why I had chosen it. Barry agreed without asking any questions.

I wanted the break to be clear, but compassionate. I still had strong feelings for Gordy, but knowing they were tied to him saving me allowed me to be clear about what I needed.

I needed to save myself.

The rest of the morning consisted of prepping for the week. It amazed me how much I could get done now that my thoughts were less cloudy. Clarity. Grace talked about it all the time, but I never really understood what she meant until now. Clarity meant you focused on what you wanted in your life and ignored the other stuff.

I arrived home and changed into my running clothes while I waited for Gordy to come over. My plan was to get out and run after we talked. I've had so much nervous energy since Tony left, and couldn't wait to run on the beach again.

But first, Gordy. The doorbell rang as if on cue, and

my heart started racing. My thoughts were crystal clear of what I wanted, but saying this to his face was going to be difficult. This much I knew.

Opening the door, he pushed his way in and pulled me into a hug. I relaxed into the hug and took a deep breath. He had never been here before, but I needed him to see the why of my decision. I purposely left artwork and books laying on the kitchen table. This was my family I had been screwing around with, and he needed to know this is where my heart belonged.

I broke the hug and led him to the kitchen. He slid out of his coat and hung it over one of the chairs at the island.

"Beautiful home," he said, wandering around the kitchen. He looked at the beach from the window above the sink. "I haven't been to many homes on this side of the lake. It's a totally different view from here."

"Yeah, same lake, minus the lighthouse." I didn't know how to jump right in, but I didn't really want to drag this out either. "Can I get you something to drink?"

"Nah, I'm good," he said, turning around, arms crossed. "Mostly, I just want to see what you need from me. I know I was an ass last night. Charlie let me have it, but I don't regret one second. Especially the kiss." He started to walk towards me, but I stopped him.

"Can we sit? I need to say some things and clear the air between us. And I need you to hear and understand what I'm saying."

His eyes clouded over, and he started to say something but stopped himself. We both sat down, and I started to stack all the stuff and move it to the other side of the table.

"Linny, before you say anything, I want you to know that I took the job with the engineering company. I'm going to be moving back here for good after Christmas."

I smiled to myself. Of course he would move back. I was still being tested.

"Gordy—I can't do this anymore," I said, bluntly. "You and I are not going to happen, and I need you to process that information and respect my wishes."

He closed his eyes and shook his head. "You don't mean that, Linn. We can finally be together. This is exactly what we've always wanted."

"I do mean it, Gordy," I implored. "And I can't have you trying to undermine my marriage every time I see you. I want you to let me go."

He pursed his lips together. "I know you think this is what you want, but you're not going to be happy with Barry. I know this."

I sighed. This was so unlike the Gordy I fell in love with. "Why are you fighting me on this? What is going on?"

He stood and went back to the window, looking at the lake.

"I just had it in my head that we would be together," he whispered. "I never imagined you wouldn't want us to be together. There hasn't been a day I haven't thought about us since last April. Even when I couldn't reach out, I was still thinking of you. Of us."

"Back in the spring, I would've jumped at this, but things have changed, and I have to choose what is going to make me happy."

"I used to make you happy. That kiss last night... I felt it. You felt it. We still have something, Linn."

"No, we *had* something, and the lust still remains. But I want something more than just the attraction. I want it all, and now I'm willing to fight for it. The husband, the kids, the house, the business... these are all things I dreamt about growing up. I'm not willing to throw it away because of one kiss."

"And when Barry goes back to work? He's just going to hurt you again," he said, turning to meet my eyes. "I won't pick up the pieces again, Linn."

Who was this person? I knew he was hurting, but he began to piss me off. "I would never ask you to pick up the pieces. From here on out, that's my job, not any man's."

"So this is it." He folded his arms and leaned back against the counter. "You're just done with me, and I don't get a say?"

"Did I have a say last spring when you wanted to fix your marriage? I don't think so. And I gave you the space and respect you needed." Frustration crawled up my spine. How dare he question this after what he put me through? "Look, Gordy, I know this hurts... I've been there, but I'm in a different place now. And I want different things."

"I think this is a huge mistake you're making. Am I just supposed to pretend I don't have feelings for you when I see you?"

"Can you, for one second, stop thinking about yourself and what *you* want? This was not an easy decision for me, but I am trying to do the right thing."

His entire body closed off. His head dropped. Arms crossed, shoulders squared off. I still wanted to comfort him, but knew I couldn't. He needed me to be distant and cold. If he was going to move on, then I needed to be heartless.

I looked at my watch. "I hate to rush this, but I need to get my run in before Barry gets home with the kids." Cold and heartless. These words ran through my head. My heart broke for him, but it was the only way.

His eyes snapped up to mine, disbelieving. "What happened since last night to make you act this way?"

"Clarity happened," I said. "And I knew that you needed this clarity too. You needed to see that I'm serious."

"Message received," he sniped. He grabbed his coat, not bothering to put it on, and walked towards the front door. "I hope you and your clarity have a nice life."

"Gordy, don't do this—"

"Do what, Linn? Be mad?" he snapped, turning to face me. The anger in his eyes startled me. "You'll have to forgive me for not wishing you the best."

He turned and walked out the door, leaving me to stand there and wonder what the hell just happened. This was not the Gordy I knew, and I'd have to accept my role in his heartbreak. A part of me wanted to text Gracie and warn her about his well-being, but he wasn't my responsibility anymore. I needed to be clear with all of my actions to move forward. Actions and words, aligned.

I didn't know where this choice, this clarity, would lead me, but I had to go with my gut. And my gut said Barry and my life with him was the direction I needed to be going towards. A wave of calm washed over me and I smiled to myself. The anxiety turned to peace.

I laced up my shoes and headed out, running towards my future.

Part Three: Love

Chapter Twenty-Seven

"So, how did it feel to cross the finish line?" A coy smile played on Tony's face.

"Unbelievable," I gushed. "I was not prepared for emotion at the end of a race, and I was overwhelmed by all these feelings I had."

Barry and I did the Frosty 5K yesterday morning, and I continued to bask in the runner's high. Barry walked the whole race, but I did my run/walk and finished in thirty-seven minutes. I didn't care how slow that would be to anyone else. I felt so much pride running across that finish line. After I was done, I looped back and walked the rest of the race with Barry, who also seemed pretty proud of himself for finishing.

"The first race is pretty powerful. It's also an indication of whether or not it's something you want to do again," he said.

"It's funny you say that," I said. "Last night, all I could think about was crossing the finish line for the marathon. Obviously that's so far away, but I could actually see it in my head."

He leaned forward, resting his elbows on the table. "That's good, Linn, exactly the motivation you need to keep up with the training." He took a drink of his water. "I have to say, you're looking more relaxed these days.

Almost happy."

I leaned back in my chair. It would be hard to explain to anyone, except for Tony who has seen me at my lowest. "I can't quite explain it, but it feels like I'm finally doing what I'm supposed to be doing. And it's easy. Well, no, not easy, but clear I guess. I don't have all this other stuff in my head wondering and questioning, so I know exactly what needs to be done. Does that make sense?"

"You're a woman on a mission. It's a beautiful thing to behold."

"Yes! A mission to bring back happy into my life," I said. "And once I let go of all the resistance in my way, it has been so enlightening to go through each day."

"I was thinking…" he stalled. "I've been wanting to start a new page on my website, highlighting clients and progress. One aspect I'm really interested in is doing a client of the month, featuring someone who has excelled in their training, whatever that may be. It doesn't have to be about weight loss or workouts, but more of how they are staying inspired to achieve their goals. I'd love it if you were my first one."

"Gee, Tony, I don't think I've been anyone's first." I regretted it the second it popped out of my mouth. He turned crimson. "Sorry. Sometimes my filter doesn't work as well as it should."

His eyes were still downcast. "It's fine. I shouldn't be embarrassed anymore."

"Ha. The answer is yes, I would love to be the first client. What do you have in mind for the piece?"

"I'm thinking of a Q and A type article, sort of like something you'd see in a fitness magazine. I'll send you a list of questions and you can just send back the answers." He stopped again, his eyebrows raised. "I implore you to answer with the least amount of snark possible. This is about inspiring other people, not making them laugh."

"I'm offended you think I'd be snarky about this," I said.

"Linn, let's be real. I rarely get a straight answer out of you. I'm only asking for something that people would want to share on Facebook or Twitter."

"Got it. I can do this, Tony. A slice of honesty, hold the humor."

He shook his head. "I'll send the questions tonight. If possible, I'd like to post it between Christmas and New Year's to inspire people for resolutions."

"You're turning into quite the marketer, Tony. I'm so happy for you."

"I'm not sure what sent me in here that day a few months ago, but it was the best choice I've ever made."

"Aww, I'm so glad you did too. I know Aiden thought I was crazy that day, but I had a good feeling about you from the beginning." I stood to refill my coffee. I didn't want this conversation to end. "If it weren't for you, I think I'd still be stuck in my old life, miserable."

"You've done all the work," he said. "I think you just needed someone to talk to."

"It's more than that, what you've done for me." I sat down and looked out the window. The snow falling reminded me of a snow globe. "You gave me my confidence back, and the crazy thing is, I didn't even know I had lost it. I was floundering and didn't know why."

He smiled. "The second you told me that running a marathon was your goal, I knew you were strong inside. A weak person doesn't pick marathons. It excited me to work with you for that reason alone."

"It wasn't my charm and good looks?"

"Well… that too," he said. "I wish you could've seen my face when you sent that first set of questions back. I had no idea what I was getting into with you."

"Thank God you didn't judge me based on that."

"If I hadn't met you first, I would've dismissed you immediately. In person, you still have that edge, but you're so much more. I don't know anyone like you."

"It's funny, Barry used to say the same thing when we were dating."

"How are things now with him?"

How were things with him?

"Definitely better now that Gordy is out of the picture. It's baby steps, but I wake up every day excited about the possibilities. And doing the race with him was pretty cool. Something I never thought we'd do together." I smiled at the memory of crossing the finish line with him. He had stopped just past the line and kissed me. Really kissed me, and I didn't hesitate in responding. His eyes twinkled as he looked at me. In that moment, with hundreds of people around us, it was just the two of us. No one else mattered. That was when I knew.

"That look on your face says it all," he mused. "You look like someone falling in love."

I felt my face flush. "I never thought it would be possible to have feelings like this for Barry again. I find myself thinking about him at random times during the day. Excited to go home again. It's like a second chance for both of us."

Full on smile. Rare, but there it was. "Sometimes you get a second chance to travel down the same path," he said.

"Do you have a book of quotes you study every night?"

"I do read a lot," he said, blushing again. "And I may or may not have daily emails sent to me with quotes."

I shook my head. "Let's play a game. I'll give you a word, and you give me a quote in five seconds or less."

"Done and done." He set his water down in preparation.

"Strength."

"That which does not kill us makes us stronger." He cocked an eyebrow, gloating.

"Good one," I said. "Truth."

"Never tell the truth to people who are not worthy of it."

"Oh wow... I love that," I gushed. "And you're right. Some people don't deserve to know everything about you. This is fun.... How about failure?"

"Our greatest glory is not in never falling, but in rising every time we fall."

"Hope." He was freaking me out a bit, but I couldn't stop.

"And now these three remain: faith, hope and love. But the greatest of these is love." He leaned back and folded his arms. "I think I've proven myself?"

"Proven you're a freak, yes," I said, laughing. "But in a weird way, I'm extremely impressed. My favorite was the falling one. I may have to print that out and hang it in the kitchen."

He stood. "As fun as this is, I do need to get going to my next appointment."

I followed him to the door. "I won't see you until after the new year," I said. "Bring it in, I need a hug."

He pulled me in without hesitation. "Dream big for next year," he whispered.

Tears sprung to my eyes as I clung to him like a lifesaver. "Thank you for everything," I whispered back.

He pulled away without looking at me, turned, and walked out the door. Halfway down the block, he turned and gave me a small wave.

I locked the door and turned to see a small gift on the table. How did he leave that without me seeing? The small box was wrapped as if Trevor did it, but the intention touched me. Layer upon layer of tape forced me to find scissors and cut my way into it. I was grateful he wasn't here to watch me breaking into my gift. Relieved of its wrapped prison, the box opened easily. Inside lay a tiny silver washer attached to red cord bracelet. A single word, SAVOR, was stamped into the circle. My heart fluttered. I hadn't received a gift with so much meaning behind it in a long time. Maybe never.

I slid it on to my wrist and tightened the cord, and I immediately felt like he was with me. I had seen articles about having a word for the year but always thought that was for people who needed help. I smiled as the irony washed over me. I grabbed my phone.

> ME: *Tony, Tony Tony*
>
> TONY: 😌
>
> ME: *My heart is full. Thank you.*
>
> TONY: *Merry Christmas Linn*

On my way home, I found myself smiling and singing to the Christmas songs on the radio. A hard contrast to last year when I felt trapped by my own doing. A loveless marriage. Another man I couldn't have. Two kids who only needed their mom to be sane. I had come so far, anchored by Barry who vaulted us into this crazy second chance. I will never understand what or how it happened when he came out of surgery, but fate had other plans for us.

And for that, I was grateful.

Chapter Twenty-Eight

The wind was harsh on Lakeside's rooftop in December. Being so close to the water, the air was sharper, more cutting than anywhere else in Frankfort. And Barry and I were up there decorating for Charlie, who wanted to surprise Grace with a rooftop proposal on the winter solstice.

The rooftop oozed romantic charm with the lights and lanterns. The tables and chairs were all still in storage, so the open space was floating in the bouncing light and shadows. Barry and I were decorating a Christmas tree with even more white lights and silver bulbs for reflection. The entire scene may confuse Santa flying by in a few days.

Julia had Grace tied up for another hour, so we had plenty of time to finish decorating. The plan was to meet them here for dinner, then Charlie would get us upstairs, somehow.

"This is pretty amazing up here," Barry said, his eyes twinkling in the light.

I pulled my focus away from the tree and looked around. My breath caught, "Oh my... it *is* amazing. Gracie is going to love this." This felt like something you'd see in the movies, not here in our little town. The fact that it was snowing lightly made it even more magical.

"This makes my proposal to you seem so ordinary." His eyes, still dancing around the space, settled and locked on mine.

"Oh Barry, you can't compare the two," I comforted. "Ours was very romantic."

I remembered it as if it were yesterday… Candlelight dinner at our favorite Italian restaurant. Ring resting in the bottom of my champagne glass. Barry, down on one knee before I even realized the scene around me.

A slow smile crept on his face. "I guess ours had a certain charm of its own," he admitted. "We were so young back then."

"I remember being the happiest girl in the world that night. I couldn't believe you were asking me to marry you."

"I'd ask again tonight if Charlie wasn't stealing my thunder," he mused.

"Aww, let them have their time. They're so happy and deserve it." I went back to hanging Christmas bulbs on the tree. "Besides, we're an old married couple. They get the fresh start tonight."

Charlie busted through the door. "Oh. My. God. She is going to die when she sees this."

"It's pretty frickin' romantic, if I say so myself," I said. "Any thoughts on getting her up here?"

"Yes, that's why I came up." He rubbed his hands together and blew heat into them. "I am going to be checking on a leak when she arrives. You and Barry will be downstairs, already waiting at the table. Jimmy is going to interrupt you and tell Grace that I need her help with something on the roof. After that, I'll take over."

Even with the frigid air, I melted inside. Excitement started to bubble up inside me, but I would have to contain it or she would know simply by looking at me.

"Linny, wipe that look off your face. You have to pretend this is any normal night." Charlie's eyes zeroed in on mine.

"Got it, Charlie," I said. "But damn, is she going to be happy. Thank you for letting us be a part of this."

"Wouldn't have it any other way. She would want the most important people in her life to witness this. I'm sure of it. Plus, would you be able to video this on your phone when I get started? I want her to be able to remember it after."

"Of course," I said, happy to have a responsibility.

"I'll take a few pics as well," Barry said, waving his phone. "Can't capture enough memories for moments like this."

"Julia is staying, correct?"

"Definitely, she is going to pretend to stay for a glass of wine before we order dinner." He shrugged. "I wanted her here for this. She is really excited too."

"Well," I said, looking over the tree. "I think our job is done up here. We should turn off the lights so she doesn't see them when they drive up."

Barry walked over and pulled the plug from the outlet. I threw the boxes away from the decorations and gathered my things. "The lanterns will be fine until we come back up."

Charlie eyes glanced around the area. "I really can't thank you both enough for helping with this," he said.

I pulled Charlie into a hug and felt him shiver, from excitement or the cold, I wasn't sure.

"Let's get downstairs and warm up before they get here," Barry said.

We wandered downstairs, Charlie heading in back. A table was set for us already, and Jimmy followed us with a glass of wine for me and club soda for Barry.

"Everything all set up there?" The bar was pretty empty tonight, so Jimmy pulled up a chair and sat with us.

"It's stunning. Gracie is going to freak," I said.

His face broke into a smile. "Charlie is so glad you two were able to be a part of this. It's going to be awesome," he said. "You two need anything else while you wait? I'm going to get behind the bar in case they're early."

"We're good," Barry said. "Thanks Jimmy."

Jimmy met my eyes for a beat, then he retreated back behind the bar. While Barry knew about Gordy, I never admitted to the slip Jimmy and I had when I was at my lowest point. Looking back, I had no idea what I was thinking. He was such a comfort to me at a time when

I needed someone, anyone, to notice me. To make me feel like I mattered. I know now I was just lonely and searching for someone to take my mind off Gordy, but the guilt still haunted me.

"You look sad all of the sudden," Barry said.

I forced a smile. "Not sad, just thinking about how far we've come," I lied. He would never know about our indiscretion. "This is going to be the best Christmas ever."

His shoulders relaxed, and his face warmed into a smile. "I don't know what I did to deserve all of this back into my life, but I am so grateful to you."

"Me? What did I do?" I took a sip of wine.

"You were able to leave the past behind us, all of it, and agree to share your amazing life with me again. I can't tell you what that means to me." His eyes were watering in the corners. "And I'll spend the rest of my life showing you my love and appreciation."

I had to admit it… Sappy Barry was growing on me. He looked at me as if no one else existed, even when the kids were around. He doted, pampered, and smothered me every day, trying to calm my doubts and fears.

My phone chimed.

> JULIA: *We are a few minutes away!!*
>
> ME: *OMG! This is happening!*
>
> JULIA: *See you soon.*

"They're on their way," I said. Barry's face lit up. "I have to calm down, otherwise she's going to know something is up."

He grabbed my hand across the table. "Have I told you how beautiful you look tonight? You were positively glowing upstairs."

"Ha! Good lighting is the best filter."

"I was going to say that happiness was," he said. "At least that's what I think is lighting you up."

"I will admit to being happier than I've been in a long time, years even," I said. "I have to remind myself that this is my life now."

"And you have no doubts or hesitations?"

"I don't think it's that I don't have any, but I firmly believe that I am exactly where I'm supposed to be. I know it'll take time, but I don't doubt us for a second." My phone beeped.

Julia: We're here!

I slid my phone into my purse. "It's show time!" I gave Jimmy a thumbs up behind the bar. His arms folded as he imitated the look of a bored bartender.

Gracie and Julia walked in, a dusting of snow layered on both of them. She waved to Jimmy, and he winked as he wiped down the bar. Julia, who looked like she was going to bust, would need to bring it down a notch. I stood to hug Gracie and gave Julia the stink-eye as I did. Her face relaxed into calm composure instantly. Barry hugged both of them and we all sat down as

Jimmy brought over wine for both of them.

"We have a leak in the back... Charlie is investigating but will be right out, Gracie," he said. "Julia, are you staying for dinner?"

"Oh no, just catching up for a bit," she said. "I have to get back home soon."

"We've had quite the day of shopping," Gracie said, taking a long drink of water. "I'm exhausted and starving. I don't know how you're still upright, Mom."

"Good living," she winked, sipping her wine.

Jimmy's phone chimed and my stomach clenched. It had to be Charlie. He looked at the message, wrinkled brow forming.

"What is it?" Gracie looked concerned.

"Charlie said there's a problem upstairs on the roof," he said, sliding his phone in his pocket. "I'm going to check it out."

"I'll come with you," Gracie said, standing.

They headed for the stairs. We waited a beat, then bolted behind them.

When we reached the top of the stairs, Gracie was standing in the middle of the rooftop, circling slowly and mouth gaping. Charlie walked out from behind the bar, smiling, but Gracie hadn't seen him yet.

"What is going on?" Gracie whispered to me.

Unable to hide my emotions, tears rolled down my cheeks. I nodded to Charlie. She turned and brought her hand to her mouth.

"Charlie?"

He reached for her and walked her over to the tree. I noticed it then, a small box with a red bow rested on one of the branches. Julia snuggled up beside me and grabbed my hand. I shivered from the inside out, and Barry put his arm around my shoulders. Julia noticed and winked at me.

I grabbed my phone and hit record. Gracie was crying now, and Charlie was talking softly to her. We couldn't hear, but we didn't need to either. Gracie's eyes never left his, locked on her future. Her everything. He knelt on one knee, and she began to cry harder.

He reached for her left hand and held it to his lips before speaking again.

"Yes!" Her voice, loud and clear, a statement to the world. "Yes, yes, yes," she repeated, bending down to hug him.

He stood, Gracie still wrapped around his neck, and swung her around. Squeals of laughter could be heard for blocks, I imagine.

"I'll be downstairs," Jimmy whispered in my ear before descending the stairs. I knew how Jimmy felt, and a small part of me felt it too. Bittersweet. This kind of love was the dream. The pinnacle. What everyone wished for when they imagined the love of their lives.

This was how I felt ten years ago, but I didn't know if I'd ever feel this kind of love ever again. It was new and fresh, without the daily trials of life, year after year, fading its sparkle. Like anything new, eventually, it just becomes old. A "before" in the "after" of life.

Gracie's hand was shaking uncontrollably as she showed me the ring. The emerald cut diamond, he told us earlier, was his mother's that she wanted passed on to Gracie. Nothing could have been more perfect for her.

I pulled her into a hug. "Dunham, you got this," I whispered.

She laughed through her tears. We both did. "I did, didn't I?"

Next, I hugged Charlie, and he lifted and swung me around too. "I can't thank you enough for all your help."

"Believe me when I say it was my privilege, Charlie," I said.

"Damn, it's cold out here," Charlie hollered. "Let's get downstairs and celebrate!"

Julia and Grace, arm in arm, led all of us downstairs, where Jimmy had glasses of champagne waiting for us. At the opposite end of the bar stood Gordy. His eyes flashed to mine, then Barry's, and guilt seeped into the lines on his forehead. He walked towards Gracie and Charlie, casting nervous glances our way before his eyes landed on his sister. He lifted her into a bear hug, whispering something to make her cry harder. Next, he shook Charlie's hand and pulled him into a hug.

Barry glanced at me. "You okay seeing him here? We can go if you want."

"I'm okay," I said. I wasn't going to ruin this for Gracie, and I refused to believe Gordy would cause a scene on this night. I reached down and grabbed Barry's hand. He squeezed it, and I met his eyes. "You have nothing to worry about. I made my choice, and he's respected it so far." Barry nodded.

"Linny, Barry." Gordy came up behind us. "I just wanted to say hi," he said.

"Gordy," I said, holding tight to Barry's hand. "You look good. How is your job going?"

His eyes flickered to our hands then back to me. "Everything is good. Can't complain." My heart sank as I watched him struggle to accept the sight in front of him. "I just want you both to know that I am happy for you. I know it seems like the last thing I'd ever say to you, but all I've ever wanted is for you to be happy, Linn."

Barry looked at me, then back to him. He reached out his hand to Gordy. "I hope you know we both wish you well," Barry said. Gordy shook his hand, stone faced.

"I appreciate that," he said. "I'll let you go. I only wanted to let you know there were no hard feelings after our last meeting. I understand what you're going through."

I smiled and longed to hug him. I knew that couldn't happen, but it didn't stop the division in my heart. He held my eyes for one more moment, then turned to stand by Julia.

Jimmy stood on the bar and whistled for the entire restaurant to hear. "Ladies and gentlemen, my brother is finally engaged!"

The confused looks turned into delight and laughter throughout the bar.

"Please raise your glasses… To Charlie and Gracie. May your love be everlasting…"

Charlie just shook his head, but the rest of us toasted to them. Grace still had tears streaming down her face as she sneaked glances at her ring. The world seemed to be in slow motion, like a dream sequence in a movie.

Barry snapping pictures of happy faces.

Jimmy hugging Charlie.

Grace leaning into her mom, resting her head on Julia's shoulder.

In that moment, I felt connected and alone, simultaneously. Similar to every New Year's Eve party I've ever attended. With the group, but lonely, somehow. I shook the thought away, pasted a smile on my face, and carried on with the celebration.

A moment like this is once in a lifetime.

Rarely, does magic happen twice.

Chapter Twenty-Nine

Today was not going as I had planned. We were unusually busy for a Saturday morning in January. Mostly, people stayed inside during the winter months, but we had a few regulars, and also the occasional weekend tourists. Today felt like a spring morning, when the snow had thawed and the townies ventured out to see the world again.

Don't get me wrong. We had our share of outdoorsy people who love winter and all that it brings, but those were not usually my clientele.

At precisely noon, Aiden kicked me out of my own bakery.

"I understand your confusion, but I have strict orders from the boss man to send you home."

"The boss *man*? Do you mean Barry?"

"You're the boss lady. He's officially the boss man by default. Obviously, you win in a real battle, but in this case, I'm on his side." The smirk on Aiden's face said it all.

"What is he up to?" I pressed him for information, hoping he'd crack under pressure.

"Barry made it clear that if I told you, he'd have to kill you," he joked. "And I love you too much to kill you, so just get out of here. Go." He shooed me away like an unwanted cat.

"But we're swamped," I objected. "I haven't seen a lunch crowd like this since October."

"Yup, and I have charmed every customer here already. I got this, boss lady."

Grudgingly, I grabbed my purse and coat. "You're sure you have this under control?"

He rolled his eyes.

I took the hint, leaving him to run the bakery, and called Barry as soon as I started my car.

"You probably have some questions," he answered, his voice bordering laughter.

"What is going on? I can't have employees kicking out of my own store!"

"It's one day, Linn," he said. "And I have to say, Aiden is a tough cookie to crack. Pardon the pun."

I smiled, in spite of myself. "I'm assuming you had to bribe him in some way to kick me out?"

"Indeed. He's a loyal one, that kid."

I felt an odd relief in knowing that Barry and Aiden were in on something together. Barry had never shown any interest in any of my employees, let alone gotten to know them. I loved that he felt comfortable going to Aiden behind my back. I also knew that Aiden wouldn't agree to anything with Barry unless he approved.

"Don't overthink this, Linn," he said. "Just come home. I have a fun surprise."

His voice was different today. Lighter, buoyant. Whatever he had planned, he was excited about it, and the curiosity overwhelmed me.

The house was quiet when I entered. No music. No TV. No Cupcake. *What was going on here?*

Barry walked out of the spare room with my overnight bag.

"Okay, what gives? Why do you have my bag?"

He smiled. "I have made some plans for today," he conceded. "I hope you will accompany me."

His eyes read a mixture of apprehension and excitement, like a kid about to jump off the high dive and was thrilled and nervous at the same time.

Butterflies bounced around my stomach just from looking at him. With as busy as we had been since the holidays, I hadn't even noticed he had lost some weight. Twenty pounds, at least. His jawline was more prominent. And his waist. I could see a waist under his sweater. He wore jeans, something I hadn't seen since our early days. He even looked taller.

"Are you checking me out?" Amusement danced in his eyes.

"When did you lose all this weight? And where did you find those jeans?"

He chuckled, setting my bag on the table. "I've steadily been losing since my heart attack. I knew I had to change the way I lived in order to keep living." He leaned against the counter, folding his arms. "As for the jeans, they have these cool places called malls. I had only heard about them before, but wow, are they great for shopping." He cocked an eyebrow.

"Well, aren't you feeling full of it today?" I unzipped my bag, a black and white Vera Bradley I had for years. Inside were clothes I had forgotten I even owned.

"I hope you don't mind I took the liberty to pick out your clothes for today."

"I hope you don't mind, but I'd like to know what I'm dressing for today."

"No, I don't mind," he said. "And I could tell you, but—"

"You'd have to kill me. Yes, I know. Your minion at the bakery had the same line." We hadn't bantered like this in forever. "Can you at least explain why we are the only two people in this house? Where's Cupcake and the kids?"

"Your mom is still recovering from bronchitis, so Gracie has them for the night."

"The *night*?" My heart sped up. "As in *all night*?"

His smile grew wide. "We're knocking a few things off our list today," he said.

"But I have a meeting tomorrow morning. Will we be back?" How could he just take over my life like this?

"Taken care of. I met with Tony and he said you're

set for the week. He will email you the training plan."

My mouth dropped open. "What do you mean you *met* with Tony?"

"About that…" He took a deep breath and blew it out slowly. "I hope you don't mind, but I hired him as well." He looked down but peered up at me through his eyebrows. Sheepishly. "After I saw the changes in you, I wondered if he could help me get back on track, health-wise." He came and sat down at the table. "I met him Thursday, initially just to talk about this weekend and my plans. But after talking with him for a few minutes, I started asking him questions about his business. We turned that meeting into my first session. I can see why you started with him."

"But how did you even know how to find Tony?" I was flabbergasted at the lengths he went for this.

"Aiden." He cringed as he looked back at me. "Pretty sure he could steal your identity if he wanted to. That kid is something else."

I sat down with Barry. "So what is all this? What are we doing today?"

He raised his eyebrows.

"You won't tell me anything?" I whined.

"Adorable, but no," he said. "You'll be surprised all day long. That's what this is about."

"I don't like surprises," I objected.

"No, you don't like *bad* surprises," he countered. "Today is about good surprises. I promise you will love them." He reached into the side pocket of my bag and pulled out an envelope and slid it over to me.

The cream-colored envelope with gold foil interior felt weighty. I pulled the card out, a single one-sided ivory card stock and read:

> *Linny ~ Today is about savoring*
> *the flavor of Michigan…*
>
> *Love, Barry.*

My hand flew to my mouth. "Is this a date card?"

He shrugged. "I thought it might add to the charm of today." The smile on his face was all pride. He knew it was a home-run move. "Those guys at *The Bachelor* know what they're doing in the romance department. I've paid attention."

"Barry—" I was at a loss for words. "How long have you been planning this?"

"Not that long, actually. You'd be amazed how things fall into place when you need them to." His eyes locked on mine for a beat, then he winked.

I sighed, taking it all in. "When do we leave? I'll stop asking where, but can I get a timeline?"

"Oddly enough, there aren't any timelines to be had today. We will leave soon, but that's all you're getting out of me. The only thing I need you to do is pack your toiletries. I wouldn't even pretend to know what you'd want for that."

I blew out a breath. "I guess I better get moving, but a timeline would definitely get me moving faster."

He rolled his eyes. "Good lord, Linny. You have ten minutes. Then we're leaving... how's that for a timeline?"

I giggled and jumped up. "I need to shower first, Barry. Give me twenty minutes, at least."

"Then go! This bus is leaving at one o'clock with or without you."

I smirked. "I don't remember threats for the one-on-one dates," I said. "Sort of kills the mood, if you ask me."

"Tick-tock, Linny." His smile lit up the room.

"So, it's obvious were checking spontaneous road trip off our list today, but what other ones do you have in mind?" I held the crumpled list in my hands. "I certainly hope we're not camping," I said.

"No, camping is usually a family trip. When we do that, the kids will be involved." He was driving north, following the coast.

"I guess this could be your surprise date," I ventured.

"Will you put that list away and just enjoy the moment? I know that's hard for you to do, but seriously, let the day just unfold."

Ignoring him, I pulled out my date card again. *Today is about savoring the flavor of Michigan.* I looked at the list again, a slow smile growing on my face. "Wine tasting?"

He looked at me over the rim of his sunglasses. "Is that on the list? Huh, I hadn't noticed."

"Yessss, wine tasting! I'm so excited," I squealed. "But you don't really drink anymore, Barry."

"Oh, a sip here and there isn't going to kill me. Besides, I wouldn't anyways, since I'm driving." He focused on the road again. "That is the last of the answers you'll get out of me. Stop trying."

I smiled, turning the heated seat on high and settling in deeper. Contentment settled in my bones and I couldn't remember a time like this with Barry since we've been married. Tension fueled any trip we ever took with the kids, and eventually we stopped doing that all together. This past year, I don't think Barry and I were ever in the same car.

"What is that look on your face? Happiness?" He looked at me, pleased.

"I was thinking I couldn't remember the last time we were in a car together, let alone on a road trip."

A cloud passed over his expression. He still had his sunglasses, but his smile faltered. "Linny, I know my faults in all of this. I know that living with me hasn't been easy."

"Barry, we have both had our issues. I certainly haven't been a saint either," I said, looking out the window. "For Christ's sake, I brought another man into the marriage. I don't know how we have been able to rise above it all."

"And I know it's not perfect yet, but it's certainly better than it's been since the beginning."

"There's no such thing as a perfect marriage," I said. "That's not what I want anyways. I want give and take. Ups and downs. That's what life is about."

"Let's aim for more ups and less downs, if it's okay with you."

"Deal," I said. "This is beautiful up here. Where are we? I haven't been paying attention."

"This little town is Omena and it will be our first stop." He took a right turn and Grand Traverse Bay opened up on the left. With the trees and water covered in snow and ice, the view was breathtaking. Most people travel here in the summer and fall, but I had to admit this was stunning. "You'll be happy I packed your camera too," he said.

"I was thinking that this is so beautiful," I said. "I can't wait to see where we are going."

He smiled. "You don't have to wait too long." He flipped on his blinker and turned into a parking lot. "Leelanau Cellars" the sign out front read. The large, slate-blue building sat on the water's edge, and I could see the back patio that opened up for summer seating.

"Barry, it's beautiful. How did you find this?"

"I seem to recall you've enjoyed their wine from time to time. I looked them up, and once I saw the pictures online, I knew this was the place we needed to be. It looked beautiful on the inside as well."

He parked, our car facing the bay. Excitement bubbled up inside me and I couldn't wait to get inside there.

The first thing I noticed when we walked inside were the views of the bay. If it was this pretty now, in the dead of winter, I couldn't imagine how beautiful it would be in the summer.

"We're gonna have to come back here in June," I whispered to Barry.

He nodded. "And again in July and August." He observed the tasting room with the eyes of a child, eventually they landed on the floor to ceiling stone fireplace. A beautiful bar covered the length of the room on one side with wrought-iron shelving with rows and rows of bottles in various reds and whites. In the center, a display of their infamous seasonal wines with odds and end gifts for the wine lover. The entire room could be described using two words only: Calming lightness.

It was serene, yet held great energy. You could feel it the second you stepped through the front door… peace. I wanted to get our bags and ask if we could stay the night. I couldn't imagine a better place to get to know your husband again.

"You did good," I said, winking. "You may have to carry me out of here, but you definitely did good." He gave me a small nod as his eyes held mine. It felt exactly like the first night we met, and my stomach flip-flopped.

The server behind the bar had been cleaning glassware since we came in. "I'm guessing you folks aren't from around here," he said, smiling.

"Good guess," Barry said, walking over. "We're from Frankfort, about an hour south."

"Of course, love that town." He sported a navy-blue button down and khaki pants, looking as if he just stepped off the yacht. "Are you familiar with our wine?"

I smiled. "Definitely. Spring Splendor is my favorite, but I'd love to try some others."

"Good choice, but I'll start you with a Winter White today. Similar but a little less sweet than the Spring."

We went on like that for about an hour. Barry would take a sip of his, but I mostly drank whatever he set in front of me, with the exception of the apricot wine. Crunchy Italian breadsticks sat on the bar in tall tumblers, and I found myself munching on them in between each glass of wine. I knew that an early dinner was going to be necessary to make it through the evening. My stomach grumbled, and my head felt a little woozy from all the wine. Other customers strayed in and sat alongside us. The classical music playing overhead matched the theme of the winery: calm. I couldn't find another word for it.

Barry generously bought a case of wine in my favorite bottles of the day, along with some beautiful wine glass dangles in various nautical themed shapes. The anchor, my favorite, would always remind me of this day.

As we left, I found myself sad to be leaving a place we both connected with so well. It was rare for us to enjoy a Saturday afternoon like this, but maybe this would be our new normal.

Maybe the rebuilding of a relationship, a marriage, would feel like dating again. When you saved trinkets from every place you went together, to remember that precise moment you started to fall in love. The anchor would hold that moment for me. It would connect me to this very minute, where I felt reluctant to leave this space in time that held so much promise for us.

Driving away, I watched the winery grow smaller and smaller in the rearview mirror. I had taken a few pictures, but nothing would match this feeling I had right now.

Bittersweet.

Chapter Thirty

The spontaneous road trip continued, heading back south. He hadn't said anything, but I guessed Traverse City even before we left the winery. And I was right.

He pulled up to a bayside resort that rivaled any hotel I'd ever been in. Given the month, the parking lot was nearly empty. A few rugged jeeps and SUVs dotted the parking lot, but there were more vacant spots than filled.

He pulled under the entryway and allowed the bored looking valet attendant to park our car. "Might as well let them get a little work done today," he said, grabbing our bags out of the trunk.

The lobby was open and bright, welcoming us to a winter wonderland with back windows overlooking the bay. I felt my breath become shallow, and my stomach fluttered with nerves as he checked us in. I wandered over to the windows to look out at the vast scenery of snow and ice. I shivered. Even with the warm and fuzzy feelings still lingering from the winery, apprehension began to creep in at the thought of spending the night with him in a hotel. We still hadn't shared a room at home.

One could say I didn't want to disturb him by waking up before the crack of dawn, but deep down I knew. I wasn't ready to jump in the deep end yet. We hadn't had sex in over a year, and even though things were progressing nicely, I still didn't feel ready for that all or nothing step.

I turned just as he was walking towards me, smirk planted on his face. "Are you ready?"

I swallowed, hard. "Sure," I managed to squeak out. "Lead the way."

His smile grew wider. "I know what you're thinking, by the way." He pushed the button for the elevator.

I looked over at him. "What do you mean? I'm not thinking anything!"

He leaned in, close to my ear. "Yes. You are," he whispered. "You're afraid to spend the night with me. Alone… in a room." He chuckled to himself.

I scoffed. "Don't be ridiculous, Barry. We've been married almost ten years." I threw my bag over my shoulder and folded my arms. "What would I have to be afraid of?"

He raised his eyebrows and smiled. "Precisely."

I sighed as we entered the elevator. Tension built with every floor that passed. Finally, the elevator dinged at the tenth floor, and the doors rolled open. I followed him down the hall, dark green carpeting hushing our steps. He stopped at 1010 and slid the key card in, smiling to himself again. The wine and the butterflies battled to see which would take me out first.

As he opened the door, I noticed two things: one,

there was room service already waiting for us. And two, the door to the adjoining room was open.

He grabbed my hand as the door shut behind us with a thud. "My dear, did you really think I wouldn't give you the option of sleeping in your own room tonight?"

I looked from the identical room open to us, then back to him. "I don't understand. You booked two rooms?"

He nodded, setting the bags down. "I did." He slid off his shoes and untucked his shirt.

"But... why?" My mind was spinning with relief but also confusion.

He grabbed the tray of cheese, fruit and crackers, and set it in the middle of the king size bed. "C'mon, sit down. We both need something after all that wine."

A carafe of water sat on the table, and I poured two glasses, gulping mine down in one drink. Barry shook his head that he didn't need any. I pulled my boots off and climbed on the bed, sitting next to him.

"So tell me what's going on," I said. I grabbed a cracker and topped it with a slice of Colby-Jack. "Why did you get two rooms?"

"Because I know what we are doing is going to take some time. If we had just started dating, I wouldn't expect to stay in the same room with you. I figure this is sort of like starting a new relationship, and I don't want to make any wrong moves."

I relaxed my shoulders for the first time since we

arrived. "I don't know what to say," I said. "I know this is hard for both of us, but you're making everything so easy."

"What's hard about spending the day fulfilling your every whim? I didn't know enough when we were really dating, but now I do. I've been paying attention at home, and all I want is to see your face light up again and again," he said. He plucked a grape from the bunch. "This wasn't about getting you back into our bed. Obviously, I'll look forward to that when you're ready, but I'm working on forever, here. Not just tonight."

I looked him in the eye, and he smiled back at me. Curious, I held his gaze longer than usual. My heart was racing out of my chest as I leaned into him.

"Butterfly kiss?" he asked, his voice shaky.

I sighed a smile. Charlotte loved butterfly kisses. "I think we can do better than that," I said, my voice nothing more than a whisper.

We sat like that for seconds, both waiting for the moment of contact. His breath raspy. Every sense in my body on high alert. I never thought I would feel this again with Barry, this hunger for touch. I ended the longing by leaning in and brushing my lips against his. Not a true kiss, but enough to spark a response from him. He reached for my hand and squeezed, before pulling me into a real kiss.

A moan escaped me, threatening to reveal my

weakness. His lips were so soft, gentler than before, or maybe I had just forgotten what it felt like to kiss him.

As fast as he swooped in to kiss me, he stopped. He grabbed the remote off the nightstand and turned on the TV. I stared at him.

"What are you doing?"

"I just thought we could watch a little something while we snacked?" He looked at his watch. "We have a few hours before we have to leave for dinner."

I blinked, unsure of what just happened. "I thought we were kissing. Having a moment."

He smiled. "Oh, yes. That was nice moment for sure." He chuckled at my frustration.

"You don't want to keep kissing me?" I couldn't help but feel the sting of rejection.

His head snapped up, eyes steady on mine. "Let me be clear about that kiss," he said, softly. "I don't think I have ever kissed you or been kissed like that in my entire life. Not kissing you is tougher than you training for a marathon in the winter. Not kissing you is going against everything my body is telling me, which, by the way, is still in working order." A smile spread across my face as he continued. "I told you earlier, we are not going to rush any part of this process. You will have to beg me for the next kiss," he said, smirking. "Until then, we can progress with the rest of our day."

"Beg you? I'm sorry, I don't beg anyone to be kissed." I slid off the bed after grabbing one more cracker, frustration bubbling in my belly. "I'll be in my room if you need anything. And for the record, I don't beg for kisses or *anything* else. Never have and never will."

I swore he was chuckling again as I crossed over into the other room, but I wouldn't give him the satisfaction of looking back. Who did he think he was? Men beg *me* for kisses, not the other way around.

I threw my bag down by the bathroom door and plopped down on the bed. My breathing had settled down, but I was still playing the last five minutes in my head. That kiss. Who knew we could kiss like that?

My phone beeped in my coat pocket.

GRACIE: *Trevor is saying he's allergic to milk. Is this true?*

ME: *No, he just doesn't want to drink it anymore. He's telling everyone that.*

GRACIE: *LOL, that's funny.*

ME: *Not really, but he's a crafty one. Charlotte okay?*

GRACIE: *Yes ma'am. Cupcake is a spaz.*

ME: *Cupcake is a TOTAL spaz. I expect her trained by tomorrow.*

GRACIE: *We thought Sadie might help, but it backfired.*

ME: *haha. As long as they're still alive tomorrow, you're good.*

GRACIE: *Everything going okay there?*

ME: *It was till 5 min ago.*

GRACIE: *Uh oh* 😔 *Hang in there. His heart is in the right place.*

ME: *Pun intended?*

GRACIE: *Ha! Gotta go!*

Sitting on the bed, I thought about the kiss again. Maybe waiting for more was the sensible thing to do, although it was rarely my first choice. I always wanted everything all at once, including now. It was like an itch to scratch. Once I became aware of it, obsession took over.

Looking at my bag, curiosity made me wonder what he actually packed for me. We were in such a hurry, I never looked. My makeup bag and toiletries were thrown in on top. I gathered them up and set in the bathroom. Next I pulled out all the clothes he had brought for me. Pulling items out, one by one, I didn't recognize anything, including the black suede ankle boots in the bottom of the bag.

"Barry," I yelled from my room. "I don't think you got the right things. These are not my clothes."

He stood in the doorway, arms crossed. "Sure they are," he confirmed. "You just haven't seen them yet." His eyes twinkling.

"What do you mean? Where did you get these?"

"Remember that cool place I told you about? The mall? I thought I'd buy you some things there too." He smiled proudly.

Looking back at the bed, I held up a black, long-sleeved top with shoulder cut-outs. Simple, classic, and exactly the size I would've gotten. Next, were black leggings, stretchy enough to want to sleep in. A gorgeous silver wrap tied the outfit together with the suede boots. Tears sprang to my eyes.

"You bought me an outfit?"

"Keep looking," he said. "There's jewelry too." He came in and sat on my bed, watching me closely. "I put them in the outside pocket."

Unzipping it, I found a small black box, and my breath caught. "Barry, what did you do?"

"Nothing I shouldn't have been doing all along," he said.

Inside the black velvet box were the most beautiful diamond hoop earrings I had ever seen. They must have cost a fortune. I wiped a tear trailing down my cheek. "They're beautiful," I whispered. "But it's too much. I can't accept them."

"Sure you can," he said. "You deserve those and so much more." He took the box and admired them. "Are they big enough? You'll wear them, right?"

I choked out laughter. "Wear them? Of course I'll wear them! I may never take them off."

A look of doubt passed through his eyes. "All I want is to make you happy again, Linny. I know it's an uphill battle, but I promise you, I'm not going to stop trying."

"Come up here," I said, scooting back towards the pillows. "Before you object, I'm not wanting anything more than for you to hold me. I just want to lie down in the same bed with you."

He eyed me carefully, his smile giving him away.

He lay down beside me, and I rested my head on his chest. He pulled me in tighter, our legs intertwining.

"It's been a while," he whispered.

I nodded into his chest. "It has."

"This might be better than the kissing thing we did in there," he joked.

"Just wait until we combine the two."

He smacked my bottom. "All in good time, my dear. This is all part of the master plan of winning you back for good."

Little did he know that I was already back. I knew what was at stake, and I wasn't going to throw it away this time. We both had too much invested.

I drifted off listening to the sound of his heart. That perfect heart that saved us both.

Chapter Thirty-One

The bakery was quiet this morning, too quiet for a Saturday, but Aiden and I were making the best of it. Shelly asked for the day off, so it was just us, and I was testing a new cookie recipe while Marvin Gaye serenaded me. They wouldn't sell yet, but I planned to use these cookies throughout February. It was a white sugar cookie dough with a red heart cut out in the center. They were a new addition this year, thanks to Aiden and his Pinterest obsession, and I was just putting the finishing touches on the recipe so we could make the dough in bulk weeks in advance.

A knock at the door caught my attention. I ignored it, thinking a toddler had gotten away from his mom. When the *rap-rap-rap* became insistent, I investigated. Didn't Aiden hear it as well?

Opening the door, I found Trevor smiling broadly. "Monkey-butt!" I shouted. A few customers looked over, then smiled. Barry was sitting at a table by the front window, getting Charlotte settled with hot chocolate and a scone. Her penchant for scones led me to believe she was an elder British woman in her past life. The wrinkle in Barry's forehead gave her mood away. Charlotte was still struggling most days, and while her bullying days were behind her at school, she was now taking it out on those who love her most.

Mr. Murphy assured us this is completely normal.

It's her or me, ran through my head on any given day.

"Can I come in back with you?" Trevor squeaked.

Aiden smiled at us. "Sounds like we might have a new hire, boss lady."

I scooped Trevor in my arms and wandered to the table. "We'll go in back before you leave, Bud. Let's sit with Daddy and Char, for right now." In the center of the table was a plate overflowing with treats.

"Aiden seemed to think filling them with sugar before we head home was a fabulous idea," Barry snorted.

"That's why he gets paid the big bucks," I said. "Coffee?"

"Please," he said. "I didn't have enough hands."

I grabbed two mugs and filled them both with coffee. His black, mine with cream. When I sat at the table, Charlotte started in.

"Mo-om," she whined. "Trevor is so annoying. Why can't he stay here with you for the rest of the day?"

Barry raised his eyebrows as he took a sip of coffee. "I'll let you handle this one."

"Charlotte, this is Mommy's work. Trevor would be so bored after five minutes."

"So?" she replied, the worst comeback ever. "You could give him jobs."

"Not gonna happen, Peanut. You're stuck with him

until I get home later."

As we bantered back and forth about Trevor, a woman walked in, looking upset. The hairs on the back of my neck stood up on alert. I glanced at Barry, who noticed her as well.

Aiden's eyes bugged out of his head the second he spotted her. I jumped out of my chair, knowing exactly who this woman was. His mother. I pretended to make myself useful behind the counter.

"Mom," Aiden stammered. "What are you doing here?"

She had a look on her face as if she just had a strong whiff of a dead fish. "Aiden, you've had enough time to play around in this *bakery*. It's time to come back home and work for the family business."

"Mom, you know that's not going to happen," he said, eyes downcast.

"Your father is working too hard, and he's lost two employees in the past month," she said. "It's time to give up this little fantasy land you're in and show some responsibility."

"Responsibility?" His tone was incredulous. "I've been living on my own for six months, Mom, and I haven't asked for one penny. And as I seem to recall, it was *you* who asked *me* to move out in the first place."

"Yes, well, I'm hoping you got whatever it was out of your system and you came to your senses now."

Her too-short bob for her overly round face was the least of her issues. I wanted to smack some sense into her. A couple customers walked in, the bell over the door startling us back to the moment.

"Why don't we take this in back," I suggested. "Aiden, I'll cover out here."

"I don't need to take this conversation in back," she sniped to me. "What is it to you, anyways?"

"Mom—"

"No, Aiden, I can certainly handle this," I whispered. "Why don't you handle the customers, and your mom and I will have a little chat."

I grabbed a mug and filled it with coffee. "Do you like cream or sugar?" I asked, sweetly.

She looked at Aiden, then me. "No, black is fine."

I led her to a table far away from any other customers and sat down. "I think you misunderstand Aiden," I started, gently. "He is happy here, and I certainly don't want to lose him as an employee."

"Your business with my son is just that. Your business. He has responsibilities to our family, and it's time he started to contribute."

"Forgive me, Mrs. Nash, but Aiden seems to think you don't approve of his being gay."

She leveled her gaze on mine. It was hatred staring back at me.

"I don't know who you *think* you are, but you have absolutely no right to talk to me about my son like that.

He is not gay." She said the word as if it were poisonous. She spat it out.

"Who *I am*, is his boss and his friend." The calmness in my voice surprised even myself. "And for the last few months I have worked on building up your son so he knows he's worthy of love again. If you could stop with your hatred, you'd see he is an amazing and talented young man. You should be proud of him."

"*Proud*?" The venom in her voice chilled me to the bone. "Proud? You've known him, what, five minutes? Why don't you let me handle my son my way, and you can go about your little business."

"If you are done, I think it's best you leave. Aiden is where he belongs where people love him." I stood, dismissing her. "Please don't ever come back here."

She sat there, mouth gaping, as I walked away.

The color from Aiden's face drained, and his eyes were round as saucers. "What did you just do?" he whispered.

"What should've been done a long time ago."

His mom sat there, motionless. She glanced up at him after a beat. "Aiden, you're really not coming home?"

Thankfully the other customers in the shop had left. It was just Barry and the kids by the front, and they couldn't hear anything. By the look on Barry's face, I could tell he was anxious about the situation.

Aiden stood rooted to his spot, only shaking his head slowly. "No, Mom, I'm not. I didn't realize until now how much I've changed since I left, but I can't ever go back to that life." I expected him to be shaking or upset somehow, but maybe I was just feeling my own anxiety. I pressed my hands on the counter to stop them from jittering. Who was I to tell another mother to leave her son alone? I hadn't walked in her shoes. But I did know that Aiden was an exceptional person, and that is what I was standing up for. She didn't know him the way I did, and couldn't possibly love him then. She had limitations to her love, just like I did for Barry for so long. Like we did for each other.

The realization hit me in the chest. All anyone wants is to be accepted for who they are, without the limitations or expectations. Once you have that, you have everything. You don't have to agree on everything, but respect is the common thread in any lasting relationship.

Aiden's mom didn't respect him, and that became clear to him as soon as she walked in today. He stared for a moment longer, never breaking his steely eye contact, then he casually took his apron off, hung it on the hook by the swinging door and walked in back.

She sat there, blinking. I looked at Barry, who could only shrug at this point.

"I suppose this is where you tell me 'I told you so,'" she said, her voice so shaky it was barely a whisper.

"I would never tell another mom that. But I will tell you if you don't learn to accept him for who he is, you'll never have him in your life again. That kid has the biggest heart of anyone I've ever known. And yes, that is something you should be proud of."

"My husband will never accept him the way he is." She stared off into space, shaking her head. "Never."

"Give it time," I said. I walked back over and sat down with her. "Time has a way of changing how we feel." I looked over at Barry and realized I had been talking about us, too.

Her eyes haunted me. Dark circles shaded under those aquamarine blue eyes, and Aiden had her coloring and face structure. He resembled her quite a bit.

"Are you hungry? I can get you anything out of the case if you'd like." Sympathy tugged at me.

She looked at the case. "I don't think so. I need to get going," she said.

"So that's it? You're just going to leave?"

Her back straightened and the pinched look washed over her face again. "Did you think a cookie would make it all better?" She stood and walked out the door, leaving the echo of the bell behind her.

Dazed, I looked at Barry. He whispered to the kids, and they came bouncing over. "Can I have another scone?" Charlotte asked.

I must have nodded, because she walked behind the case and used the little wax paper to reach for one herself. She looked like she owned the joint.

"How did Aiden come from that woman?" Barry said. His eyes followed mine and he grinned at Charlotte. "That's your mini-me, you know. When we were over there, she gave me the recipe for those."

I knew what he was trying to do, but my heart broke for Aiden. Finally, Aiden walked out from the back, coat on. His eyes were red-rimmed and distant. I stood to hug him, but he stopped me.

"I need to get out of here," he said. "Thank you for trying, but I knew as soon as I saw her how it was going to end."

"Aiden, you shouldn't have to change for your mom to love you. The problem is hers, not yours."

"Is it?" The hollow expression chilled me.

"Aiden, stay, come hang out with us today," Barry said. We both looked at him, slack-jawed. "You haven't even met Cupcake yet, and she would love a new person in the house to pee on the floor for."

One side of his mouth lifted.

"And we have two episodes of *The Bachelor* on the DVR." I chimed in.

"Charlotte's only half-way through the second Harry Potter book…"

"And—"

Aiden lifted his hand to stop me. Full on smile now. "I can't tell any longer if you're tempting me or pushing me away." He pulled up a chair and sat down with us. "I know what you're doing, and it's sweet, but really, I'm okay. This isn't anything I haven't dealt with before. The fact that I have a support staff now is all I need."

"Shelly's home?"

"Yes, we're supposed to have plans tonight."

"Okay, but if she bails…" I trailed off.

"I know, you have lots of ways to distract me," he winked. "*The Bachelor*? *Really*?"

"Have you seen him? He's adorable," I said.

Barry rolled his eyes. "On that intellectual note, I'm going to bundle these monsters up and take off."

The bell chimed, announcing an elderly couple entering the bakery. I leaned in and squeezed his shoulders. "Call if you need anything," I whispered.

Behind the counter, I fell into my all-business mode. The couple, having shed their hats and scarves, were regulars. The Robinsons. Barry waved from the door, winking before he turned to leave. "Bye Mom-meeee," from the kids. Aiden trailed behind them.

"Lovely family," Mrs. Robinson said. "I bet those kids love coming to see their mom at work!"

"Ha," I retorted. "It's more like 'how many treats can I get before we leave?'"

They ordered—a banana chip muffin for him and little birds for her. I gave them their coffee and offered to bring the goods to their table.

Watching them, my mind kept replaying the last half-hour, but the Robinsons gave me hope. I believed there were more people like them in the world than the Nashes. I had to believe that. Just like I had to believe that eventually Aiden's mom would come around.

He didn't need that, but I did.

This compassion, the weight of it, felt new to me. I wanted to save the world with love and understanding. Every time we choose fear over love is a missed opportunity, and I was tired of missing anything. Mrs. Nash lived in fear. The look in her eye spoke volumes of her home life, and it looked eerily similar to mine a year ago. That's why I wanted to save her. To save them.

This morning opened my eyes to how much everything had changed in my life. Having Barry stop by, unannounced, is everything I never knew I wanted. Correction: I knew what I wanted, but didn't think I'd ever get it, or even deserve it. I could see Barry and me growing old together like the Robinsons now, which is something I had never thought before. The future never seemed clear to me. It always included the bakery, but oddly enough I pictured myself alone.

Is that what I thought I deserved? I erased the thought from my head and began to create a new picture in my head of the future. Your life becomes what you focus on… I had heard this so many times from Grace, but never really understood it until now.

I planted the seed of that memory and would nurture it until it became true. It was so clear to me, and the flutter of hope made me smile to myself. I pulled out my phone and texted Barry.

ME: *Thank you for coming in today!*

BARRY: *Are you missing me already?* 😉

ME: *Maybe…*

BARRY: *I get that a lot.*

I giggled. This was the man I married.

After the Robinsons left, I flipped the "closed" sign and cleaned up. Some days it's good to be the boss and close early for no reason other than to get back home. Some days the decisions were simply that clear.

Chapter Thirty-Two

Five. Six. Seven. Eight.
Running makes me feel great.

This was my chant today while I ran. In the past month, I had switched completely from the run/walk to strictly a slower jog for the majority of the training time. It was still only running two miles at a time, but a part of me was encouraged by the fact I didn't need to shift gears every ninety seconds. I warmed up and cooled down with a five-minute walk, otherwise, I was running.

Tony mentioned repeating a word or phrase to encourage my rhythm and breathing. It was another positive aspect from doing away with the intervals. Every run was something different. Sometimes, I just counted, and other days I'd repeat "I am a runner," hoping the subliminal message seeped into my brain. The mental strain to get me out the door was exhausting, but as soon as my warm-up was completed, I was ready to go.

My head was clearer, and I was not as wound up after I ran. Gracie said this is why she continues to run. When in doubt, Tony said to imagine myself crossing the finish line. That is another vision I kept in my head while I running. It reminded me why I'm doing this.

Cupcake greeted me with a puddle when I got home. "Cupcake! Bad girl," I scolded. She sat and cocked her head to one side.

I shook my head, knowing it was a battle I wasn't going to win today. A pink sticky note caught my attention on the countertop:

Took the kids to the store! Text me if you need anything...

What could he possibly be getting? I had gotten groceries on Thursday, knowing the kids would be home from school for winter break. Even Trevor's pre-school was taking advantage of the long weekend. If you asked me, it was a conspiracy, but Barry seemed thrilled at the idea of having them home a couple extra days. He also got excited at snow days.

My phone pinged with another weather advisory. More snow. It was as if we're all being punished this weekend. Cupcake's collar jingled as she follows me to the bathroom. I turned the shower on hot and stripped down to weigh myself. It had become a daily thing, weighing myself. I liked to see the digital display jump and wonder where it will land. Most days I know exactly what it will say, but today surprised me. Down one and a half pounds.

I hadn't lost much yet, just ten pounds total, but it felt like thirty. My body moved easier and all of my clothes were bigger now. I scanned my body in just a sports bra and underwear, and noticed my legs looked leaner too. Longer. The muscles, still warm from the run, gave my legs definition. Cupcake barked her approval.

"Thanks Babygirl," I cooed. "I think I look pretty good too."

By the time I was out of the shower, I heard bustling around in the kitchen. Charlotte whining and Barry consoling. Cupcake was barking at the door to get out and see her people, her stubby tail wagging excitedly. She squeezed through the opening before I could pull it open all the way. Her nails rattled on the hardwood floor, and Trevor's high pitch "Cuppy," echoed throughout the house.

The moment caught me off guard and my heart swelled. When did this become my life? The perfect family image I used to carry in my head didn't resemble what we looked like now. This was messy and busy but filled with love. It didn't matter that Charlotte's whine could be considered an Olympic event. Or that Trevor's screen time was in the double digits some weeks. I didn't care that we ordered pizza every single Friday. Or that my kids knew how to order candy and Pokémon cards on Alexa. Behind this insanity is where the magic lives. You find it in the crevices and cracks, the glue that holds the whole ship together. It's how a family can withstand all the pressure of everyday life. It's love.

I threw on pajamas and towel dried my hair, rushing the post-shower ritual I normally had. Like Cupcake, I wanted to see my people. Entering the kitchen, I noticed two things: a mountain of junk food on the counter, and next to it, a square ivory envelope. He had done it again.

His eyes met mine, reflecting humor and charm.

"It seems there's a delivery for you," he jested.

As I walked closer, I notice a single red rose laying behind all the junk food. My hands flew to my mouth. "Is that what I think it is?"

"If you think it's a group date rose, then yes, you would be correct." His eyes twinkled. "Although, I'm fairly certain I reduced my choice by one at the store."

"Daddy bought you a flower, Mommy," Charlotte piped in. "I told him to by a lot, but he just wanted one."

"One is the perfect number, Char, and I love it," I said. "But what is this about a group date?"

"You were lucky to get the one-on-one date last time, so naturally, this is a group date tonight."

A slow smile spread across my face. "What do you have in mind with these hooligans? They're not exactly date-worthy."

"I could tell ya, but then I'd have to kill ya." He walked up close, leaned in, brushing his lips against my cheek. My knees went weak. He had been doing that ever since we got back from Traverse City, small doses of intimacy. Enough to drive me crazy, and I had to admit, he played me like a fiddle.

"If you don't mind," he said. "I have some business to take care of in the basement. Give me a half-hour?"

Business? He rarely worked on the weekends at home anymore. "Whatever you need. We will get this stuff taken care of while you're down there."

"Don't miss me too much." He smirked, the door snapping shut behind him.

"Mom, we also got a bell for Cupcake," Charlotte said.

Trevor, who was unsuccessfully playing fetch with Cupcake, looked over. "A bell? Can we play with it?"

Charlotte put her hands on her hips. Classic big sister pose. Or Wonder Woman. Same thing.

"No, Trevor, it's to help with potty training."

"Are you sure, Charlotte? Daddy didn't mention this to me."

"We stopped at the pet store, and one of the really old workers there said this trick always worked. Especially for the dogs who aren't too smart."

I sat down and pulled her up onto my lap. "Okay, you have my attention. What did the really old worker say?"

"She said to tie this bell to a string and hang it from the door. Every time we take Cupcake out, we ring the bell. Then, sooner or later, she will start ringing the bell when she wants to go potty." She finished with a nod.

"Okay, I guess we better find some string then," I said. "Maybe we should test it out too."

Her face lit up. "Can I hold the leash?"

"Of course you can. And I think the leash holder should also be the bell ringer."

"I wanna ring the bellllllllll." Trevor had a way of not being part of any conversation, but he also never missed a beat.

"Not this time, Bud," I responded. "You'll get the next turn."

Triumph registered on Charlotte's face as she hopped off my lap and reached for the leash on the hook by the back door. I rummaged through our junk drawer until I found a roll of twine from Christmas. I looped it through the top of the silver bell and tied a knot. Curious about the noise, Cupcake wandered over to me and sat down. I tied the twine around the door knob, leaving enough room for her to reach it.

We threw our winter coats and boots on. Michigan winters aren't for wimps, and this one had been worse than usual. The one good thing Cupcake taught us was to deal with weather, no matter how bad. Puppies didn't care if it was raining or snowing. Dog owners have to brave the weather, and as a parent, this was a valuable lesson.

Inside, Barry was waiting for us, excitement bubbling from his every move. He was smiling bigger, eyes alert, as he was packing a picnic basket with all of the junk food. A cooler also sat on the bar filled with wine, sodas, water, and juice boxes.

"What is going on?" I raised my voice for effect, but that just made him chuckle.

"Did you ever open your date card? I don't think so," he said.

Of course, I had forgotten to open the date card. That would explain this. At least I hoped it would. I slid my finger under the flap. The envelope, just like the last one, was gold lined and weighty. The card had one sentence:

If you don't have enough,
perhaps you should ask for s'more.

Camping.

"But wait—" I said, finishing my own thought. "We are not going camping outside."

"Oh heck no," he said. He looked at me like I was crazy. "Why don't you grab the basket, and I'll get the cooler. Let's head downstairs."

Intrigued, I grabbed the basket in one hand and Cupcake in the other. She still hated the stairs to the basement and would only bark at the top until we picked her up.

The kids, feeding off Barry's excitement, raced downstairs before we even got to the doorway. I heard Charlotte gasp and Trevor yell, "Cooooooooooool."

Downstairs, I gasped myself. Twinkle lights crisscrossed the room, and in the center stood an enormous tent. All the furniture had been pushed to the perimeter of the room. Outside on the walk-out patio, he had a fire going in a portable fire pit. The speaker had the sound of crickets and owls hooting playing softly. He had thought of everything.

"Well," he said, "I knew we couldn't go camping before our anniversary, so I figured we could camp in the basement tonight. I have everything to roast hotdogs and s'mores and more junk food than we will need in one night."

"Daddy, this is so cool! Can I go in the tent?" Charlotte's eyes sparkled as she took it all in.

"Of course, sweetie. The zipper is at the bottom. Careful not to let any bugs or critters inside."

Peals of giggles. "Is Trevor a bug or a critter?"

Trevor stood in front of the patio door, staring at the fire. "Daddy, is that a real fire?"

Barry chuckled. "It sure is, Bud. That's how we're going to cook dinner and dessert."

"Can I have a snack?"

I barked out laughter. "Trevor, don't you want to see where we're sleeping tonight?"

He looked at the tent as if seeing it for the first time. "We're sleeping in *that*?"

"Yes, come check it out," Barry said. "Everyone has their own sleeping bag, and yours has Thomas the Train on it."

"Coooooooool," he said.

"I can't believe you did all this," I said.

"Truth be told, I think I'm more excited than the kids. And this summer, we're going to take them camping for real. Getting all this stuff was like Christmas for me." He grabbed my hand and squeezed. "I wasted too much time working. This is what life is all about."

"We never camped growing up," I said. "This is new for me."

"I want these kids to know what it's like to take real family vacations. Camping. Disney. Road trips to the Grand Canyon. I have so many plans for us," he said. His eyes took on a dreamy, faraway look, as if he was staring directly into the future. I believed he could see us doing all those things.

My thoughts flashed back to months ago, saying goodbye to Gordy and yes to all this. I was heartbroken, but hopeful. Now, I could see the future as clearly as Barry could, and every day felt like a gift. Second chances don't always work out, sometimes they're just another stepping stone to something better. But when they do work out, it's as if the past falls away completely, and you can only see what is in front of you.

Letting go of the past is the first step, always. The second step is to move forward. It's as if running has become a metaphor for my entire life, and I wondered if fate intervened on that day when I crossed paths with the marathon. Tony's quote in his email today said, "*Pain is inevitable. Suffering is optional*," and I believe that to be true. If someone had said this to me a year ago, I would've laughed at them, but now I get it.

What I would do with it had yet to be seen, but knowing it gave me a strength I didn't have before. A knowledge that inspired me to rise above the little issues of everyday life and embrace all of it. The good, the bad, and the ugly.

I knew there would be very little sleep tonight, being cramped in a tent with the four of us, but I also knew that the memories we would make outweighed the discomfort of another tired Monday.

I leaned in and kissed Barry on the cheek. "This is amazing, by the way."

He wrapped his arm around my shoulder and kissed the top of my head. "It's not Yellowstone Park, but it'll do for a snowy night in Michigan."

"Are you kidding? We have our own bathroom. This is better than Yellowstone to me."

"I'll make an outdoor girl out of you someday," he bantered. "Just you wait. You're going to love sleeping under the stars."

"If you say so," I agreed. "But don't underestimate the lure of a private bathroom."

He chuckled and hugged me. Cupcake wrestled out of my arms and scampered into the tent. Charlotte and Trevor squealed with joy. It was the sound of happy, I decided, and I wanted it to fill every room in this house.

Life with Grace

Valentine's Day

February 14 at 11:41 a.m. || 34 Comments

"Magic is when you live your life the way you didn't picture it and leave nothing behind."

— Robert M. Drake

Valentine's Day is a tricky holiday. It's a Hallmark holiday, no doubt. But over the past year, I've grown to believe it is so much more than that.

I think it has to do more with being in love with your own life than with someone else. When someone is so happy with their own life, the world becomes lovelier and people become more lovable. It fills a void in your life, and searching for that one love/job/outfit becomes irrelevant. Everything you have is enough. You are enough.

It happened to me last year, and I have had a front row seat to watch it happen in my friend's life as well. It is something to behold, the power of owning what you want and having the courage to see it through.

Is it easy? Not on your life.

In fact, it's the hardest thing you'll ever do, but I believe it's the path, the only path, to a happy life.

Most people put their happiness in other people, things, or even careers, never looking inside themselves. Some search their whole lives, finding disappointment at every turn. Or they find a fleeting moment of getting what they want, only to want more the next day. It's an endless cycle of wanting and receiving, without ever appreciating what they have.

I'm here to tell you there's another way.

And when you're ready, your life will open up to all the good this world can give you. Love will find you, no matter its form, and every day becomes an adventure.

If you find yourself alone this Valentine's Day, don't worry, you are exactly where you need to be. Use this as your wakeup call and make a change you've been pondering for a while. The scarier the better. Those dreams that make us pause are the ones that really

Life with Grace

count. Make a list of things you love about your life. Then make a list of things you want to add or change. It's okay to not know what you want. Just keep looking at the good things, and a shift will take place. Eventually, you'll look for the positive before the negative. It takes time and can be frustrating as hell, but this exercise will change your life for the better.

Which is something we all want, isn't it?

As for my friend, I can't tell you enough how brave she is. Once she realized (or remembered, as I like to tell her) what she really wanted, the choice, while not easy, became clear to her. She took the leap and landed exactly where she wanted to be.

Happy. In love.

I wish that for all of you as well.

Happy Valentine's Day, my friends...

Monday, February 14

I gotta hand it to the creators of The Bachelor. *The series finale on Valentine's Day? Drama, love, beautiful locations overlooking a crystal blue ocean.*

Friggin' genius.

Who wouldn't fall in love?

I've been thinking about the show constantly and how it's applied to my life lately. I always used to say that it would be so easy to fall in love on that show. Who wouldn't? Mansions. Dream dates. Endless supplies of wine. But it's no secret the success rate once the show is over is slim at best, and it has proven time and time again that the women choose more wisely than the men do.

I chalk it up to the fact that the women will do anything to snag the bachelor. They drop everything, including their core beliefs, to "win" the prize of getting engaged. Only when they get out in the real world do they understand they simply don't work any longer without the bubble of the show to seclude them.

But if taking the couple out of the show doesn't work, would adding the show to a couple save a marriage? I never really thought about it until tonight, watching all the drama unfold, Barry by my side. He spent the entire time trying to guess, never realizing that the editors slant the final show on purpose to surprise the viewer. The underdog always wins. The dark horse. Everyone wants that fairy tale ending with a sparkly Neil Lane three-carat diamond on your hand.

Gracie argued that you can't save a marriage just by elaborate dates, but I'm still not convinced. Granted, Barry and I have been through so much, but I have come to see how much those dates meant to me. The fact that he planned them so elaborately felt like proof that he was into saving this marriage 100%. It felt real.

As I'm sure it does do all the contestants.

So what does any of this mean? Why am I still up at midnight pondering this? Truth is, I want it all. I want the real-life marriage and all that comes with that, but I also want the fairy tale. The over-the-top evidence that my husband wants to be with me.

Let's be honest, a Neil Lane diamond wouldn't hurt either.

My journal closed with a satisfying *thunk*. My tea was lukewarm and Barry was long asleep. I couldn't sleep when I got in bed with all of these thoughts circling my brain. After I had read Gracie's post, I wanted to sort it out in my head. I wanted evidence, the *why* of my happiness. Up until today I would've told you it was because of Barry, but now I think he might just be a lovely repercussion of choosing the life I wanted.

Did it really matter? I'm exactly where I want to be, and I haven't been able to say that for years. Too many to count.

The tea splashed in the sink and I rinsed out the cup, setting it on the rack to dry. I tiptoed into our room and curled into bed silently, with only the soft snores from Barry in the room. I had stopped sleeping in the spare room recently and found it difficult to fall asleep ever since. I found myself wanting to be back in the other room, longing for the silence and peace. The bed creaked as I rolled over, and Cupcake whimpered in her crate.

Oh hell no. I couldn't let my sleeplessness wake her up. If ever there were motivation to fall asleep quickly, it was the rustling of a puppy. Lying still, I focused on my breath and slowed it down to match Barry's.

In and out. I felt my shoulders relax and my eyes shut. Cupcake heaved a big sigh and quieted back down. Suffering is optional...suffering is optional... suffering is optional. I repeated this to myself until I drifted off into a dreamless sleep.

Chapter Thirty-Three

As I crossed the finish line, I have never felt more exuberant in my life. *I just ran a 10K*, kept circling my thoughts. Barry and the kids were waiting for me as I cross the line. Tony stood with Gracie, who jumped up and down like I'd won an Olympic event.

The moment felt surreal, like I was watching it happen from afar. Faces flashed before me, Barry, Tony, Gracie, Charlotte and Trevor hugged me. I felt like there wasn't anything I couldn't do. Even though I knew the marathon was going to be hard, it was still doable.

It was Gracie's idea to head to the bakery to celebrate, and the kids chimed in with their approval. The storefront sign had already been turned to "open" when we arrived, something I rarely missed when I closed up. Perhaps Aiden missed it yesterday?

I looked at Barry, who was grinning ear to ear, and the hairs on the back of my neck stood up. Something was going on. Charlotte pulled my hand, "C'mon, Mommy, let's go."

Balloons were the first thing I noticed when I stepped through the doorway. They covered the floor and floated in bunches at the front counter. Trevor immediately began kicking each one to fly into the air.

On every table, a tray held all of our favorite goodies, baked fresh. Aiden must have been up all night to bake this amount of food. Once our friends were all inside, Aiden switched the open sign to closed again. Flutes of Mimosas were on a tray by the register, along with chocolate milk, water, and orange juice.

I eyed Barry again, certain he was the one who had orchestrated this.

"Don't look at me," he said, holding his hands in surrender. "This was all Gracie."

I scanned the crowd and noticed she and Charlie were behind the counter pouring more drinks. Jimmy and Julia, not far from him, were talking to Tony, who seemed to be in his glory.

"Why did she do all this? It was just a 10K," I said, overwhelmed.

"Someday, hopefully soon, you will understand how much you are loved," he said. He kissed me on the cheek. "By the way, we have plans tonight, so don't go making any other dates."

I gave him the side-eye. "Plans? Would this have anything to do with our anniversary?"

He bumped his head with his hand. "Is that today? I completely forgot."

"Liar. What do you have planned?"

With the race today, I hadn't even thought about our anniversary. It lingered in the back of my mind all week, but the race took precedence over all other thoughts. I became obsessed with making sure I had every opportunity to succeed.

"I could tell ya…" he started.

"Yeah, yeah, I get it. You're not going to tell me anything."

"Bingo."

Gracie walked over with a Mimosa for me. "What are you two lovebirds talking about over here?" she asked, hugging me. "Come, join the party. This is all for you!"

"You did not have to do this, Dunham," I said.

"You know I wasn't going to let your first 5K go by without a celebration. Besides, I had more help than you think. Aiden is Superman. Whatever you're paying him, it's not enough."

"He is Superman," I agreed. "Saved my life more than once."

"This means the world that you would go to this trouble for me," I said, pulling her into one more hug.

I spent the next hour talking and laughing with the people I love the most. My mom and dad showed up after church, giving me flowers. It seemed like such a big deal for a little race, but who was I to complain? Maybe this would be the new normal, this celebrating life.

Before it ended, Aiden pulled me aside. "I know today is a big day for you, and also your anniversary, so I wanted to let you know that I have tomorrow covered. You get the day off." He smiled broadly.

"You're giving me the day off?" I hadn't taken a day

off since I opened.

"Yes, ma'am," he confirmed. "If you show up, I will have you dragged out."

I pulled him into a hug. "I don't think you'll ever know how important you are to me," I whispered. "Thank you for everything. This was amazing."

"Anytime, boss lady."

Barry and I helped clean up so Aiden didn't have to do it all, and by the time we got home, I was bone-tired.

"Why don't you go sleep for a little bit. We don't have plans until later, and I don't want you to be exhausted."

My internal radar pinged. "What exactly do you have planned?"

"It's a surprise," he shrugged. "I'm not sure why you think I'll tell you, but it's annoying you keep asking."

I sighed, knowing I wouldn't win. I closed our bedroom door, keeping the kids and Cupcake at bay, and fell into a deep sleep. When I woke up, the sunlight slanted through the shade, invading my darkened room. Checking my phone, I was startled that it read 5:03 p.m. I had slept three hours, at least, and a part of me could've slept longer, but I knew we were supposed to have plans tonight.

I threw on yoga pants and padded out to the kitchen. On the bar was a single ivory envelope, propped up in front of a crystal vase with one red rose. I opened the envelope and it read:

Let's get this party started...

A beach party? There's no way he would plan that in March, but as I looked out the back window, there he was, with the kids, bonfire roaring. Tiki torches flickered in the falling sunlight, and Charlie and Jimmy were there helping Barry with a makeshift bar, complete with a keg. I shook my head. *What have you done, Barry?*

Opening the sliding door, I walked out, feeling the ache in my back from the run earlier. I cupped my hands around my mouth. "Hey!"

The three of them stopped what they were doing and looked in my direction.

"Surprise!" Barry yelled over the rush of waves. Jimmy and Charlie both waved at me. "Come out," he shouted.

I held my index finger out, the universal sign for "one second." Inside, I piled my hair on top of my head and jumped in the shower. Once out, I rolled through my makeup as fast as I could. A healthy dose of dry shampoo also did the trick, making me look fresh as can be. I slid into new jeans, a smaller size thanks to all the running, and pulled on a grey sweater. I wrapped an emerald green infinity scarf around my neck and went in search for my Uggs and winter coat. My stomach had butterflies at the thought of a party, but I knew he had thought of everything.

The weather today for March far exceeded normal temperatures that usually range between twenty-five and thirty-five degrees. We topped out at fifty, but with the sun going down, that would drop quickly, especially by the lake.

The sun had already set by the time I found my way down to the beach, torches blazing now. Charlotte and Trevor were playing with Gracie, who was playing fetch with Sadie and Cupcake. Music was blaring Bob Segar, Barry's favorite, from a wireless speaker on the bar. The damp air sent chills down my spine, although I was certain it was mostly nerves. Barry was talking with my dad about the stock market when I walked up.

"Hey," he said, pulling me tight for a kiss on the cheek. "You're here! I was worried you'd sleep through the party."

"I can't believe you pulled this off," I said, wrapping my arms around his waist.

"Happy Anniversary," my dad said. "I love how happy you both look."

"Aww, thanks Pops," I said, hugging him. "Where's Mom?"

He glanced around the crowd. "Oh, she's here somewhere. Probably gabbing with one of your friends. She drops me like a hot potato in a social scene."

"I saw her with Aiden, comparing recipes," Barry interrupted.

"Of course! I should have known. She loves that Aiden character," Dad said.

I scanned the crowd, noticing people from the law firm and even cousins of his I haven't seen since our wedding ten years ago.

Jimmy came up behind me with a red solo cup of beer. "Thought you could use one of these," he said. He tilted his head and smiled, eyes locked on mine. "You look good, Linn," he said. "Really happy."

I matched his smile. "Jimmy, can you believe it worked out like this?"

"Not from where we were last fall," he snickered.

I shot him a death stare, and he chuckled. "Linn, don't worry. That will go to my grave." He crossed his hand over his heart. "But I can still think about it now and then, right?"

Gracie, who came up beside us, punched him for me. "Get your mind out of the gutter, Jimmy."

"How could you even know what we were talking about?"

"We always know, Jimmy," Gracie said, winking. "How are you feeling tonight? Legs sore?"

"Honestly, they're not too bad," I said, taking a gulp of the beer. "My back is pretty tight though."

"Your face was priceless when you crossed the line," Gracie said. "It was the perfect mixture of relief and pride."

"My face hurt from smiling earlier. I felt like I could do anything." I also felt like I could talk about this for years, and never come up with the exact feeling I had about it.

"Gordy sends his best," Gracie said. "He knew enough not to come tonight, even though Barry was gracious enough to invite him." My heart constricted at the sound of his name. "He only wants you to be happy, Linn. I hope you know that."

I leaned in to hug her. "I know that. We did get a chance to talk at your engagement, but it still breaks my heart," I whispered. "I want nothing but the best for him as well."

Jimmy rolled his eyes. "It's always a matter of time before it turns mushy between you two," he said, walking away.

"So this is pretty frickin' amazing," she said. "I'm gonna have Charlie take romance lessons from Barry before the wedding."

I choked on the sip I had taken. "Who would've thought we'd ever say those words? Sometimes, I wonder how this all fell into place the way it has."

I scanned the crowd for Barry and found him, looking at me. Our eyes connected, and he winked. He nodded for me to come over. I squeezed Gracie's hand as I left to make my way through the crowd. Standing in front of him, the entire party faded away. He reached for my hand and pulled me to the side.

"I have one more surprise for you," he beamed.

My head tipped. "Barry, you have to stop doing all this."

"Oh honey, I have big plans for us," he said.

Charlie swooped in, kissed me on the cheek and took our beers from us. "I'll just refill these for you," he said, winking.

Turning back to Barry, he was down on one knee before me. Tears sprang to my eyes. "Barry—"

He reached for my hands. "Linny, I know it hasn't been easy, these last ten years, but I'm wondering if you would still be interested in spending the rest of your life with me?"

He pulled out a small velvet box from his pocket. My hands covered my face. *Is this really happening?* Looking back down at him, he had tears streaming down his face. "I took the liberty of picking a new ring for you," he said. "I hope it brings us both more joy than we thought possible." He opened the box, and inside sat the most exquisite princess cut diamond I had ever seen.

"Oh Barry," I whispered. I pulled him up and leapt into his arms. He spun me around easily, and I realized how strong he had gotten.

"Is that a yes," he whispered, laughing. He set me down and kissed me.

I heard cheers and yelps.

"Yes, of course it's yes," I said. I pulled my mitten off and moved my original wedding set to my right hand.

He pulled the ring out of the box and reached for my hand. "With this ring, I promise to make all our dreams come true," he said. My heart fluttered. He slid the new diamond on my hand and lifted to kiss it.

Staring at the ring, I was mesmerized. The setting was platinum, and the center diamond had to be two carats, minimum, but then there were smaller diamonds surrounding it.

"I don't know what to say," I said. "I can't believe you did all this."

"Pretty sure we accomplished everything on our list." He pulled me in for a hug.

"Pretty sure I'm going to show you how much I appreciate all of this later tonight," I said.

"That sounds promising," he mused.

Charlotte and Trevor ran up and hugged us both. "Mommy, let me see the ring," Charlotte squealed. "It's so big!"

Charlie brought our beers back, refilled, and gave me a long hug. "Damn, he's good," he said.

I giggled. "It's insane how good he is."

Barry whistled loudly to address the crowd. "I can't thank you all enough for being a part of our anniversary celebration. Linny and I continue to be blessed, and having all of you here to celebrate with us makes it that much more special." He raised his glass, "To love."

"To love," they repeated and cheered.

He pulled me into a side hug and kissed the top of my head. Charlotte wrapped her arms around my waist, relishing in the moment.

"Do I have to go to school tomorrow?" Her unblinking eyes stared up at me.

"Do ducks quack?"

"Yes, Mommy, but what do ducks have to do with

school?"

"Nothing, but the answer is the same. Yes, Char, you have to go to school." Her analytical brain would ponder this more later, I could tell.

"Smile!" Gracie stood in front of us with her phone. I looked at Barry, and he looked so happy. This moment would be in my memory forever. "Great picture," Gracie approved. "I'll send it to you, Linn."

I didn't want this night to end, even though it was technically a school night. The fact that I had the day off tomorrow made tonight even more fun, but morning would come early to get the kids to school. People were starting to scatter already. The chill in the air sent people home earlier than if this were a summer bonfire. The muscles in my back and legs stiffened in the cold, and I looked forward to going inside.

I loved every second of this party, but I couldn't wait to get on with the rest of our lives either. My eyes were drawn to this new ring from Barry, and I wondered how long he had planned this entire night. It was as if he had planned the whole list in advanced. It felt like a dream, only we wouldn't have to wake up from this.

Inside, Barry fussed around, getting the kids to bed, and insisted I open a bottle of champagne for us. Butterflies multiplied in my stomach and my hands were shaking. We hadn't been intimate in over a year, and this felt like it was the first time. My breath came out in puffs just thinking about it.

I covered the bottle with a hand towel and shimmied off the cork. The towel muffled the pop and caught the champagne that flowed out of the top. I poured two flutes and arranged cheese and crackers on a plate. Even with the nerves, I knew my body needed some nourishment.

Barry sauntered in, looking like the cat who ate the canary. "Both kids are out. They could barely keep their eyes open."

"Good, they'll be exhausted, but we'll get them to bed early tomorrow."

I stood at the kitchen counter, nibbling on a slice of cheese, when he came and stood behind me. He didn't touch me, but I could feel him there. His presence. His breath.

When I first met Barry, one of my favorite things about him was his height. I was always taller than most of the boys in high school, and Barry, six-foot-two and broad shouldered, made me feel more feminine beside him. A flush of heat rolled through my body as he rested his hands on my shoulders. He lifted my hair away from my neck, and his lips sent shockwaves through every cell. My breath pitched as his hands traveled down to my hips and pulled them closer to his. He turned me slowly to face him, his lips trailing kisses along my neck and collarbone. A moan escaped his mouth as he leaned in and his lips met mine. His actions were hungry, forceful, and I don't remember feeling like this since our honeymoon, when we couldn't keep our hands off each other.

His hands cradled my face as he drew away. His eyes were misty. "I don't ever want to lose you again," he said.

I pulled him in and kissed away his tears, then found my way back to his lips again. I pushed him back against the counter behind him and wrapped my arms around his waist. I didn't want to waste another minute being sad or reliving what we've been through. Tonight, our lives started over, and I would do everything in my power to help him forget.

His shirt lifted easily out of the waistband of his jeans, and I slowly unbuttoned it, brushing kisses on his chest after each one. His breath became more shallow the lower I unbuttoned and kissed. He pulled me back up, and his eyes darted between mine and my lips. "We should probably continue this in the bedroom," I said, pulling his shirt off.

"Wait now, slow down," he said. He picked up both flutes and handed one to me. "Once again, to love." His smile said it all. He stole my heart with that smile so many years ago, and I never want to go another day without it.

"To the one I love," I said, raising my glass to clink his. The soft *ting* echoed as we both sipped the sweet bubbles. I leaned in and kissed him, nipping at his bottom lip.

"You seem to be in quite a hurry," he said between kisses.

My head fell to his chest and I hugged him closer. "I think I'm just nervous," I admitted.

His hand lifted my chin. "You have nothing to be nervous about," he said. His eyes reflected love and passion that I hadn't seen from him since our honeymoon. "Tonight is going to be extraordinary, and I don't want to rush one second of it."

I rested my head on his chest again, pulling him tight against my body. "I just want everything to be perfect," I said.

"Then I think we both want the same thing," he said. He reached down and lifted me, cradling me to his chest.

I threw my head back and laughed at the romantic gesture. I felt alive and free, knowing this was just the beginning again. He carried me back to our bed where we both allowed these feelings of the love we rebuilt sustain us through the night, and it was *perfect*.

This was our life.

For better or worse.

In sickness or in health.

And now these three remain: faith, hope and love.

But the greatest of these is love.

Chapter Thirty-Three

The alarm went off and I was shocked. Not that it was going off, but that I was still in bed at all. Barry was still sleeping, so I grabbed some clothes and sneaked out of the room, closing the door behind me. After last night, he deserved to sleep in.

My mind began to go there, with him, but I knew I had to get the kids up and out the door in a short amount of time. I pondered letting them sleep in, but also would have liked to have Barry to myself today, even for a little bit.

Cupcake danced around my feet as I began to rouse the kids. Charlotte awoke with little prodding, but Trevor was a different story. He was whiny and dramatic about being "toooooo tiiiiiiirrrreed" to go to school. Cupcake kissed him until he was in fits of giggles. One point for the pooch.

"It's storytime and coloring," Charlotte fussed with an eye roll.

"Charlotte, that's enough," I scolded her.

For the first time in my life, I throw Eggo waffles in the toaster, and serve them up with butter and syrup. I don't have time to bake, and I know they would scoff if I made eggs.

Eggos received cheers that are usually reserved for

cookies after dinner. I didn't care at this point. I just wanted to get them off to school and back home. I ached from the tips of my shoulders to my toes, and I downed a couple Motrin with my coffee.

Once the kids were bundled up with their coats, boots, and backpacks, I grabbed Cupcake and took her with me.

"Cuppy's coming?" Trevor's eyes were as wide as saucers.

"She sure is!" I announced.

"But Daddy never lets us bring her. He says she'll pee in the car," Charlotte looked worried. Not about the pee, but about what will happen if she does have an accident.

"Charlotte, she'll be in my lap the whole time. Don't worry." She nodded her head, but the anxious look lingered in her eyes. "How about this… if there is an accident, I'll be sure to clean it before Daddy finds out."

Her face relaxed into a smile. "Okay, cool," she agreed.

The smile couldn't be wiped from my face this morning. It had been so long since I have taken the kids to school, and my heart was thrumming with love. Even Trevor had a skip in his step as his teacher helped him out of the car. It felt like magic was in the air.

Back at home, I put a fresh pot of coffee on for both of us and rummaged through the freezer to find something to pop in the oven for breakfast. Chocolate croissants would be the perfect treat to start our lives together again. I couldn't believe he was still sleeping. I looked at the clock: 9:08 it read. Feeling giddy, I thought maybe waking him up would be the best way to start the day.

I tiptoed into the bedroom, Cupcake behind me, but I instantly knew something was wrong. The one thing I'll always remember is the *ting* of her tags on her collar when I attempted to be so quiet. Barry wasn't just sleeping soundly, he didn't seem to be moving at all. The color was drained from his face, and when I touched him, he was ice cold.

"Barry," I shouted. "Barry, wake up. Barry!"

I shouted his name over and over again, but I couldn't reach him. My stomach lurched, and I started to pant. Cupcake, sensing danger, whimpered beside me. Without hesitating, I called 911.

"Barry," I couldn't stop shouting his name.

"911 Operator, how can I help you?" She sounded muffled, not nearly as alert as I needed her to be at this precise moment.

"I can't get my husband to wake up," I screamed into the phone. "He's pale and cold, and I can't wake him up."

She notified me that an ambulance was on the way and asked if I could unlock the doors for them when they arrived. I rushed to the front door and opened it completely, then rushed back to his side.

"Ma'am, have there been health concerns in the past

year the EMTs should be aware of?"

I racked my brain. "Yes, shit, yes. He had a heart attack last fall, I can't remember when. At least six months."

"Okay, that's good information, ma'am. Can you tell me if you find a pulse?"

I didn't want to touch him again. In my heart I knew, and I crumpled to the floor, sobbing. "Nooooo," I screamed, primal and raw.

"Can you tell me your name? Ma'am?"

"It's Linny. Lynette Sinclair," I mumbled.

"Good, Linny, good." She sounded like a teacher talking to an upset child. "Linny, I want you to put the phone down but don't hang up. And then I want to see if you can find a pulse either in his neck or in his wrist."

"Nooo, I can't. I can't do it," I wailed. "I don't want to touch him."

From a distance, I could hear sirens coming closer.

"Linny, can you hear them? Help is on the way. They're almost there."

I ran to the front door, still clutching the phone. I didn't know her name, but she was my lifeline at this point. Outside, the sound became deafening. An ambulance followed by a fire truck and a police car. Cupcake danced on the porch, barking ferociously at anyone pulling up.

Three men got out of the ambulance, two of them wheeling a gurney into the house.

"Has he regained consciousness? Any changes in his

behavior?"

I stared at them. "He's cold and not moving. I don't know what to do," I stammered.

"It's okay, Linny, we're here to help," the first paramedic responded. "Take us to where he is, please."

I ran ahead of them and heard them following me. Barry was still motionless and white.

"It's probably best if you wait out here," the second paramedic said to me. "Sometimes, what we do looks worse than it is."

I looked at my phone in my hands. The operator had disconnected and my screen saver—the picture Gracie took last night—stared back at me. I texted my mom.

ME: *Can you come over right now?*

MOM: *At the store. Is everything okay?*

ME: *No. I need you.*

MOM: *On my way.*

I stood outside my door and tried to hear what is going on, but the voices were quiet and steady. There was a police officer standing in my kitchen, and the firefighters stayed outside. I knew it was standard for all of them to come, but couldn't understand why. Cupcake wouldn't stop barking in the kitchen, stressed with the intruders in our home.

The door opened and all three paramedics stood there looking somber. I looked past them, and they had covered Barry with a sheet. Our sheet.

"Ma'am, I am terribly sorry, but it appears he expired several hours ago, most likely in his sleep. You never would've noticed anything."

I felt lightheaded, like I might fall over. This can't be happening. We just started over.

"Let's go sit down in the kitchen," he said, grabbing my elbow and leading me away. "I've contacted the ME's office, and they are sending someone soon."

"Can I just go lie down with him? Just one last time?" My mind was spinning, only wanting one thing: to lie by my husband's side.

They looked at each other like it was the worst idea ever, but the first guy shrugged. "Is there someone we can call for you?"

I shook my head. "My mom is on her way," I choked out.

They stood out of my way, and I walked into our room. Silence. I looked at our bed, the sheet covering over his head looked like a prank one of the kids would do.

Oh, fuck, the kids.

I crawled onto the bed, careful not to move too much. I pulled the sheet down and the blanket up over his shoulders. "Oh, Barry," I whispered. "Why did you leave me?"

I lay close, but didn't touch him, never wanting to feel that coldness ever again. Curled up on my side, I started talking to him, telling him about our morning.

With tears running down my face, making the pillow damp, I told him how worried Charlotte was about taking Cupcake. How snarky she was with Trevor. Barry would've loved her comment about storytime and coloring. I told him how Cupcake, our fierce watchdog, was currently barking at everyone in the kitchen. Soon, all I could hear was the hitching in my voice, my breath catching between sobs. I felt my mom's presence in the room, and she grabbed my hand, gently leading me off the bed. She enfolded me into her arms, and repeated, "Shhhh, it's okay."

But it wasn't okay, and it wouldn't be okay, ever. I stood there, in her arms, my head heavy on her shoulder. I felt her crying with me, but never did she loosen her grip.

"What am I going to do?" I whispered.

"What you've always done," she whispered back. "Live. Linny, your kids need you to live. Barry needs you to live."

"How am I going to tell them?"

I felt her shake her head and a sob escaped her chest. "I don't know, honey. We will figure it out with you."

A knock at the door startled both of us. "I'm terribly sorry, but the ME is here."

My mom grabbed my hand and led me out to the kitchen. She picked up Cupcake, who was frantic and distressed. She seemed to calm instantly in her arms, resting her head on my mom's forearm.

"Ladies, the ME's office will take it from here. When

she is done with her part, you'll be notified if an autopsy is required or if he can go directly to the funeral home. It's best to contact them early, though, just in case an autopsy isn't necessary."

"So what do we do now?" My mom squeezed my hand as I spoke. My voice didn't sound like my own.

"Just wait for the medical examiner for the next steps. She will explain everything," he said. I stared at his gold name badge as he talked to us, not able to face the pity in his eyes. I wondered if Officer J. Thomas had a wife and kids, and how many times a day he had to console someone who lost a loved one. How could he get up in the morning if this was a part of his job? It was beyond my comprehension that some people dealt with death on a daily basis and managed to survive. "Again," he continued. "I am terribly sorry for your loss, Mrs. Sinclair."

It dawned on me that I had no idea what he was saying to me.

My mom looked at me. "Let's go in Charlotte's room, Linn." She grabbed my hand. "Thank you, officer."

"No problem, ma'am. I'll let the ME know where to find you," he said, shaking my mom's hand. "You take care."

We shut the door, and I sat on Charlotte's bed while my mom slid her back down the door until she was sitting on the floor. Cupcake settled in her lap, visibly shaking. My mom looked at the time on her watch.

"I will pick up Trevor in an hour when he's done and keep him until Charlotte is done too. Then I'll bring them home when you are ready to talk to them. Your dad and I will both be here for you."

I felt my face crumple into more tears. How could I possibly tell my children their father is never coming home?

Cupcake's ears perked up. She heard something in the kitchen and started bouncing on my mom's lap.

"Shhh, sit down," she said. Cupcake looked at me, then back at my mom. "Let me out," her face seemed to say.

A rap at the door jolted my mom. She stood and opened the door.

"Ma'am, I just wanted to let you know we are done." The woman's eyes darted from mine to my mom's.

My mom looked at me as I sat up on the bed. "Will you be needing an autopsy?" she asked the officer.

"The ME Office will not be requesting an autopsy. Given his history with heart problems, it is apparent his death is from natural causes. At this point, you can contact the funeral home, and they will come to transport him."

My mom took a deep breath. "You've been helpful, thank you."

She nodded. "I'm sincerely sorry for your loss, Mrs. Sinclair." Her footsteps echoed in my head as she walked towards the front door. I shuddered at the sound of the front door closing.

Pools of tears flooded my eyes. "What am I supposed to do?"

Sheer exhaustion lined my mother's face. "I'm going to call the funeral home," she said. "Why don't you come out, and I'll make some tea?"

Instead, I curled up on Charlotte's bed, clutching her favorite stuffed bear. I stared at the picture on my phone from last night. The four of us standing there, so in love, so full of hope. Gracie snapped the picture at the exact moment I looked up at Barry. I have never seen a picture of myself with this look, a mixture of gratitude and happiness stretched across my face. Barry, tall and handsome, looked proud. Like he had the world in the palm of his hand.

And he did.

I heard my mom's voice in the kitchen, and I knew she was calling Dad, making the news real to the world. Not just in the bubble of this house. I rolled over and faced the wall, unable to share in making anything real. I wanted to stay in this bubble. I wanted Barry to come wake me up and tell me I fell asleep in Charlotte's room. I wanted him to make love to me again. Last night happened too fast, and I wanted more. More talking, more kisses, more laughter.

I remembered falling asleep next to him, his breath steady and slow, thinking we were going to be like that forever. We had beat the odds of a failing marriage and found our way back to love. That never happens.

And now he was gone.

My eyes fluttered shut, and I tried to relive every moment in the last six months. The look on his face when we kissed again for the first time. The wine tasting in Leelenau. I recalled the day he brought me the list, when I was sitting out by the beach. He always knew he'd win me back. He had set the plan in motion so many months ago and made me fall back in love with him, a different love than before. A love that would never have been broken by too much work and frayed anxieties.

This love would've lasted a lifetime.

I heard voices again, and I didn't know how long I've been laying here. I just knew I couldn't face the world yet.

"Linn?" It was Gracie. The pitch — the breaking of her voice — questioned whether I'll ever be okay again. All in one syllable.

The bed squeaked as she crawled up next to me. I felt her hand on my shoulder, sending me further into a reckless hysteria. She was crying too, softly, but steady. Nothing else was said for minutes. We just lay there, crying and holding. When she did speak, she simply whispered, "Over a cliff." My heart continued to shatter into a million little pieces.

I thought about the kids, Charlotte especially, who had grown so close to Barry in the last few months. How would I save them? How could I possibly be a single parent?

"We're all going to help you through this." It was as

if she is reading my mind. "Stay put. I'm going to talk with your mom before she leaves."

I listened to her, only because I didn't have the energy to get out of Charlotte's bed. Barry lying in our bed pops into my mind, how peaceful he looked before I realized what happened. My heart raced again, thinking about trying to wake him up. Holding on to hope the entire time the operator tried to keep me calm. I think I already knew at that point, but I needed someone to tell me. Someone to bust the dream of happily ever after we had planned for the last six months.

Why did I have to fall back in love with him? Everything would've been so much easier if he woke up from his surgery the same old Barry, and we would've just gone our separate ways. I will never understand why we went through this just for him to die and to crush my heart in the process.

This is how a heart breaks. Piece by piece, I replayed the memories of us, and my heart shattered over and over again. I wanted to wake up and have this be a horrible dream of an overactive imagination. Someone who worries too much and will now make her husband go get his heart checked... once we wake up.

But this wasn't a dream, and I could never sleep in that bed again. I don't know if I can even go in that room ever again, now that the memory of the worst moment of my life lived in those walls. I thought of his wedding ring, and suddenly had to know if he had it on or if it was on the nightstand.

I jumped out of bed and raced to the kitchen, startling my mom and Grace.

"His ring!" I cried.

"Linny, it's too much. Let's go lie back down," my mom said.

"His ring," I said louder this time. "I don't know if he had his ring on this morning."

Gracie took a deep breath. "Where would it be if he didn't have it on?"

"On the nightstand. I can't remember seeing it, though." My voice didn't even sound like my own. It was borderline hysterical, and I think my mom and Grace would have done anything to make me stop talking.

"Have a seat, sweetie," she said. "I'll go check and come right back."

My mom pulled out a chair and guided me to sit down. She poured a glass of water and brought it over to me. I stared at her, amazed she thinks I want water. "Is there any coffee left?"

She blinked rapidly. "I dumped it out after it turned off an hour ago. I can make some more, though." She paused, staring at me. "The funeral home said they would send someone over soon."

I stared back at her, understanding the depth of her words, but unable to react.

Gracie walked towards me, holding his ring like a prized possession. "It was right on the nightstand where you said it would be," she said. She sat next to me and placed the ring in my open hand.

Tears streamed down my face as I smiled at it. "He hated wearing this thing," I said. "Said his hands swelled too much at night to keep it on all the time."

Gracie wiped her face with a tissue and slid the box over to me. "Do you want me to call Aiden and figure out what to do with the bakery? I don't want you to worry about anything."

I put my head in my hands, not wanting any part of that conversation. "Yeah, I guess," I said. "Whatever he wants to do is fine with me. If he wants to close for the rest of the week, whatever." The bakery, my lovely little bakery, would be fine in the end. Right now, I couldn't think about it.

"Okay, I'll take Cupcake out for a walk and call him," she said. My poor dog looked so stressed, ears pulled back, tail limp. "C'mon, sweet girl. Let's go outside." The hint of a wag shifted her tail.

The door shut, and my mom met my eyes. "What can I get you?"

The coffee gurgled behind her, and she turned to pour me a fresh cup. "This is all I want," I whispered. "I'm not hungry."

A piercing throb had developed behind my right eye, and I rubbed it trying to ease the pain.

"Do you think he's in heaven?" My lip started to quiver, thinking about him all alone.

She had been wiping down the counter and froze,

looking back at me. "Oh Linny," she said, hugging me from behind. "Of course he's in heaven. He's watching over you right now. You and the kids. I can feel it."

"But he hadn't been to church in years," I explained. "Neither of us have."

She was shaking her head before I finished my sentence. "God loves you no matter what. It's not even a question of where he is."

Her conviction felt like a balm. I wanted so much to believe he went to a better place and didn't suffer, but I couldn't help but wonder if he felt scared or upset about not being here. *Why did he have to go?*

Gracie walked back in, wiping her face with her sleeve. Cupcake stopped when she saw me. She sat and whimpered until I picked her up. Her fur was cold from outside, and her feet were still wet. I nuzzled her neck, smelling the outside puppy scent.

"Well, that sucked," Gracie said. "But he is going to handle the bakery—whatever that may entail—until you are ready to come back. He's up for the task and is obviously heartbroken for you."

"Yeah, I don't think I could tell anyone," I said. I took a sip of coffee and flinched. Barry would've called this cowboy coffee.

"I hope you don't mind, but I called Charlie too." She poured herself a cup of coffee. After adding creamer she took a sip and made a face. She added more creamer. "He's bringing food over in a while. And obviously my mom is going to intrude and help wherever possible." She shrugged.

I attempted a smile and nodded. I didn't want to see anyone, and certainly didn't want any food, but I knew the kids would require some normalcy. And that included food.

My mom looked at her watch. "I'm going to head over and get Trevor." She pulled her coat on and leaned over to kiss the top of my head. "I'll call after I get Charlotte and see how you're feeling."

"Okay, Mom," I said. "Thank you."

Gracie stood to hug her, but Cupcake barked at a knock on the front door.

"That is probably the people from Hayes Funeral Home," Mom said. "I'll let them in on my way out."

Gracie and I stood in my kitchen and listened to the voices. We heard the stretcher being wheeled in, two men walking behind it. They stopped once they got to the kitchen.

"Mrs. Sinclair, we are so sorry for your loss," the one pushing the stretcher said. They both had on black pants and white button-down shirts. I'd laugh at the dress code cliché any other time, but now I wanted to scream at them. "If you could direct us to the body, we will be out of here soon."

"The *body*?" I snapped. "That body is my husband."

Gracie shot me a look before directing them back to our room. "He's this way," she said, leaving me in the kitchen. When she came back, she pulled me in a hug. "Do you want to go in Charlotte's room when they wheel him out? They said it's easier for the family to not see that happening."

The only thing I remember after that is Gracie helping me to the spare room and tucking me in.

"I'll be right out here if you need me, but try to sleep. It will be your only friend for the next few weeks," she said. She shut the door softly, and the room went black.

Darkness had fallen when I woke up. Not nighttime darkness, but the kind of gloom Michigan weather brings when a storm is present. Rain pelted the window—at least I hoped it was rain and not sleet or snow. Voices muffled in the kitchen, and I knew I had to go face them, but all I wanted was to stay in this bed, away from anyone who would remind me Barry was gone.

Opening the door, I could hear the voices clearly now. Charlie and Jimmy were both here with Grace. Would Barry know about our indiscretion now? I stood at the entry of the kitchen until Charlie noticed me first. Without saying a word, he walked over and wrapped me in a hug. The tears started to fall again as he pulled me in tighter.

"Your mom called a while ago," Gracie said. "Both kids are with her at home. She said to call when you're up for it."

Jimmy had tears in his eyes as he approached me. "I

am so sorry, Linn," he whispered, as he pulled me into him. I broke his hug, not wanting to feel anything I used to for him. I never wanted to be reminded of that night ever again. Hugging Jimmy felt like a betrayal.

I sat down at the table and Grace handed me my phone. "I only answered when I knew it was your mom. Most of the other calls left voicemails."

I scrolled through my notifications... Aiden, Tony, Shelly... all left several texts and voicemails. I laid my phone down, unable to process any of the messages. I felt lightheaded and tried to remember the last time I ate anything.

"Can I fix you a sandwich or something?" Jimmy read my mind. "We brought some food over, plus Mom's going to start planning meals for you this week. You won't have to worry about that for a few years," he snickered. His half-smile gave away how uncomfortable he felt.

"Yeah, I don't feel great right now," I said. "I don't want much but I should probably eat something."

Jimmy set a turkey sandwich and some pretzels in front of me. On any given day, I would inhale this given how hungry I was, but a sandwich wasn't what I wanted.

"Honey, you have to eat something," Gracie said, grabbing my hand. "I know this is killing you, but your kids are going to need you, Linn."

She was right. "I guess I should call my mom now," I said. My stomach clenched at the thought. I pushed the plate of food away, suddenly nauseous again.

Gracie leaned forward to meet my eyes. "Hey, we're here with you," she said. "And if you want us to leave, we'll leave. Just tell us what you need."

"I need Barry to be alive."

She closed her eyes and tightened her grip on my hand. "Barry is still with you. Just in other ways, now."

"Forgive me if I don't care about the other ways," I snapped. "I'd prefer he were here to hold me right now." I pulled my hand away, and she gave me a sad smile.

"I'm not going to say I know what you're going through, Linn, but you have to believe that if Barry could be here, in this moment, he would. He loved you so much."

I stared at the table, not wanting to meet anyone's eyes. Hearing how much he loved me felt pointless and cruel. Every thought in my head, everywhere I looked, reminded me he wasn't here any longer. I looked at the clock, 5:15, and knew I had to tell my kids. My mom answered on the first ring.

"...ello," she answered. For as long as I can remember, my mom would answer the phone before it reached her ear, so you'd only hear the second half of hello.

"Hi Mom," I said. Hearing her voice activated my tear ducts again.

"Oh honey, I've been so worried about you today." I could hear my dad talking and Trevor giggling in the background.

"I think it's probably time to bring the kids home. We can't wait any longer."

"Okay," she said, gently. "Your dad and I will bring them over soon."

We disconnected after saying our byes, and I looked at Gracie. "Do you mind staying a little longer? I want the kids surrounded by love when they are told."

Her chin quivered as her eyes filled up. She swallowed hard and nodded. "Do you want my mom to come over?"

"Nah, I think we can handle this." I looked at my phone again, memorizing the picture from last night in rich detail. I didn't know how Gracie did it, but she had managed to catch the twinkle in Barry's brown eyes. He stared back at me, forever in love, and I knew we'd never be that happy family ever again.

The house was quiet. The kids were finally asleep. Charlotte took the news the hardest, being older, and Trevor reacted like I thought he would. With a request for a snack. I knew he understood what we were saying, but the gravity of the situation was lost on him, thank God.

I was curled up on the couch with a blanket and sleep was elusive, something that came in bits and pieces. Gracie and my mom spent much of the evening moving my clothes into the spare room. I never wanted to go in the bedroom again.

My phone chimed with a text.

TONY: *You awake?*

ME: *Yup.*

TONY: *Linny, I am so sorry.*

ME: *I'm not sure how to handle any of this.*

TONY: *Do you want to talk? You can call me if you want.*

ME: *Honestly, I just want this day to end. I can't talk or think about it anymore.*

TONY: *I get it. I'm here if you need ANYTHING. I will check in tomorrow.*

ME: 🤍

TONY: 🤍

I fell asleep clutching my phone. Any time I woke up, I'd look at the picture to remind myself that love was real. All you had to do was look at our faces, in our eyes to see that love.

It broke my heart to know I'd never see that look again.

Chapter Thirty-Four

"I'm not sure why you thought coming out here on karaoke night would be a good idea," I said. Gracie rolled her eyes at me. The one-month anniversary loomed in my head all day, and I just wanted to be home, curled up on the couch.

Jimmy set five shots down on the bar in front of us. Pink shots.

"For one, it's Aiden's birthday." Aiden elbowed me in the ribcage as she continued. "His twenty-first birthday, to be exact, and we're celebrating. And secondly, today marks the anniversary of finding out my husband was a pedophile. This day deserves to have shots involved in its memory."

"Here, here," Charlie said grabbing a shot glass. "Happy birthday, Aiden!"

We all raised our glasses and drank down the pink mixture.

"Aww, thanks everyone," Aiden responded, wiping his mouth. "You guys are the best."

The three of us sat at the bar with me in the middle. Gracie had to keep leaning over to talk to Aiden without yelling too much. After my month of solitary confinement, being here felt invasive on every sensory level.

"Did you get to do anything fun today?" Gracie shouted.

Aiden's face lit up. "Boss lady gave me the day off, so Shelly and I went to Traverse City to shop."

I thought of our date there a few months back. The single red rose on our table at the restaurant. The annoying twinkle in his eye.

"Linny?" Gracie and Aiden were looking at me, raised eyebrows.

"I asked how business had been going. Where were you just now?"

I shook the memory off. "Oh, business is booming. Aiden here is a social media genius, and sales are up from last year. I'm still trying to figure out how to balance the kids and work right now, but I guess there could be worse problems."

"I keep telling her to bring the kids in after school," Aiden piped in. "It's a totally different vibe there in the afternoons, and they would love it."

Gracie raised her eyebrows to me. I shot her a look back. *No judgements*.

"And they could see their mom in action, which would be good for them too," he continued.

Being around Aiden sometimes made me feel like everything would be okay. I took a sip of wine, savoring the buzzed feeling in my head.

"And training? How is that going?" Gracie wouldn't stop with the questions.

Aiden leaned forward. "She hasn't run in the past

310

month. *And* she stopped meeting with Tony."

"What?" Gracie's eyes were saucers. "Linny, you were so excited about the marathon. What happened?"

"Uhh, my husband died?" This started to feel like an intervention.

Gracie reached for my hand. "We know that." Her tone was softer, eyes shiny. "You can't give up on yourself, though. Barry wouldn't have wanted that."

"We don't know what he would want, because he's not here," I snapped.

Gracie turned back toward the bar and eyed Jimmy, who leaned on the bar in front of us. "How are the kids doing?" he asked.

The muscles in my shoulders relaxed. "They're actually doing pretty well," I said. "Considering life has been so different."

"They're doing well, because they have you for a mom," Jimmy said. "But I think we're all concerned about you, however." His eyes never left mine, and I felt a pull to stay focused on him. I knew Gracie and Aiden were both listening, but in this moment, it was just me and Jimmy.

"I'm so worried they're going to be screwed up for life because of this, I can't even think about myself." Tears filled my eyes, and he slid a clean napkin over to me. "I can handle this… it's them I care about saving."

He shook his head slowly. "It doesn't work like that, Linny. If you don't take care of yourself, you'll have nothing left to give them eventually." Gracie tightened her grip on my hand.

"Word," Aiden chimed in. "Could we also touch upon the music issue we have at the bakery, as long as we're here?"

We all looked at Aiden.

"We have listened to Coldplay and Sam Smith for the last month."

"Woof," Gracie joked.

"You know I love you boss lady, but enough is enough. I'm bringing back Lady Gaga starting tomorrow. The doom and gloom duo are giving me hives."

Gracie giggled behind me, and despite myself, I did too.

"Jesus Aiden, why didn't you just say something?"

"I tried to change it a few times, but you kept switching it back," he said.

I sighed. "Fine, you pick the music from now on."

"And the training? Are you going to start running again?"

I shook my head slowly. "I can't even wrap my brain around that right now. I know I made the commitment, but that was before."

Gracie nodded, not pushing me any further, but I knew this would not be the last of our conversation about it.

By the time I got home, my head was pounding. The kids were already in bed, Cupcake was sleeping, and my mom eyed me carefully.

"Are you okay? You look so pale," she said.

"I'm fine, just sensory overload," I responded. "How were the kids?"

She melted into a smile. "I think this was good for them tonight. They were happy and relaxed. We played Monopoly for an hour. Not surprisingly, Charlotte bought everything."

I smiled. "Of course she did." I poured myself some water and gulped down two Motrin. "They ate okay?"

"We ordered pizza," she said, nodding. "They ate a ton. What about you, did you eat anything?"

"We split the mushrooms," I said. "I wasn't really hungry."

"Linny, you have to eat better," she chided.

"Mom, don't start tonight," I snapped. "Everyone there treated me like it was an intervention all night. I can't take anymore judgement about how I'm handling all of this."

She raised her hands defensively. "No one is judging you. We are all just trying to help you get through this."

I took a deep breath and blew it out slowly. "I think we're doing okay," I said. *I didn't ask for anyone's help!*

She pulled on her coat, eyes looking defeated. Tired. Pulling me into a hug, she whispered, "I'm sorry. I know how hard this is for you."

Tears sprung to my eyes again, and I pulled away. "Thanks, Mom. For everything."

All I wanted was sleep.

"I'll see you in the morning," she said.

I put water on for tea and found my journal. Opening it up, I realized the last day I wrote in here was Valentine's Day. I had all but forgotten about this journal until Gracie said something that triggered the memory. "Writing something down helps me remember details I had forgotten," she'd said. I don't even remember what we were talking about, lists I think, but on my way home, I thought of my journal and knew it was time.

April 18 - One Month Anniversary

Where do I even begin? How do I write about something that is still too painful to even think about? When will I ever feel happiness? I had it once, briefly, and I'm truly afraid I will never be genuinely happy again. I feel glimmers of lightness when I see Charlotte giggle, or Trevor belly laugh, and those are the moments when I know they will be okay. Losing their dad has been so hard on them, but they are better at finding joy in life despite the pain. They still want to laugh and have fun. I want that for them too. I just don't know how to bring myself to let go of him. Everything reminds me of him. The way Charlotte snickers and Trevor's brown eyes. I can't even clean up Cupcake's accidents without hearing Barry chuckle in my head.

It's as if the longing will never go away. We had just

gotten to a place where happiness felt so right, and now I'll never feel that way again. I don't even want to try. There are moments I wish we had never tried again. In some ways, it would be so much easier if we had parted months ago. My heart wouldn't be crushing me, now. But, even with this broken heart, I know the love we recreated mattered. It was something to be proud of, something Charlotte and Trevor can hold onto. Something to strive for later in life.

My life will forever be divided into before and after. Before he died and after. How I view anything now in the "after" will look far different than it did before. The kids will be different. My priorities... everything. And I would just give anything to have one more moment with him. One more conversation. One more kiss. One more before.

What if none of it was real? Gracie keeps asking if he's in my dreams, and he isn't. I don't remember dreams at all, never have really, but would give anything to see him again... even in a dream.

I closed my journal and rested my head on my arms. Cupcake's collar jingled as she shook off sleep. She walked over and sat by my feet, blinking. Then she stood and walked to the front door and jingled the bell hanging for her. I smiled, remembering the day Charlotte hung it up, so excited for Cupcake to learn something.

Again, I saw Barry's face smiling at me. He was here

with me, I knew that, I just wanted more. Always wanted more.

Getting up, I resigned myself to the fact that life would simply be like this in the after. I didn't need happiness like others did. I could manage, keeping my family upright and loved. I would become the poster child for survival.

Coming back in the house, I locked up and turned out the lights. Settling on the couch with my blanket pulled up to my chin, I finally drifted off into a dreamless sleep.

Chapter Thirty-Five

Have you ever listened to a Sam Smith song and not wanted to weep? No song in particular… he has a theme of writing about heartbreak that makes you feel understood and wholly connected to that pain. They are beautiful and melancholy at the same time, and I don't know if he's helping or hurting, but I don't care, either.

It was a quiet Sunday afternoon, and I had Sam singing to me—loudly—and Aiden wasn't here to complain or subtly change the music to something else. Gracie and Charlie offered to take the kids to skating, and I was prepping for the week.

The ringing of the bell startled me. Was Aiden here? He was the only one with a key. I wiped my hands on my apron, about to walk through the door, when Tony walked through.

"How did you get in here? I know I locked the door," I questioned, stopping in my tracks.

"Oh, hi Linn," he said. "Good to see you, too."

"Tony." I walked over and gave him a hug. "I didn't know how much I missed you until just now," I said, wiping tears away.

"You're officially on break," he said, pulling my hand towards the front. "Can I make you some coffee?"

"What planet are we on, when you offer to make me coffee?"

"Is that a yes?"

I rolled my eyes. "Yes. That's a yes. Do you know how to work that coffee maker?" I flipped the light switch for the overhead lights.

"I'll figure it out," he said. "How about finding something a little more upbeat to listen to? Or silence. Silence would be good."

I stuck my tongue out at him as I walked in back. Seconds later, we were listening to Ed Sheeran. "Will this do?" I asked, walking back up front.

"This is perfect," he said. With the coffee brewing, he grabbed a bottle of water out of the cooler and walked over to the corner table. "Sit."

I crossed my arms.

"Adorable," he said. "Please, sit. Join me."

I pulled the chair out and plunked myself down with a thud.

He stared at me for what felt like ten minutes.

"So what brings you by the bakery today? And how did you get in? You never explained."

"Gracie texted me and thought that we needed a meeting. She told me when to be here, and Aiden met me out front to let me in."

"So this is why Gracie was so willing to take the kids to skating lessons," I mused. "I wish people would just let me be."

"And by letting you be, you mean not taking care of yourself?"

My head dropped to the side. "I'm trying to keep my family from falling apart. I hardly doubt a month or two of not running is going to kill me."

"It's not about the running, Linny," he raised his voice, exasperated. "It's everything else. You're shutting everyone out of your life and sinking into depression. And the worst part is you don't seem to care!"

"I *don't* care!" I shouted back. "I don't care about anything anymore. Is that what you want to hear?"

"Yes, that's exactly what I wanted you to say." I never imagined calm, cool Tony could lose his patience like this. "Now, you're at least being honest with someone."

I shook my head and looked out the window. It had stopped raining, but the glass still had rain drops running down in tiny tracks. "I don't know what to do, Tony. All I want is to sleep. Kids, work, and sleep: that's my To Do list every day. And I really don't give a shit about anything else."

"So you're just going to give up?"

"Give up what, exactly?" Exhaustion seeped into my voice.

"Give up on living. On feeling. On connecting with other people. Is that how you want to raise your kids?"

"You don't have one clue about what I'm going through," I shot back. "Don't you dare judge me. Why don't you just go and forget you know me."

A small smile crept onto his face. "That's exactly what you want, isn't it? You want everyone to simply leave you alone to wallow in your misery."

"I just don't have the energy to be challenged right now. Not mentally or physically. I don't have it in me to fight back." I rested my head in my hands.

"It takes more strength to hang on than it does to let go." He reached for my hand. "You are hanging on to Barry, and he's not here. You have to let him go, Linny. He would never want you to live like this. I wish you had known how proud he was of you taking on the marathon and how you were finally taking care of yourself."

My chin quivered as I met his eyes. He nodded.

"I'm so tired, Tony. I don't know how to take care of myself anymore."

"Let's focus on the basic human needs, Linny, food, water, and sleep. But, by the looks of you, the first thing we need to tackle is sleep," he said. "I don't think you're getting enough."

I snorted. "I barely sleep anymore," I whispered. "I can't sleep in our room ever again, and I fall asleep on the couch every night."

"That stops tonight. You have a spare room, correct?"

I nodded.

"From here on out, that is your room, your sacred space to rest."

"It's not the same," I said.

"Let's just be clear about the future, Linny. Nothing is ever going to be the same. It's going to be uncomfortable at first, but you have to find a new normal. You have to find a way to live in this world without Barry."

"Why are you being so heartless? I just want to be left alone."

"Because there is a small part of you that still wants to live, and that's who I'm talking to. You know I haven't said anything you don't need to hear, but you're too afraid to move forward. You're afraid to be alone, but here's the thing, Linny. You're not alone, and you never have been. Family comes in all shapes and sizes, and you're surrounded by love every single day, but you're not seeing it. It's time to create a new family for yourself and for your kids. They need a mom who is happy, not this shell of a person I'm looking at."

I couldn't hold back the tears any longer. I knew he was speaking the truth to me, but I didn't know how to let go of the past. "I need help," I said. The simple statement of admission broke me down. I doubled over, sobbing uncontrollably. I felt his hand on my back, pulling me into his chest.

"It's okay, Linn," he soothed. "Shhh, it's okay." He repeated this until I calmed down. Minutes felt like hours as the emotions flooded my body. Like a wave, they would rise and fall.

I rested my head on his shoulder, exhausted and

empty. "I don't know how to do any of this."

"I know," he said. "I'm going to help you. And I think we need to find a therapist for you. Just until you get back on your feet."

"Probably true." I nodded. For the first time in months, I didn't feel resistance to someone's suggestion.

"Did you agree with something I said?" I felt his cheeks tighten into a smile.

"Let's not pat ourselves on the back yet," I joked. "You're lucky I haven't punched you today."

"There she is," he said, kissing the top of my head. "I knew you were still in there somewhere."

"Do you charge extra for emotional outbursts?" I sat up, feeling calmer.

"Only for clients I don't like. For you, it's on the house." His serious face was back in place, but relief reflected in his eyes.

I grabbed the unopened water bottle still on the table and took a long drink. I felt like a weight had been lifted from my shoulders. "So this was all Gracie's idea?"

He smiled easily. "Let's just say it was a group effort," he said. "You have a lot of people who love you. Including me."

I blinked back more tears. "I know that. I really do, but I just wanted to sink into this hole and stay there forever."

He nodded. "We could all see that happening." He

leaned forward. "I'll send your first email tonight about how we're going to get you back amongst the living. It'll be baby steps, but these are the most important ones."

"What about the marathon? Have I missed too much?"

He rolled his eyes. "Can we focus on one thing at a time? The marathon will happen if you're ready, but I'm not worried about it."

I chewed on the inside of my lip. "Okay," I said.

"Okay, what?"

"Okay, I'll follow your recipe for living," I said, smirking.

"As if you had a choice?" He stood and stretched. "I have another client to get to at the gym."

I walked him to the door. He turned and pulled me into a hug, smiling. "Thank you for this," I whispered.

He pulled me in tighter before releasing me. "Thank you for letting me in. I know this wasn't easy."

I nodded before more tears came. He walked out, and I locked the door behind him, watching him go.

He reached the edge of the sidewalk, turned and smiled at me.

Baby steps. I felt like I had just taken the first one, but I knew it would be okay, eventually.

Epilogue

My legs don't hurt anymore. I think they're numb.

Somewhere around mile fourteen a higher power—St. Jude, my mom would argue—took over and carried me along. My hips feel like squares in round sockets, and I've heard my ankle pop for the last mile. It's helping me keep my rhythm now.

I have seen Gracie more today than I have in weeks. I'm not sure how she's done it, but she has managed to cheer me on at least once in every mile. Some miles she finds extra spots. At first, I smiled and cheered with her. *I'm doing a marathon! This is really happening!!*

Now, I cry every time I see her, and not the pretty tears running down my cheeks as I valiantly keep running. No, this is the ugly cry that caused people to stop in their tracks and inquire if I need medical attention. I will have to drink Gatorade for weeks to make up this dehydration.

I am in the back of the pack, with the rest of the diehard stragglers who refuse to give up. By mile twenty-three it dawns on me that I'm in the exact spot where I saw the runners a year ago. That fateful day when I boldly told Tony that I wanted to run a marathon, and I realized that I never once doubted this was going to happen.

I always knew I'd be here.

It's at that moment I dig in and try to jog again. I had been walking/crying/limping for the last mile unsure why I was doing this. Now, I remembered.

At the twenty-four mile marker, I see Aiden with Grace and Julia. Aiden holds a neon orange poster with *"Get it, Gurl"* written in glitter gold lettering. I can't help but laugh and cry, simultaneously. The laughter feels good, and I know I have more than two miles left. I had heard horror stories about the quarter mile at the end of a marathon and steel myself for the remainder of this run.

I saw Tony before the race. "Don't worry about me today. Just focus on moving forward, and I will find you in the last mile," he said.

I counted on that.

In my head, I have envisioned seeing him first as I cross the finish line. He was the one reason I chose to do this race, and he damn well better be here for me.

Mile twenty-five. Pain, mostly mental, is hitting me in waves. Julia and my mom are standing with Charlotte and Trevor. My heart bursts, and I run to hug them. "Keep going, Momma," is all I need to hear to finish the race.

I can't get Barry off my mind and prayed wherever he is, he's here watching over me. Hell, I knew he was. I wouldn't be this far if he wasn't.

Why did he have to leave me? Why did I have to take so long to come around? I wasted so much of our precious time we had left, always thinking he'd be there for me. I stop, leaning my hands on my knees, unsure I can move forward any longer. I hear footsteps behind me.

"What's the deal?" It's Tony. "We have less than a mile to go," he says. He is sweating, running bib placed on his shirt, and it hits me. He's been following me the whole time. *I'll find you in the last mile…*

I bit my lip to prevent the breakdown response I'm feeling. He locks eyes with me. "You did not run this far to quit. I'm in this with you… let's go."

The city streets are lined with people cheering, many of them watching Tony try to coerce me to keep going. I hear the announcer at the finish line calling out when someone crosses, loud music in the background. Tony is right—I didn't come this far to quit.

"Okay," I say, falling into a jog again. "Let's go, bitch."

He smiles and shakes his head. "There's my girl."

I have shooting pains from my hips down the back of both legs. Every step thundering through my body.

"Just hear the music," Tony says, breaking my thoughts. "Think about your kids watching you cross that line. How proud they will be."

The tears just keep coming, and I'm not trying to stop them. Neither is Tony. He knows what an emotional journey this last year has been, and I know he's

326

expecting it to happen. We finally pass the twenty-six mile marker, and a sob escapes my chest. Gracie is there, beside me. She grabs my hand and squeezes it tight.

"Over a cliff," she says, tears running down her cheeks as well.

I look ahead and see the finish line ahead. It still feels like it's a mile away, my body breaking down in a slow painful shuffle at this point.

"Linn, you got the rest of the way on your own," Tony says. "Grace and I are right here behind you, but you need to cross that line on your own."

I nod, knowing if I look at him, I will stop him from falling behind. I let go of Gracie's hand and hear her cheering behind me. The shuffle goes faster, like a turtle trying to run. I can feel my heart beating again, broken, but still doing its job.

Twenty feet away.

Fifteen.

Ten.

The clouds part, and a brilliant sunlight hits the sign. *Barry...*

Five.

I see Charlotte and Trevor, arms open as they wait for me. Aiden is jumping and hugging my mom.

"Number 31838, Linny Sinclair, you did it!!!"

Before I can drop to my knees, Tony is there holding me up, and wraps a foil blanket around my shoulders. Grace tries to hand me a drink, but I fall into her arms and nearly tip her over.

"I got you," she whispers. I feel Charlotte and Trevor hug around my legs and waist. My only thought is: *how am I going to walk after this*? My stomach feels like acid is burning a hole through it, and my legs start to shake uncontrollably.

"We need to get you sitting down, Linn," Tony says. "C'mon, over here."

A large tent with chairs and trainer tables are set up for runners needing assistance. I sit on a table as my stomach cramps with the sip of water I drank.

"Focus on your breath," he says quietly. "You're fine, but you need to get your heart rate back down."

I close my eyes and do what he says, listening for my heart. I'm still alive, but my heart is still breaking with every beat.

I did it, a little voice says, and I knew in that instant, life would be okay. It wasn't about the struggle and the heartache. It was about moving forward through all of it. That's what living means. That's how you survive and eventually thrive.

You keep living.

You keep loving.

And you savor the hell out of every second of every day.

The End

About the Author

Mo Parisian lives in Lansing, Michigan along with her husband and two sons. She works full-time as a nanny (triplets!) and also writes for mjparisian.com, her website. Figure skating and hockey have been a part of her life for as long as she can remember, and if she's not writing, you can find her reading or searching for the perfect chocolate chip cookie recipe.

This is How a Heart Breaks is Mo's second novel. Her first novel, *What We Know Now*, is available on Amazon.com

Acknowledgements

First and foremost, I want to thank my family and friends. Without their love and support, this wouldn't ever happen. Writing and publishing is a privilege that I don't take lightly. My biggest hope is always to inspire someone to do something or challenge themselves in ways they've only dreamt about. My family—*my people*— have always been the ones to inspire me, so this is for them.

My dad is the hardest worker I've ever known, and it is from him I gained one of my best qualities: persistence. My husband would argue that it's stubbornness (okay, *everyone* would), but it's the persistence that helped me cross the literary finish line again. Without it, the books simply wouldn't get done. So, thank you Popsie.

I am forever grateful for the day I met my editor and biggest cheerleader, Susan Anderson with Poole Publishing Services. The cover art, the editing, and the formatting are all things I couldn't do without her, and she makes it look so damn easy. Susie, these words will never be enough…

To my amazing team of "first-draft" readers… thank you. Linda and Lara, you both made this book better with every suggestion and comment. You understood the story better than I did sometimes, and always helped me keep an eye on the details. Amy, Pam, Lisa,

Kristie, and Jane, I still smile at the responses you gave me. (Even the angry ones :)) Thank you all for loving Linny as much as I did.

Often, I'll get to a section of the book that reaches beyond my own knowledge, and I'll seek out those who know way more than I do on certain subjects. My gratitude to Dave, Jeff, and Matt for answering endless questions, rewriting sentences :), but being sworn to secrecy in the process.

My world in Frankfort, MI continues to bring magic into my life. I love every minute I've spent bringing this lovely Michigan beach town to you. Anyone who knows me, understands that writing a book that takes place in a bakery is sort of like the best of both worlds for me. As a writer who also loves to bake, escaping to Bab's everyday felt like another dream that came true. I only hope you enjoyed her bakery as much as I did.

The anchor symbol you see throughout the book is something I came across when I began researching this book and the faith, hope, love theme. It's called a Camargue Cross, and it stands for the three cardinal virtues: the cross for faith; the anchor for hope; the heart for love. I fell in love with it instantly and knew it would be a part of this book somehow.

As always, everything I write has a little bit of my mom sprinkled throughout. I only wish she were still around to see these characters come to life, but her spirit continues to live on inside them.

Thank you for reading!